Praise for

THE LINES BETWEEN US

"In *The Lines Between Us*, D'Harlingue has created a captivating debut novel filled with unique characters, exquisite details, and intriguing family secrets. A diary and letters furtively passed down over three hundred years from grandmother to granddaughter transport readers back in time and move them forward as the mysteries are elegantly revealed. This book is about women's honor, overcoming heartache, and bravery."

—JILL G. HALL, author of *The Black Velvet Coat*

"Rebecca D'Harlingue's *The Lines Between Us* is a heartfelt and intelligent novel about love, family, and the ties that bind us to generations past."

—MICHAEL DAVID LUKAS, author of
The Last Watchman of Old Cairo

"In her meticulously researched epistolary novel *The Lines Between Us,* Rebecca D'Harlingue weaves a tale of familial love, brutality, and sacrifice during the seventeenth-century Spanish Inquisition. D'Harlingue's elegantly crafted, intriguing story spans the Old and New Worlds, exploring the oppression and power of generations of women bound together by a dark family secret—and their modern-day descendant's quest to uncover the truth about her ancestry."

—KRISTEN HARNISCH, international best-selling author
of *The Vintner's Daughter* and *The California Wife*

"Well-kept secrets maintain unbroken lines connecting generations for three centuries in this arresting story about women and the compromises they must make for survival. The author immerses us in 17th-century Spain and doesn't let us emerge until 21st-century America, when Rachel fills in the missing spaces. Well-written and engaging, the tale rings true and affirms women's strength, desire to be heard, and fierce love of family."

—LINDA STEWART HENLEY, author of *Estelle*

THE
LINES
BETWEEN
US

THE

Lines

Between

Us

A Novel

REBECCA D'HARLINGUE

SHE WRITES PRESS

Published 2020
Printed in the United States of America
Print ISBN: 978-1-63152-743-2
E-ISBN: 978-1-63152-744-9
Library of Congress Control Number: 2020906001

For information, address:
She Writes Press
1569 Solano Ave #546
Berkeley, CA 94707

She Writes Press is a division of SparkPoint Studio, LLC.

Book design by Stacey Aaronson

*To my husband, Art, for your love and encouragement
in all of my pursuits,
and to our children, Ben and Kate,
for giving us joy each day.*

TABLE OF CONTENTS

Prologue . . . 1

OLD WORLD

NEW WORLD

PROLOGUE

It is more commonplace in story than in life that loved ones are witness to dying words that carry meaning or forgiveness. So it was with me, for, though I heard my mother's words, they served only to confound and injure.

"I am like Ana," she had said. "I have failed Juliana."

But I knew no Juliana, nor an Ana who had disappointed. I knew only that my mother had left me and would not now explain. In my profession I interpret others' words within boundaries prescribed by a meticulous author. That world is less than real, but there is no dire consequence for turning down a wrong path of understanding.

What would come to pass would cause me to rethink my mother's final words, as when some occasion of joy or sorrow compels us to reinterpret all that preceded, as though the past could be purified or tainted by it.

Rachel Pearson Strand
St. Louis, Missouri, 2014

OLD WORLD

ANA

Madrid, 7 February 1661

Upon awakening, sequestered behind thick bed curtains, Ana couldn't place the reason for her agitation. Then it came to her. Yesterday, in the study of her late husband, Emilio, she had come upon something totally unexpected. She had found a diary, a diary she had not known existed.

It had been over a year since Emilio's death, and she had entered his study only those few times when she had needed to look for a medical reference. She never lingered. Yesterday as she had removed a volume from a shelf, she had seen a small, well-worn, leather-bound book behind it. She opened to the first page, and upon reading *Journal of Emilio Cardero Díaz*, she quickly snapped it closed. She had stumbled to a chair and after a few frozen moments had resolutely arisen and abandoned the room and the diary.

For many months after Emilio's death, Ana's grief had been a friend in its familiarity. Like a miser who cannot bear to see his riches dwindle, she had guarded her sorrow like a treasure, fearing that its waning would shrink her heart. She had lost the image of him shortly after his death, and her inability to conjure it had left her betrayer and betrayed. Nothing had comforted. The emptiness could not be touched or taken. Ana had felt herself to be a woman who had asked very little of God, and to whom God, in His turn, had given very little.

Then, slowly, her healing had come so far that she could look at loveliness and see its curvature and depth, not the featureless plane that all had been before. What would this journal do to that fragile equilibrium?

Now as she lay in her bed, Ana knew that she could not ignore the book, that she would retrieve it that night.

"The Sánchez woman has been here with her sick child already. I sent her away, but there's no doubt that she will return again. If she would harness into something worthwhile the persistence she uses in plaguing you with her problems, I've no doubt she could better her lot." Clara felt no need to knock on her mistress's door in the morning, nor to announce her presence in a gentler manner. In fact, she often employed the tactic of making some statement which was calculated to get a rise from Ana. The day was about getting down to business, and she was glad that Doña Ana had finally seemed capable of making herself useful again after the long desert of her grief.

Clara's scheme did not work this morning, however, and she detected no life behind the heavily curtained walnut bed with its ornately spiraled posts. More than once after Don Emilio had died, Clara had urged Ana to take the curtains off her bed. That way, Clara argued, when she entered Ana's room in the morning, she could determine whether her mistress was awake yet and guide her actions accordingly. Of course, this was a specious argument, for Clara's purpose in entering Ana's room was always to rouse her. But Clara was a woman who did not like concealment, and she reasoned that a widow had no need of the privacy of a curtained bed, especially in the scorching Madrid summer. Ana had proved more stubborn than Clara on this one point, and the curtains remained. Even Clara would not presume so much as to draw the bed drapes aside, so she placed Ana's breakfast tray on the bulky marriage chest and left the room noisily, her displeasure apparent in her gait.

Assured of Clara's departure, Ana drew back the curtains and endeavored to put the journal from her mind for now. Dwelling on it would gain her nothing. The bed was high, but her feet had no trouble reaching the floor. Ana was tall for a woman, a fact her father had frequently commented upon with distaste, as though her height were due to a lack of self-restraint.

Glancing toward the diffuse light from the oiled parchment windows, Ana was once again glad that she had not given in to her brother Sebastián's pressure to have glass windows installed throughout the house. Here, at least in her private rooms, the parchment blurred and softened the world's encroachment.

Ana wrapped herself in a loose robe, postponing the moment when she would don the encumbrance of the costume worn by women of her class. Recalling the comfort of the loose-fitting habit she had worn for eleven years while she lived in the Convent of Corpus Christi, Ana again reminded herself that the convent could be a refuge for widows.

She had entered the convent because, even with a father who had the king's favor and was willing to pay a generous dowry, no groom had been found. She had lived with the nuns for eleven years but had not taken her final vows of poverty, chastity, and obedience. This was unusual, but Ana's patience and kindness had deterred the Madre Superior from pressing the point.

Ana had not been alone in her lack of a special calling. For some it was an escape from poverty. Others were given to God by their families. If the family was wealthy, the convent received a generous endowment, and the girl might bring a servant with her. Life within was more restrictive, but worldly pleasures were possible. A young gallant might court one of the residents, spying on her through the grille of the choir, arranging to have poetry smuggled in, or even visiting his lady in the parlor. All of this could engender jealousy. It was possible to find peace in the convent, but also petty rivalries.

Still, Ana had been content there, discovering comfort and delight in the company of other women, having lived without mother or sister. Even so, she could not make up her mind to return, and her brother pressed her to stay out in the world. He had shown genuine sadness those years ago when Ana had requested of their father to allow her to enter the convent. It had seemed to her more desirable than becoming the maiden aunt in her brother's house, a guest on the periphery of a real family.

In some ways, she had ended with that fate after all. She had her own home, but her brother had come to rely on her to counsel his motherless daughter, Juliana, who was now sixteen. Ana loved Juliana most deeply and was more than happy to fulfill this role, though there was always the reminder that Juliana was not her child. No, Juliana very closely resembled her beautiful mother. Juliana had been told that her mother died in childbirth, but in reality she had been taken when Juliana was one year old. No one was ever allowed to so much as speak the woman's name, much less to mention the circumstances of her tragic end. Sebastián behaved as though he could obliterate through sheer will what to him was a disgraceful truth about the mother of his only child.

Despite what he had done, Ana loved her brother and knew that he had nearly been destroyed by the manner of his wife's demise. So, since Emilio's death, as Sebastián had imposed ever more frequently upon Ana to plan and supervise the elaborate dinners he gave for his political acquaintances, she willingly came to his aid.

Tomorrow was just such a dinner, and Ana sighed at the thought. She finished her breakfast of bread and let the thick chocolate drink that was so popular linger in her mouth an extra moment. She donned a plain dress, pulled her hair back into a simple bun, and went out to see what was ailing the Sánchez child.

Ana never hesitated to do all that her knowledge allowed her to do for a sick child. In this way, she told herself, she played out by proxy a woman's role, for she had never had her own child. Though they had never spoken of it before their marriage, Ana and Emilio had each held the secret faith within their hearts that there might be a baby, for why would God deny them the blessings that He bestowed so lavishly upon others? When familiarity had worn through their initial shyness with each other, they had begun to speak of this wish. Ana was past her best childbearing years, but each thought that hope might not be in vain. Time passed, and Ana became pregnant but miscarried. After that, their loving became a chore, done methodically to achieve an end, no end in itself.

As no child came, they had slowly let their hope die, to appreciate what they had, to find their love again. Still, each time a youngster was brought to them for treatment, they had carefully shielded their eyes from each other.

"The rash is nothing serious, but I have an ointment that can offer your boy some comfort."

"Thank you, señora, but if he does not need it to recover . . ." Ana suspected that her hesitation was due to embarrassment at having already encroached upon Ana's

charity. The mother had probably brought the child only because she had feared that the red marks mottling her son's
back were portents of a greater danger, for she had lost a
daughter only the previous spring. The daughter had died in
one of the hospitals for the destitute, and the woman had
confided in Ana that she no longer trusted such places and
for that reason had sought out Ana's help. Though Ana knew
from her husband that the charity hospitals varied in the
care they offered, she did not try to convince the woman to
place her child's fate in their hands again.

"In fact," Ana began, as she turned and rummaged
through the jars on a high shelf, "every day I must inventory
all of my medicines." She continued, as though the ointment
itself had now become her major concern, "I mix most of
them myself, and some of them retain their potency for only
a limited time." She retrieved a jar and held it to the light.
"Yes, this must be used shortly." Having transferred the need
from the child to the salve, Ana dipped three fingers into the
jar and placed the unction on the palm of her opposite hand.

"This may feel a little cold, child," she said softly to the
boy, gently spreading the balm across his back in a circular
blessing. As she traced his contours, the tension in the
child's body eased, but Ana did not notice when her comfort reached him. Her eyes saw only her own hand, and then
not even that. Standing where Emilio had stood, her hand
precisely miming the patterns she had seen a thousand
times, she began to sink, to become engulfed by the sense of
her dead husband. She yielded to the allure, and it was not
that he was there with her, but that she merged with him
and was subsumed in him, and there was consolation in
that fusion. She did not wish to leave. This was not the
rapture of the soul transfigured by the presence of God, as
described by Santa Teresa de Ávila or San Juan de la Cruz,
but it was consummation. Briefly she had escaped the

prison of the body, which holds the mind hostage until death. Perhaps she would find this union with Emilio tonight as she read his journal.

2

Emilio

Journal of Emilio Cardero Díaz
Age 31
Madrid
January, Year of Our Lord 1639

Today I have seen the most wonderful play, *The New World Discovered by Cristóbal Colón*, written some twenty-six years ago by our great dramatist Lope de Vega. Lope shows to us a Colón who dares to dream amid a chorus of mockery. Surely his quest was not only for riches, but for truth.

I have always had the seed of desire to go to this New Land, not to conquer or convert, but to discover it anew for myself, to see what hope it offers. I will read what I can, and record my thoughts here, in preparation for the day when, free from obligations to my parents and siblings, I might make my journey.

February 1639

I have obtained a copy of a biography of Colón, said to be written by his son, Hernando. It was published in Venice some seventy years ago and was difficult to find. It is strange that so little has been written of this man, since Spain rode to glory on the discoveries of "*el capitán de Isabel.*" And what of those cries of "gold, God, and glory" that brought adventurers and holy men alike to the new lands' shores? History will give its judgment to Colón, whose life affected the Old World and the New. Surely, though, the bringing of the Holy Faith to the poor heathens there cannot but be counted good.

March 1639

I mentioned my interest in the Indies in a letter to my former professor at the Universidad de Salamanca. He has most kindly sent me a copy of a study he had by a Sevillian physician, Nicolás Monardes. It is a survey of the medicinal plants of America and is titled *Joyful News out of the New Found World.* Though it was written fifty years ago, from what I have studied thus far, it does not seem as though many of Monardes's discoveries have been used here, though of course he mentions lignum vitae, the New World's cure for its disease called syphilis. Can it be that God has hidden in this world the cure for all our ills, if only we are brave enough to find them? If only, in our rush to tame, we do not destroy.

April 1639

A friend has directed me to a most extensive study, which, though written in the time of Felipe II, has not been widely published. The author of this impressive work was one Dr. Francisco Hernández. There must be entries for over a thousand drugs and remedies, most of which Hernández learned of from the Aztecs. Among them is the use of sarsaparilla as a diuretic for kidney and bladder ailments. It can also be taken to treat rashes.

It is a matter of amazement to me that the Aztecs could have been so advanced in the study of medicine. For, although I do not know whether all of these remedies are effective, it can hardly be said that all treatments commonly practiced in Europe are in fact curative. No, it is rather the obviously systematic study that intrigues me, for how can such steadfast diligence help but lead to greater knowledge?

At least some of the peoples of these new lands must be more developed than is commonly thought. How I would love to observe them myself! Until that time, I will read what I can of them. Surely there are more writings by learned men who go beyond the simple descriptions penned by returned soldiers and merchants.

3

A N A

Ana slowly closed the journal, refraining from looking ahead to see when her name might appear. Though she had thought that she would rush through the writings, she decided to parse them, to prolong the time that she was hearing afresh from her Emilio.

As Ana pondered Emilio's writing the next morning, she admitted to herself that she had never been much concerned with those lands so far away. It seemed that they touched her life not at all. From time to time Emilio would mention something about them, but she had often only half listened. Ana had been a girl in her father's house, a woman in a convent, a wife in her husband's home. How would thoughts of those alien lands even have entered her dreams?

Her day proceeded as usual, ministering to those who had come seeking her help. At times Ana would even skip her siesta if there were people waiting for her. Today had been such a day, and as she climbed the stairs to her room to prepare for the dinner at her brother's home, Ana again reflected on Sebastián's insistence on her presence at these periodic events. Perhaps he thought that she would feel needed to have a man to cater to, and this annoyed and touched her. Though he had not always succeeded, Sebastián had always tried to read her heart. If he truly thought that he required her aid, how could she deny him? If his motive was to make her feel needed, how could she rupture the complicity that is required when those we love seek to succor us?

Still, she wished that Sebastián were less demanding in his attempt to rescue her, even directing how she was to dress.

"You must look the part of the hostess of a house such as mine," he had complained in the early days of her assumption of that role.

"But why must I wear the elaborate and extremely uncomfortable costume with which the wives of your acquaintances choose to adorn themselves? My apparel is in every way modest."

"It is not about modesty. It is about what is expected in the household of someone of my rank. What you wear reflects upon me. After all, I am an important member of the Cortes of Madrid."

And so Ana had acquiesced, though the hours of discomfort she endured had hardly seemed justifiable in light of the very few moments she was actually seen by her brother's male guests. At his side, she briefly greeted the guests as they arrived, and then she and any ladies who had accompanied their husbands would retire to an adjoining room, where they dined separately from the men, ostensibly so they would not have to endure the masculine discussions of politics and the state of the country. Ana knew that for some of the women a dinner at Sebastián's was a treat, as most husbands did not necessarily bring their wives to social events. Sebastián's table was also always generously laid with marinated meats and stews, with fruits and almond cakes for dessert.

A few months before, Ana had brought up the subject

of the furnishings in the room where the women dined. It consisted of the traditional accoutrements of mats, low tables, and large cushions. Ana had mentioned to her brother the opinion of her late husband, who had traveled in France and Italy, that the Spanish custom was a holdover from seven centuries of occupation by the Moors. Emilio had argued that, although the Catholic monarchs Ferdinand and Isabel had long ago rid the land of the last occupying Moors with the capture of Granada in that momentous year of 1492, and even the Moriscos, those of Christianized Muslim descent, had been expelled early in the present century, some Spaniards unwittingly clung to Moorish ways.

When Ana had broached the subject with her brother, he had replied, "Sister, I know that Emilio had an unusual arrangement in your home, and though I loved and respected him, he had some opinions with which I did not agree. We follow the custom of our own pure-blooded forefathers." Ana had bitten her tongue and subjugated her opinion to her love for her brother, for he and Juliana were her only hope of escaping her loneliness. Then unexpectedly, some weeks later, Sebastián had installed chairs in the room, which surprised the women, but to which they happily adapted.

Three weeks ago, Sebastián had again shown his ability to alter his customs, and for the last two dinners, the men and women had eaten in the same room. Ana had noticed that the ladies, no less than the gentlemen, seemed uncomfortable, but Sebastián had announced his belief that the new arrangement would prove edifying for the women, allowing them to observe the serious nature of their husbands' discourses. It would also curtail the idle gossip that he believed was the main focus of the ladies' dinners. Finally, there was no need to further safeguard the modesty of the ladies, since all were proper wives with honorable husbands. Juliana, however, would no longer be allowed to attend.

Ana had mused that in some ways her brother was more open-minded than most of his peers. It seemed that at times he liked to flaunt his slightly unconventional ideas, including his belief that women should be educated, which in reality their father had instilled in him. Perhaps Sebastián felt that this image fit in well with his work as an *arbitrista*, those self-appointed creators of solutions to the country's myriad problems.

As she now opened the door of her *armario* to choose which gown she would wear, Ana had to admit to herself that she had taken more care of her appearance for those last two dinners than she had done previously. It was not the case that she expected to attract the eye of one of the gentlemen, for she knew that she could not, even if she had aspired to it. No, her wish was simply that the guests might think, *Sebastián's sister looks less ill-favored than usual this evening.*

Ana caught her reflection in the mirror above the paneled drawer fronts that served as her dressing table. The fingers of her left hand grazed her face lightly. She was again surprised at the discrepancy between the face she saw reflected back and the softened, more delicate version her imagination had soothed her mind into remembering. When she had been young, some days she had been able to unearth some pleasant aspect, if not beauty, but when she had entered the convent, Ana had forgone the use of a mirror, though many did not. Now she regretted those lost years, for when she had returned to the world, she had not been able to discover any kinder traces of the past.

Though he had cared for her deeply, Emilio had never called her fair. While she told herself that she was glad Emilio had loved her for herself and not her face, part of her would have relished inspiring love with beauty. Such beauty does not last, she knew from church and poetry and life, but it might have outlived her beloved. Surely, to have added loveliness to the world through her mere presence would not have been an evil gift.

Ana had loved Emilio, and his loss was a dagger in her heart, which only time would scar over. Still, she sometimes found herself wondering about another life that might have been. If she had been more comely, she might have married young, had children, and someday grandchildren to comfort her in her old age. "God made me thus," was her oft-repeated chastisement and consolation when she sank into these musings, "and if my life has followed from the plainness of my face, then that, too, has been His will."

Embracing this philosophy, and because of her status as a widow, Ana did not resort to the use of elaborate cosmetics: no ceruse foundation cream, over which pink or vermillion paint could be applied. She wore no wax upon her lips. There was something of submission to God's will in this, but at the same time a kind of pride that said, *I will not stoop to the futile indignity of trying to create a face that others will find more pleasing.* She did spray herself with rosewater and spread almond paste upon her hands.

Unable to postpone it longer, Ana called Clara to her room to help her dress. She did not wear the most elaborate version of the *guardainfante* framework of whalebone hoops and osier twigs, but donning even a modified form required aid. Clara began her familiar refrain.

"I find it shameful that Don Sebastián should subject

a respectable widow to the humiliation of dining with men not of her family." Clara's continuous reference to Ana as a "respectable widow" had begun to sound like advice, rather than description.

"It is Sebastián's wish, and there is nothing immodest about it. In truth, I have found the political discussions particularly interesting," Ana replied, as she stepped into the mass of hoops, which Clara then lifted to her waist, tied, and covered with a cinching corset.

"Interesting! Yes, I suppose that many improper things might be termed interesting," retorted Clara, with an extra tug at the corset strings. Both women concentrated as they lifted the black silk dress over the underpinning they had just constructed. The skirt cascaded down the petticoat, and the hem gathered in folds upon the floor. Even when she had her leather shoes on, the hem would drag on the ground, the price a lady paid for keeping her feet concealed.

"You cannot tell me that those men are not harboring indecent thoughts when they see displayed before them women in disarray," Clara continued, as she adjusted the ballooned sleeves, slashed at the wrists to reveal a lining of pale blue, the only relief to the widow's black of Ana's costume.

"I would hardly call it disarray to be sitting on a chair at a table." Ana laughed. "Besides, you needn't worry about me, since I am hardly likely to be the object of the gentlemen's desires."

"And what of the others?" Clara asked, as she continued to adjust the fall of the dress, and Ana could not help but feel some pain that Clara had not bothered to politely contradict her.

"Emilio approved," Ana replied simply, using her proven weapon against Clara's scolding. Ana knew that Clara had always held Emilio in such esteem that she would have counted him a living saint had this not seemed heretical to her.

"Well, Don Emilio—God rest his soul, though I'm sure he doesn't need my blessing—even Don Emilio could be subject to some odd ideas from his readings about heathen lands."

"Heathen, all under the mantle of Holy Mother Church? For shame, Clara!"

Clara did not respond, but pulled a little harder as she braided, twisted, and pinned Ana's hair into place. Next she wrapped Ana's manta over her body, covering her from head to foot, and silently walked with her to the door. Many fashionable ladies wore mantas of tulle or transparent silk, but the effect of these was often more one of coquetry than of modesty. Ana preferred her brown watered-silk manta, which allowed her to conceal the fact that at times she left the house wearing her comfortable but plain gowns.

Hoping to restore harmony, Ana said, "Besides, if I didn't go to these dinners, how could I tell you about the ridiculous plain-lensed spectacles that Doña Elvira wore last week?"

"I thought that fashion was losing favor," said Clara, conspiring with Ana to ignore the unpleasant moment of their discussion of each other's virtue.

"Though she prides herself on wearing the epitome of the latest fashions, by the time she catches on, they are usually on the way out. Doña María was even more entertaining clumping about on her high-heeled chopines." Both of the women laughed at the image of the portly señora teetering on her high cork heels. "At least my height allows me to forgo that particular insanity," Ana said. She pulled the manta more closely around her face and stepped out her door and into her brother's waiting carriage.

It was true, what she had told Clara: that the gentlemen's political discourses had caught her interest. The week before, someone had cast aspersions on His Majesty's favored minister, Marquis Luis Méndez de Haro, nephew of the former royal favorite, the much-maligned Count-Duke Olivares. One gentleman claimed that de Haro's policies were what squelched trade and contributed to a series of monetary crises. While Ana had often heard her brother criticize de Haro's ideas, and most especially the unfavorable Treaty of the Pyrenees, completed two years earlier, he did not blindly condemn all that de Haro did. At the dinner, Sebastián had reminded his guests that not all of the fault could be laid at de Haro's door.

"The marquis cannot take all the blame, surely, for our dismal economy, for efforts to improve it meet only with hostility. The well-born Spaniard disdains the work of merchants as below him, and those who do successfully take it up are suspected of being conversos, with the blood of Jewish forebears running through their veins. Those of the highest aristocracy, whose wealth comes from their land, escape the stigma of work, as the very peasants who work their fields, by virtue of their poverty, it seems, boast of their *pureza de sangre*, pure blood untainted by Jew or Moor. These are hardly the attitudes of a society that would prosper in the world of trade, where only the ignorant peasant works and those successful men of higher birth are subjected to accusations of tainted ancestry."

For a few moments no one replied to this attack upon the mores of the land, but then Sebastián's guests had indulged in a heated defense of the superiority of Spain's beliefs, of its love of honor, and of Catholicism.

Ana believed that Sebastián's arguments had been in defense not only of de Haro, but of the programs of His

Majesty's government. As conditions in the country deteriorated, many whispered, then spoke aloud, uncomplimen-
tary comparisons between Felipe IV and his grandfather
the great Felipe II, or even between the current monarch
and his father, but Sebastián was never one of these.

Many *arbitristas* freely disparaged His Majesty, but
Sebastián, though his recommendations for change could
be seen as an implied criticism of the king's government,
had once told Ana that he saw them as a kind of homage
to Felipe, the offering of the product of his intellect to his
most sovereign lord. Ana and Sebastián had often heard
their father say that to speak ill of the king was to speak
ill of the monarchy, of Spain itself, and Ana knew that Sebastián's honor would never allow him to sink to the level
of the complaining malcontents. Her brother had always
been thus inclined, and his constancy had been repaid and
reinforced by the monarch's uncustomary indulgence upon
the death of Juliana's mother.

Yes, Clara, Ana thought, as she entered Sebastián's
home, *I have found the discussions of my brother's guests
most enlightening, and I hope to do so again tonight.*

But the evening had not been what Ana had hoped. The
men seemed in a mood to make claims without providing
reasoning, and the discussion soon descended into acrimony.
As honorary hostess, Ana had felt it her duty to spare the
ladies this ordeal and had reluctantly interrupted the discussion, begging the gentlemen to postpone their debate.
Chivalry had at once ruled, and most of the men had
apologized, offering the quite plausible excuse that they
were not accustomed to dining with ladies and had fallen
into their usual habits.

Upon arriving home, Ana pled a headache, so as to

limit discussion with Clara while the maid aided her in removing her encumbering garments. Having dismissed Clara, Ana retrieved from the chest at the end of her bed Emilio's journal and pulled back the leather cover to reveal his fine hand.

4

Emilio

I had hoped to be able to return to these pages with the answer that has so occupied my mind. But, alas, I find that the more I read, the less I am able to form a view of the natives of those lands across the sea.

I have taken advantage of the few political contacts that I have to get hold of manuscripts not generally available. One acquaintance, a secretary to a member of the Council of the Indies, has been most helpful in allowing me to borrow reports written for the council. When I expressed my concern that his position might be jeopardized if it were discovered that someone outside the official sphere was reading the papers, he answered that, for the man who had done such a great service to his family in treating his ill father, he was bound by honor to perform a service for me. Besides, he added, perhaps to further ease my discomfort, the manuscripts, some already decades old, were so numerous and so unorganized that no one would ever notice that any individual study was missing for a brief period of time. In the unlikely event that the file that I was reading should be asked for, he could readily retrieve it from me.

In final answer to any anxiety I might feel on his

behalf, he said, "Don Emilio, we trusted you with the life of my father. How could I not trust you with some papers?" At times I feel both blessed and unworthy to practice my profession. It offers me so much: a livelihood, the gratification of being able to help others, intellectual stimulation, and this gratitude from patients for simply performing the duties of my position, as does any man.

But to my subject, where I confess that my readings serve more to broaden than to dispel my confusion. Who are these people I would know? Are they barbarians, as described by so many returning conquistadores, who thus justified their slaughter? Or should we see in the very difference of those races an innate nobility that we have lost, as Peter Martyr d'Anghiera wrote in *Decades* over a century ago?

Juan de Betanzos, in his *Narrative of the Incas*, says that the conquistadores could not understand because they did not choose to do so, and that simply learning the language of a people can open the door to their ways. What does it say of those in the area of Brazil that they pierce their lips and cheeks with pointed bones or green stones, or paint their thighs and legs with dye, as Jean de Léry wrote? Though de Léry was both French and a minister of the heretical Calvinist group, his descriptions are intriguing, and the fact that he does not condemn even more so.

Perhaps we can see only what we already know. If we did not know a sailing ship for what it was, might we not, upon seeing it in the distance, think it some gigantic water bird, its head concealed by spreading wings? We might fear it for its power, or disdain it for its bestiality, but we would hardly ascribe to it complexity or sophistication, or any affinity to men such as ourselves. So it is with the men of the Indies, who might be other than we see, with our quick labels of savagery or nobility. Perhaps they are neither so base nor so exalted, but merely men, who have constructed for themselves ideas and rules to try to understand and tame the world around them, as we have constructed country, honor, and perhaps even religion (though it would be construed heretical to say so) to explain and complicate our lives.

November 1639

I despair of ever understanding the population of the New World. It is not only that the European writings contradict one another, but also that the number and variety of the groups of peoples there is so vast. If a stranger from a faraway land came to what we call Europe, what would he see—one group: Europeans; dozens of groups: French, Dutch, Spaniards, English; hundreds of groups: Andalusians, Neapolitans, Lombards, Scots; or thousands: Castilian hidalgos, Roman priests, Venetian beggars, English tradesmen? Stranger still, would they classify us in ways we have yet to imagine? Thus I wonder whether we have clustered and arranged those inhabitants of the Indies as they divide or unite themselves.

Some even put forward the theory that the Indians were made by nature to be our slaves. It is doubtful that before we invaded the lands of the Indies, their inhabitants saw themselves as slaves to men whose existence they did not imagine. Yet what they are now will forever be a reaction to what has happened to them since we strangers came. The peoples who were there are no more. And what of the tens of thousands we have killed with our greed, our diseases, and our swords?

March 1640

Though I have not altered my belief that we have forever changed the true face of the Americas, I am told that there is still much to be seen there that is fantastic and novel, both the peoples and the landscape, which is said to be passing strange.

I have thought of a way that I might make my journey, by putting on as ship's physician in some trading fleet to the Indies, though this must remain a future dream. For now, my duties to my family must prevail. I shall hold close and secret my vision of a voyage to those lands.

July 1640

I will be traveling much sooner than I had anticipated, but not to my desired destination. My brother has asked me to go to Naples for him, to oversee the selling of some of his assets there. I cannot deny that I undertake this trip with some reluctance. I have little experience with matters of business, but my brother has taken pains to explain to me in some detail the nature of my task there, and I believe it will not lie outside the realm of my competence.

The other reason for my hesitance is one that I would confess only to myself, for I fear that it betrays some smallness of character on my part. Does it not seem presumptuous of my brother to ask me for help, when his business was given to him exclusively by our father? It is true that our father felt that to divide the business would have provided neither of us with sufficient income to live in a style suited to our birth, and that he paid generously for my education. Neither has my brother become fantastically wealthy, though he and his family live very comfortably, while I have had to earn my way as a physician, a profession that many of my birth would disdain. Though I find my occupation's rewards go far beyond the monetary, this is simply a happy circumstance. I might just as easily have found myself earning my way by some more irksome means.

Still, my brother will pay for the journey and compensate me well for my time. He says there is no one else he can trust in these dealings, and so he relies upon me. I shall go by sea and thus test my constitution for the rigors of such a voyage.

5

ANA

If there had been witnesses, they would have seen the jerking movements sometimes made in sleep, a physical connection to the world of dreams, unlooked for and disconcerting, emissaries that, when they awaken us, add to our unease. Ana knew that the dreams had commenced at the time of her sister-in-law's death, some sixteen years earlier, yet in the dream she was always a child, not understanding the source of her terror but perceiving the dread and fascination of those around her.

Ana put the dream from her mind, as much as she was ever able to do. Life may be a dream, and even that dream composed of dreams, as Don Calderón de la Barca suggested in his play, but Ana had found that often dreams were more intense, not more ephemeral, than waking reality. Too frequently sleep did not offer the desired oblivion.

Nor had her dream put out of her mind the pages she had read the night before. Emilio had continued with his speculations about the New World, and though the pages dated from before she knew him, she could not help but feel hurt by the fact that he had never spoken in any depth to her of these studies and speculation. Neither had he ever spoken of his desire to venture across the sea.

Putting these thoughts aside, Ana pushed back the bed

curtains. It was early, for the light had barely begun to show itself through the opaque windows, but she decided to rise and manage her dress alone, since she did not wish to hear Clara's prattle this morning, her sermons of responsibility. Ana had done her share of duty.

Yet she recognized that solace could be found in helping others, as she had learned at the convent and in her work with Emilio. Those who came for her help were those who could only rely on her charity, for they had no other resources. Ana did not live lavishly and so could use what she had to help others. Her brother had objected to his sister's doing such work, though he had kept that to himself while Emilio had lived, but in this Ana had not allowed him to overrule her.

As she approached the part of the house that had been reserved for her ministering, already there were people waiting for her in the courtyard. She greeted them all, assuring them that she would give to each what help she could. She silently prayed that it would be enough, if not to save, at least to mitigate pain or postpone tragedy.

The day went quickly as she immersed herself in the maladies of others, and at its end she asked to have a simple meal brought to her room, as she had no energy for anything more formal. The quiet of her room was a welcome shelter, and she ate and then readied herself for bed.

Juliana had asked to meet her the following morning for Mass, and Ana wished to be well rested for her time with her beloved niece, with whom she expected to spend much of the day. She knew that Sebastián had treated his daughter to an afternoon at the theater that day, and she hoped that the girl would wish to share her experience with her aunt.

Sebastián, though strict with Juliana, was not of the opinion, as were so many fathers, that to educate a daughter was to invite rebellious behavior. He had declared that, were a student to receive proper guidance, education would not only enlighten the mind but refine the sensibilities, sharpen the understanding, and instill a respect for propriety. The course of Juliana's studies had been quite dry, and Ana had suggested to her brother that some lighter reading, such as works of fiction, would not only be enjoyable but could be edifying as well.

Finally, Sebastián had relented. "Very well, but I will select the books. Heaven knows what you might see as fit reading for a young girl, Ana. Undoubtedly, you would think that even a picaresque novel—*Lazarillo de Tormes*, perhaps, or a ridiculous tale of chivalrous knights—would be appropriate. Cervantes had it right when he skewered those fantastical works, which pose for their heroes some simplistic problems, inevitably solved with a sword, and set women to dreaming of brave and handsome fools. Still, neither would I have my daughter read *Don Quixote*. Though the object of the parody is well deserving of the treatment it receives, I'll not have my daughter learn that subtle form of disrespect."

"No, I would not have had her read any of those works," Ana had replied, though it was more the disillusion of the second part of the *Quixote* from which she would desire to shield Juliana. There would be opportunity enough later in her niece's life to understand the poignancy of the fate of the would-be knight errant.

Sebastián had decided upon works of some fairly contemporary playwrights, who conveyed the types of lessons he wanted his daughter to learn. He had given Juliana a beautiful leather journal on her birthday, believing that it would be an added inducement to a serious study of the morals to be found in the works. Ana had been touched to see how pleased her niece had been with her gift, a far cry from the new gown or necklace that other girls of her age and class would have received.

Ana again considered a comment her niece had made the week before. Juliana had not shared very much with Ana about her studies, and Ana had felt a little hurt. She had waited for the girl to mention something about her readings, but when she hadn't, Ana had brought up the subject. A murmured "My father is not satisfied with how I view the plays," was the only response she had received, and Ana did not press her, for she knew that Juliana loved and respected her father and wished to please him.

The previous evening, as she had bidden farewell to Sebastián, Ana had commented on the upcoming trip to the theater. "I have put it off for as long as I could, being reluctant to expose Juliana to the gaze of so many young men, but I hope that seeing a play performed will give her a better understanding of its intended message," her brother had replied seriously, and Ana had recalled Juliana's words.

As she pulled out Emilio's journal, Ana brushed aside any disquieting implications of these remarks and hoped that the experience of having seen a play performed would make Juliana more loquacious about her studies. She smiled to herself in anticipation of the time she would spend with her niece, as she opened the book on her lap. She would read only a little while. She had gotten to a section where Emilio had inserted some extra sheets. This would work out well, for they were brief, and Ana could read them and then rest. Emilio must not have taken his journal on the trip of which he had spoken, for these sheets were written in Padua. In his enthusiasm for the medical discussions he had engaged in there, he seemed not to have been able to wait until his return home to record his thoughts.

6

Emilio

Having concluded my brother's business in Naples, I traveled north to Padua, desirous as I was of attending some lectures at the university here, this great seat of medical learning, where Andreas Vesalius himself studied and gave us his great work, *De Humani Corporis Fabrica Libri Septem*, on the anatomy of the human body. I treasure my own copy of this book, which my mentor gave to me upon completion of my studies at the Universidad de Salamanca. His grandfather had known Vesalius when the great anatomist had been at the court of Felipe II, and so he valued the book all the more, and the gift touched me greatly.

As exciting as Vesalius's refutation of Galen's view of human anatomy was for the last century, I believe that the work of an Englishman named William Harvey may be to ours. I had heard of a book he published a decade ago, but many refuted it at the time. Harvey received his doctorate in Padua in 1602, and some here still remember his brilliance. They tell me of Harvey's exciting work on the topic of human blood. Making use of the description of the valves in the veins, done by his teacher here, Giralomo Fabrizio, and of his own extensive observations, measurements, and calculations, Harvey has shown that the blood cannot be constantly made in the liver and sent to the tissues, as Galen taught. Harvey believes that the blood is constantly circulated throughout the body, and that this is the reason for the beating of the heart! I do not know how this new understanding might one day affect the way we practice our profession, but these new discoveries are like finding another world within us.

ANA

It had been a long time since Ana had anticipated a day with true delight, but the prospect of seeing Juliana afforded her great pleasure. Ana set aside the nagging doubt she had experienced the previous night upon reading of Emilio's excitement about the future of his calling. She had known that the ministrations she offered were merely pale imitations of what Emilio would have been able to employ. Still, she decided to forgive herself for not having the training that would never have been allowed her as a woman anyway, and turned her thoughts to her niece.

Juliana had been not merely ardent in her request, but insistent that they attend Mass at the Iglesia de San Nicolás where Ana, but not Juliana, usually worshipped. Ana suspected that there was a certain young man there whose smile Juliana sought, but she could see no harm in this, though she knew that Sebastián would not tolerate even this small liberty to be taken with his daughter. Still, Ana could not reproach herself. Accompanying her niece to Holy Mass could hardly qualify her as a go-between. She was also anxious to hear Juliana's impressions of the theater.

Ana would take Communion at Mass and so would not breakfast. Having dressed and descended, Ana instructed Clara that dinner should be light, donned her manta, and left the house.

As Ana approached the twelfth-century Iglesia de San Nicolás, she studied the brick tower with its horseshoe arches. The Mudéjar architecture was unmistakable, and she had even heard it said that the tower had originally been the minaret of a Moorish mosque. Some were scandalized at such a thought, but Ana believed it and even found it fitting that the beautiful structure had, like so many of the Moors themselves, become part of the one true faith.

Ana thought that she saw Juliana, though it was difficult to distinguish one young lady from another in the sea of mantas. In Ana's youth, one would have seen many women wearing the *tapado*, the veil that revealed only a hint of the face beneath. More than twenty years ago His Majesty had prohibited that covering attire, and he had not been the first to try to forbid it. Those who defied the law risked a fine of a thousand *maravedís*, and double that for second offenders. Still, courtesans used it to pass themselves off as ladies of quality, and even highborn women sometimes made a clever use of the *tapado*, adding mystery meant more to excite men than to repel them.

Having finally sighted Juliana and the squat figure of Silvia, *dueña* to Juliana, as she had been to Ana in her childhood, Ana headed for the pair. As she approached, she noticed her niece looking about, the manta exaggerating the discreet movements of her head. Ana thought that she was looking for Antonio, whom Juliana had mentioned to her in passing the week before, with the hint of a blush coloring her cheeks. Nearing Juliana and Silvia, however, she noticed that the girl's movements seemed agitated.

Upon reaching her niece, Ana was taken aback. This was more than disappointment at not seeing a dashing young gentleman. Juliana's eyes were red, her skin pale and translucent. In response to Juliana's quiet greeting "*Buenos días*, Tía," Ana took her niece's hands in hers.

"Juliana, *querida*, what is wrong?" Before Juliana could answer, Silvia stepped to Juliana's side, close to Ana, nearly blocking Juliana from Ana's view.

"She does not feel well, Doña Ana. I begged her not to come to Mass, but as we were afraid that word would not reach you before you left, Juliana did not want to leave you waiting."

Ana hid the annoyance she felt at Silvia's interference as she said, "Oh, I'm so sorry that you have come. Juliana really does look quite unwell."

"Perhaps it is something she ate, or the excitement of her excursion to the theater yesterday." Again Silvia had replied, and Juliana seemed content to have it so.

"Has Sebastián seen her? I'm surprised he let her leave the house in such a condition."

Silvia and Juliana exchanged glances, and Silvia explained, "We did not see Don Sebastián this morning."

"Perhaps we should not stay for Mass but take Juliana home."

"Oh, no, Tía!" Juliana had found her voice. "I must stay for Mass, and I also wish to make my confession."

"What sins can you have, *mi amor*, that would need to be confessed?"

"Please, Tía Ana—I feel fine. Please allow me to stay."

Ana chided herself for the frivolous motivations she had ascribed to her niece's desire to attend Mass. Juliana was a serious young girl, much as Ana herself had been, and Ana remembered the need she had sometimes felt to seek comfort in the confessional for some small infraction of thought, word, or deed.

"Very well, but afterward you must allow me to go home with you and examine you, and no complaining about whatever I deem you need."

"Thank you, Tía."

Mass was about to begin, and Juliana and Silvia followed Ana to her customary place. At first her worry about Juliana disturbed Ana's thoughts, but as the priest intoned the beautiful Gregorian chant, she let its grace soothe her. Though one shouldn't give importance to such things, she was grateful that it was Padre Carrillo who was celebrating Mass today. The lines of the chant, their rising and falling notes surrounding the repeated tone of the line of prayer, seemed to reverberate deeply in his rotund figure.

Ana reflected upon how the rituals of faith contained varied treasures, depending upon the needs of the seeker. Comfort and hope, salvation from eternal suffering, redemption from the silent haunting of a deed repented. For Ana, it was beauty. The magnificent architecture of a cathedral, the delicate invitation of the chapel at her convent, the curve of the jaw of a lovely statue of Our Lady, the brocade of the celebrant's vestments, her beloved Gregorian chant. Yet Ana knew that these were but the gateways to the beauty of ideas, love, sacrifice, forgiveness. Christ had offered to Peter the keys to the kingdom of heaven, and Holy Mother Church taught that in this act, Our Lord had given us the sacrament of Penance, with its power to wipe clean our souls. But the key was something more. The key was his example and his words "Love your neighbor as yourself," which would open to us an earthly paradise. Though Ana felt herself no less guilty than others of forgetting this maxim, the idea that man could aspire to such a goal was what struck her with its splendor.

As the church emptied, Juliana joined the line outside the confessional. Neither Ana nor Silvia accompanied her, as all three had received the sacrament only the week before. Ana worried that Juliana's fervor was excessive at times. There was nothing intrinsically to be censured in devotion, but in the convent Ana had also seen the effects on those who demanded of themselves a too-exacting adherence to pious ways. The least of the dangers was a loss of joy in one's faith. The worst was a descent into fanaticism, which, while punishing the flesh, could become a kind of perverse pride in one's own piety.

Ana could not help but notice that Juliana was lingering longer than usual in the confessional, and she hoped that the priest would refrain from showing his irritation at having to listen to the self-accusations of a young girl's overly active conscience. When her niece emerged from the confessional in tears, it seemed to Ana that her worries had been justified, and by the time she reached Juliana, her indignation at the priest's lack of patience was complete.

"What did he say to you?" she blurted out, her agitation so great that she momentarily forgot the sacred secrecy of the confessional.

Juliana looked at her aunt with anguish in her eyes but replied only, "Nothing that I did not expect." In response to her questioning look, Silvia shook her head almost imperceptibly. In testament to Ana's faith in Silvia's love for Juliana, Ana simply took her niece's cold hand and placed it on her own arm. Adjusting Juliana's manta to hide her face in shadow, she led her niece out into the street. Silvia followed the pair, and on her face was etched a look of fear.

"Juliana, you must go directly to bed, and I will make you a decoction to warm you. You seem so cold, *querida*. Do you feel weak?" Ana asked upon crossing Sebastián's threshold.

"Really, Tía, I'm fine. Please, don't trouble yourself. It is simply that I did not sleep well last night."

Worried about some imagined guilt, thought Ana. If only she could impart to her niece the simple truth that she herself had learned, that God did not make us perfect creatures, and that to agonize over our faults was to question His wisdom. If the Creator had expected us to be flawless, there would be no need for the sacrament of Penance. Our Lord would not have had to teach forgiveness, both human and divine. *How can I impart to her this acceptance of herself, which took me so many years to learn?* Ana wondered. But Juliana was Sebastián's daughter, and he had never learned to accept fault, whether in himself or in others.

"Juliana, I know that I have no right to ask, but are you making yourself ill over whatever it was that you talked to Father about after Mass?"

"It is nothing for you to worry about, Tía."

"I tell you, Doña Ana, I believe that it is just something that Juliana ate, or the excitement of her attendance at the theater," Silvia interjected.

"Why would that make her cold and pale, Silvia?" Ana replied sharply. She thought she had again caught a look of complicity pass quickly between the girl and her *dueña*. "Where is Sebastián? Let's see what he has to say about this."

"No! Please, Doña Ana, you know that he would be angry with me for taking Juliana to Mass if there were any hint that she was not feeling well."

"Please, Tía, don't tell Papa. I insisted that Silvia take me. I don't mind Papa's scolding, but I don't wish to make trouble for Silvia."

"Is your father such a tyrant that his displeasure is to be so feared?" Ana asked gently. "I will say nothing to him, if only you'll rest now, Juliana, and follow my instructions."

Ana left the room and found that her threat had been an empty one, since her brother had already left the house. She went to the kitchen and prepared the mixture for Juliana, then saw that the girl was put to bed. When her niece drifted into an uneasy sleep, Ana returned home, as she had promised to see the Sánchez child again. She had told Silvia that she would come that evening to check on her niece. She did not go, however, for just as she was about to leave for Sebastián's home, she received a note in Juliana's hand.

Dearest Tía Ana,

I am sorry if I caused you any distress this morning. As I am feeling quite well now, you need not trouble yourself to come this evening to check on me. Although I would, as always, greatly enjoy your company, I am afraid that I must finish some reading that Father has assigned me, and do a journal entry. I shall see you soon.

Your devoted niece,
Juliana

Ana slowly refolded the paper. While she was relieved that Juliana seemed to have recovered, the note pained her in a way that went beyond its content or tone. It had brought home to her again the feeling of isolation that she was so often required to combat. She was only an intruder in the lives of others.

Ana told herself that if Sebastián had noted any lingering pallor in his daughter, he surely would have called upon his sister's advice. Still, it was with a feeling of unease that she opened her husband's journal to the place she had marked with a ribbon

8

Emilio

Madrid, December 1640

Although my travels for my brother have shown that I
have an affinity for sea travel, I fear that I will not be able
to go to the New World for some time. I have ascertained
that putting on as a ship's physician with a trade fleet
going there is more complicated than I had hoped. It
seems that there is more competition for such positions
than I imagined. As with all else, one needs connections.

February 1641

I have purchased a book, *The Indian Militia and
Description of the Indies*, by a Spanish captain, Bernardo
de Vargas Machuca, published at the turn of the century.
On the frontispiece is a print of a man, one would presume
the captain, holding a navigator's compass on top of a
globe, the other hand holding a sword. The man's head
looks somewhat large for his body. His ruffled collar perches
atop engraved armor. His large eyes look at the viewer with
confidence, as though he knows a secret but does not wish
to impart it. Below the picture is the inscription:

> By the sword and the compass
> More and more and more and more.

It seems that this is all that the opening of a new world means to many: conquest. How different are discoveries of the men of medicine whom I so admire. For even if one assumed that their endeavors were merely to satisfy their own intellectual curiosity, or to garner for themselves wealth and fame, the ultimate result is still a benefit to mankind.

Given the accounts of the horrors we of the Old World have committed in the New, as chronicled by Las Casas in the mid-1500s and as depicted so realistically in the illustrations accompanying the reprint of his work at the end of the century, how can one not shrink from the goal of incessant conquest? To this day, we murder and enslave. Will God forgive us that, when offered such a gift, we could only maim?

June 1641

Nowhere do I find conjectures on how America has changed the European mind. We barely question what we have believed for centuries, and many see the discoveries as irrelevant even to social philosophy. They argue that the ancients knew nothing of these lands, yet look at the wisdom they achieved. But must it not have meaning for us? We can point to this discovery and say, "This we have done. Of this the ancients did not dream." And if they in their wisdom did not dream of this reality, what awaits us, of which we have yet to dream?

August 1641

I have come across some interesting and related hypotheses in my reading. Some have proposed the theory that the Indians were, and continue to be, passing through stages, as did Europe itself. The end of that progression is what many see as Christianity, though the humanists say it is civilization. Of course, our progress was not unchecked. To our own Spain the Romans eventually brought Christianity, but we were invaded by the Visigoths. The Visigoths accepted the religion of their captured land, but we were then conquered by the Moors. They were not driven from our peninsula for seven centuries. The Catholic monarchs restored the supremacy of Catholicism in Spain, but elsewhere the Church has been torn asunder by Luther, Calvin, and Henry.

The Christianity the Indians "progress" to has often been imposed, but I wonder if they accept it in their hearts. Yet in Europe, also, religion has often been decreed. Perhaps the first who succumb to force only feign belief, but do pretense and ritual finally reach the heart? If a child sees his parents practicing this new religion, will he not accept it as truth? But I wander too far afield, and what would the Holy Inquisition make of all my musings? Yet their occupation is different from the circumstances of which I speak. It has often been said that the Inquisition seeks to bring back to the Holy Faith those who once professed it, but who have fallen into error and might lead others there as well.

Those who speak of a progress toward civilization consider that we have already attained it, yet do not our actions in the Americas undercut our right to that claim? Rather than we leading those inhabitants to civilization, have we not demonstrated our reversion to barbarity? If we speak of their own development, we can never know where that would have led, since their world will never be the same as it might have been, and nor will ours.

On a professional note, old Sor María, who had helped me in my ministrations at the Convent of Corpus Christi, passed on to what I am sure will be her eternal reward. Never have I known a gentler soul. She succumbed to a fever, the cause of which I was unable to determine. The abbess will look for a new assistant for me in my periodic visits to the good sisters.

November 1641

All of my readings have not served to assuage my desire to go to the New World myself. On the contrary, they have sharpened it. Through various avenues, I have made inquiries and requests regarding my desire to put on as a ship's physician, and finally I have received word from a friend that there might be an opportunity for me with a fleet that will be leaving in May. I will work diligently to extricate myself from my brother's business dealings. I see no need of my further service. Can it not now be the time to pursue my own desires?

I note here that my occasional work at the convent continues. The illness that began with Sor María's death spread among the sisters during the autumn months, and I had difficulty with the diagnosis. I am chagrined to admit that I am still not certain what caused the fevers, and I did lose two patients, though they had been somewhat infirm before the onset of the malady. With a combination of treatments, the other stricken sisters improved, and most returned to full health. But perhaps I flatter myself. Though we physicians often like to take credit for recovery, nothing happens without God's help and the natural recuperative powers He has given to his creatures.

I should not omit mention of Sor Ana, who volunteered to help me upon the death of Sor María. I have come to admire her greatly. She first showed bravery in offering her help, for she could herself have caught the fever, which we had already seen could be fatal. She did not shrink from even the most repugnant tasks I asked of her, and I seldom saw her lose her patience with her sisters, though surely she must have been sorely tried. I sometimes find it necessary to gruffly assert the authority of the physician over a complaining or uncooperative patient, but I never saw her resort to any like tactics.

Add to this that she is quick to learn, much more than other ladies. Though now I think on it, I do not believe that I have ever endeavored to teach a woman anything of substance. She tells me that her father allowed her to be tutored with her brother when she was young, and perhaps this habit of learning enables her to absorb knowledge now. Though she follows my instructions, when I have the time she questions the reasoning behind the treatments and often probes beyond the explanation "Because it is always done so."

January 1642

I believe that I have secured a position on the fleet leaving for the Indies in May.

April 1642

I am quite distraught. All my hopes for sailing in May are dashed. Another, it must be supposed with better connections, has snatched the post from me. I am told it will be another year before there will be such an opening again.

I have already referred many of my regular patients to other physicians, so my practice is much reduced. I do have savings, which I planned to use at my new destination, so I can make use of those if I must. I will try to build up my practice again quickly, for I do not wish to have to apply to my brother for help, now that I have disconnected myself from his business.

At least now I will not have to bid farewell to Sor Ana and the others at the convent.

July 1642

I try to find whatever means I can to comfort myself, but I must confess to my continued feeling of disappointment that I have not been able to travel to the New World. One argument I have used with myself asked whether I might not be adding to the injustices done to the natives of those lands by being part of the treasure fleet that seeks to bring their riches to our shores. I answer that I hoped to put my curing skills to good use there, and how could my remaining at home help them? Would it undo any injustices already done? If I am a man of good intent, is that not enough?

9

ANA

Ana awoke to darkness and a sharp pain in her back. Squelching a momentary panic, she realized that she was sitting in the chair in her room. In the dim light from the brazier, she saw that Emilio's journal lay on the floor. She stirred the embers and relit her candle.

She should have simply gone to bed, but she was reluctant to stop her reading, now that she had finally come to a mention of herself. Still, even after the time that they had started working together, he wrote of his bitter disappointment at the posting on the ship having been taken from him, and this exclusion from his hopes and dreams left Ana feeling empty.

She told herself to go to her bed, that tomorrow would be a busy day, but she knew that she would not be able to sleep. She straightened up in the chair and found the page where she had left off reading.

10

Emilio

August 1642

My work at the convent continues. Sor Ana has told me
that she entered the convent when she was but seventeen.
That seems very young to have made the decision to reject
the world, though I know that many girls enter that life at
a yet more tender age. I am ever more impressed with Sor
Ana's quick mind and gentle manner. I must admit, if only
to myself, that on those occasions when I have arrived at
the convent and have been told that Sor Ana has been
called to other duties that day, I have felt a sense of most
keen disappointment.

September 1642

To some the New World means little more than anxiously
awaited cargos of silver to pay off investors, or to be
confiscated by the royal treasury. Felipe looks to silver to
ease the task of keeping his empire, which spreads to
Naples and the Netherlands. To him the Indies are but a
chest that holds the means to European power. The silver
mines most easily stripped have been depleted, and more
mercury is needed to extract less silver, decreasing
shipments and profits. Spain does not look to its own

rapacity for explanation but blames the new lands themselves, that they no longer contain untouched riches, as a violated woman is blamed because she is no longer virginal.

There are those who say that our experience with the new lands has harmed more than helped us. The tide of silver has steadily increased our prices for many decades, with little recourse for the poor. In matters of trade with the rest of Europe, our position has deteriorated, as we use American silver to buy more goods from other lands, while we produce less to sell in turn. Already at the turn of the century the great *arbitrista* González de Cellorigo saw the fault of this, believing that the riches won by Spain from conquest should be used to spur agriculture, the making of goods, and the trading of them, but his wise counsel was ignored. Even our great poet of love Garcilaso de la Vega has written of the corrosive effects of a wealth won but not earned.

I do know that the hope of a better life can be found in those new lands for the man who can but muster the means and the courage to embrace it. One of my charity patients showed me a letter from her husband, who left her and their son three years ago to seek his fortune across the sea. He wrote to her from Puebla to join him there now, that together they can live in a comfortable prosperity. Some lament that the New World drains from us those with vision and enterprise, and I fear that it may be so.

October 1642

I will record here a short scene from my visit to the convent today, though I fear that my growing affection for Sor Ana prompts me to read much more into her words and manner than is meant.

When I called at the convent today, I was met at the door by the servant who usually admits me, and she informed me that, thank Our Lord, there were no sisters in need of my ministrations today, for the infirmary had been cleared out. As she was closing the door, I heard Sor Ana's voice: "Please, Juana, allow the good doctor to enter, as I have some particular questions to put to him about the care of our sisters. We will be in the infirmary, where some of us are taking this opportunity to give the room a very thorough cleaning."

It was odd to observe that all of the beds in the infirmary were now unoccupied, as I had never seen it so, and I asked Sor Ana how this had come to be.

"None of our sisters suffers from any particular sickness at the moment, thanks be to God. As for those who are infirm and usually lie within, I have asked Madre Superior if they might remain in their own rooms, where I do believe they rest more comfortably in their familiar surroundings. Of course, someone visits them and sits with them several times a day, and two of the older sisters have even been able to be carried to the garden for a short period on a mild day."

My surprise must have been evident to Sor Ana, for she followed this with "I had thought that this would meet with your approval. I had understood your opinion to be that allowing the sisters a place of quiet, away from others' complaints, might contribute at least to their ability to rest."

"Yes, that is so. Perhaps you should have consulted with me beforehand, however."

At seeing her downcast face, I instantly regretted my words. "Yet I think that it is certainly worth continuing this course for a while and seeing how the sisters fare. You said you had some questions for me?"

"Yes, I did. I confess that I mostly wished to see your reaction to this new arrangement, and in truth, I did not wish to forgo the great contentment that your visits bring."

When I remained silent, not knowing how to answer, she hastily continued, "That is, my ailing sisters always greatly appreciate your attentions."

"Thank you, Sor Ana. I myself find my visits here most gratifying."

At this, she stood and murmured that she must take no more of my time. She did not suggest that we see any of the other sisters. Is it possible that Sor Ana finds my company as pleasing as I have come to find hers? Yet the impediments to anything further between us must be many.

II

ANA

Ana awoke not completely rested, but with a sense of relief. She had made it to her bed, but the curtains were open and she could see that this time she had slept until morning. She glanced at the journal, now lying on the small table, next to the snuffed-out candle.

Emilio's words had taken her back to her early feelings for him, before they had been overlaid by the intervening years, then by his loss. She remembered the guilty attraction and the doubt. Perhaps it was true that her entrance into the convent had been but the best of limited possibilities. Nevertheless, she had begun her life there with the sincere desire to be worthy of her Lord and of her sisters. This man who had entered her protected world had disturbed her equanimity, but she had not been able to call these new emotions evil.

Prior to the day that Emilio had chronicled, Ana had thought that he could never look at her as anything other than a pair of hands to help him in his work at the convent, but on that day she had made bold to try to let him know in some small way her growing tenderness for him. She remembered her confusion and embarrassment at the time, and for her former self wished that she had known that Emilio, too, hoped that within their encounter lay a deeper meaning.

She let her thoughts linger on those memories until she heard loud voices, and Clara suddenly entered. "Doña Ana, come quickly! It is old Fernando. He is very upset, but none of us can make sense of what he is saying."

Ana put a robe over her nightclothes, quickly followed Clara, and found Fernando, Sebastián's manservant, seated on a stool. He was quiet now, having exhausted what air was left to him after his walk from Sebastián's home. When he saw Ana, he began again.

"How to explain? Gone! No one saw . . . and then I looked for . . ."

"Calm yourself, Fernando." Ana took his hand. "Look at me and take slow, deep breaths. Compose yourself and begin again, please, very slowly. What has you so agitated, my friend? Who is gone, Fernando?"

"Both, all, Don Sebastián, the señorita, and even my Silvia." At this last he could contain himself no longer, and tears welled up in his eyes. Silvia and Fernando had served in the same house for over forty years, he manifestly loving her for all of them. Though Ana believed that he had once hoped for more, it seemed that he had long since learned to live on the sisterly regard that was all that Silvia was willing to offer him. Ana had often thought this hard of Silvia, but Silvia kept her own counsel in these things, and Sebastián's household ever esteemed a circumspect woman.

Clara shook her head. "Gone? Surely the ladies just went to Mass, and surely the master has no need to make an accounting to you of his whereabouts." Ana looked reprovingly at Clara for her lack of sympathy at Fernando's distress, and even in his present state, Fernando's face made it clear that he did not have to accept condescension from another servant.

"Please, explain yourself more clearly, Fernando," Ana tried again. "What do you mean?"

"They are not just gone out for the day, señora. There was chaos in the señorita's room, as Silvia never would allow, and clothes were clearly missing."

"And my brother's room, and Silvia's?"

"Don Sebastián's room is orderly, as always, and I could not see that any clothes had been taken, but he also left before the household was up and about. Silvia's room . . ." But here the old man could not continue but simply wept, as though recalling what he had seen but could not describe.

"Well, I'm sure that there is some explanation, and that my brother will inform us of it when he returns, which will surely be today, since he at least has taken no change of attire, and we all know how fastidious he is about his appearance." Ana was certain of this aspect of her response, but it was difficult to imagine why her niece and Silvia might have left so unexpectedly.

Fernando clearly needed more reassurance than this, and Ana suggested, "Perhaps Juliana and Silvia decided to gather some old, unneeded clothing and wished to distribute it to the poor."

"But why so early, señora, and why so secretly?"

When Ana arrived at her brother's house, the young maid Constanza greeted her.

"*Buenos días*, Doña Ana. Please come in. I am sorry, but no one is in today. Señorita Juliana is not here. I do not know when she left, but Don Sebastián left an hour ago." Constanza had always seemed to Ana to possess a timid manner, but today she seemed particularly wary.

"Sebastián left an hour ago? But Fernando informed me that your master had left early this morning, before the household arose."

"Oh, yes, señora, he had. But then he returned."

"And left again?"

"Yes, Doña Ana."

"Did he say where he was going?"

"No."

"Or where he had been?"

"Of course not, señora."

"Has Señorita Juliana or Silvia returned?"

"No, señora."

"Did . . . Constanza, I am losing patience. Please tell me if you know anything about what has been going on here."

"I don't know what you mean, señora."

"Then please take me to my niece's room."

Ana stopped abruptly at the doorway to Juliana's room. Clothing and toilette articles lay scattered about, but not as though considered and rejected, as one would expect in the normal course of choosing items for a trip. Dresses lay rumpled on the floor, and a shoe's mate might be found across the room. Even the jar of hand cream, which Juliana had received from Ana with obvious delight, was broken on the floor, its contents melding with the colors of the small carpet next to it, muting the bold hues, obscuring the rigid geometric pattern. Part of Ana's mind judged that the carpet was now lovelier. She walked over and picked up a shard from the jar. "It is very thick to have shattered so. It is as though it were thrown, rather than simply dropped," she murmured.

Lying at the border of the spilled cream was a doll that Juliana had received several years earlier and cherished still. There was cream upon its face, as though it had been abruptly pushed from childhood to womanhood.

Ana surveyed the room, the general disorder breaking down into its composing parts. The pile in the far corner from the door was books. Below the desk, papers had been scattered and ink from the well was still wet upon the desk. The doors of the two wardrobes were open, and most of the clothes had been removed.

Constanza stood silently in the doorway.

"What happened here?" Ana asked her.

"Just as you see, señora." It occurred to Ana that perhaps the girl was not obtuse but frightened, and this thought startled and worried her.

"Are you afraid of something, Constanza?"

"No." Ana studied the downturned face and wondered whether there was meaning in the fact that the girl had not even asked, "Afraid of what?"

Ridiculous! Ana thought in self-reproof. *I simply feel unsettled at finding Juliana's room in such disorder. What could the silly girl possibly be afraid of?*

To Constanza she said, "I understand that Silvia also left this morning."

"She seems to have done, señora."

"I will see her room also."

Constanza led Ana to a large, airy room close to Juliana's bedroom. Silvia had always been exacting about her person and had emphasized to Juliana that there was never an excuse for not appearing neat and carefully groomed. This attitude must be reflected in one's room as well, for how could order emerge from disorder?

For this reason, something in Ana dreaded seeing confusion in Silvia's room, but what she saw was even more unnerving. Silvia's room had been emptied of all belongings, as though the occupant could no longer bear the clutter of even her own most prized possessions. No piece of clothing, no comb, no veil or needlework remained. Even the bedclothes had been removed and taken. Ana walked over to Silvia's open chest and lifted the false bottom. Even the box, the location of which Silvia had once revealed to Ana, was gone. Ana did not know what the box had contained. Silvia had merely mentioned its existence, and Ana had not wished to probe into this one place that was Silvia's own. Though she had been treated well and loved by her charges, Silvia had lived her life in her master's house, with never a refuge outside his compass. She had only this box, containing whatever mementos she had treasured. Its absence left the room barren and forlorn.

"Where are the other servants?" asked Ana.

"The master told the others to go and visit their families or friends for a few days," replied Constanza.

"And he left you in charge of the household?" Ana asked, unable to keep the incredulity from her voice.

"No, Doña Ana, but I have no family. Please do not tell the master that you found me here. I did not know where to go. The house seems frightening when it is empty, but less so than the streets."

"You have nowhere else to go?"

"No, señora." Now the girl could curb her tears no longer.

Ana sighed and reminded herself of her duty to be kind. "Would you like to stay with me until my brother's return?"

"Oh, yes, Doña Ana, and I would work very hard for you."

I never noticed that you worked very hard for my brother, Ana thought, but she instructed the girl to gather her things while she went through and did what she could to close up the house. When they stepped into the street, Ana's servant Manuel was waiting for her.

"No doubt Clara sent you here," observed Ana, and

Manuel did not trouble himself to reply. The three walked back in silence, Ana finding a refuge from disturbing questions in her irritation with Clara.

Upon arriving home, Ana gave Clara only a brief accounting, then declared that she was suffering a headache, would proceed immediately to her room, and was not to be disturbed. She tried to make sense of what she had seen at Sebastián's home. Since he had told the servants to leave, it must simply be that he had taken Juliana and her *dueña* on a trip with him. But why leave so precipitously? She prayed for guidance and tried to calm her mind, as she had learned to do at the convent.

Hours passed with Ana's thoughts going round and round, but they found no likely resting place of explanation. As the day's light grew dim, Ana sought her bed but could find no repose. In frustration, she roused herself before the room was cast into complete darkness and lit the candle to read by.

12

Emilio

There is again a possibility that I might find passage as
ship's physician in a fleet to leave in early summer, but I
do not feel the elation that I did a year ago. I would hate
to leave Sor Ana. My visits to the convent are the
highlight of my week, most eagerly anticipated. Yet it is
probably for the best that I find a passage, for what can
come of loving a nun? Perhaps it is sin even to think of it.

December 1642

I see a kind of hope. I spoke today to Sor Ana of my
interest in travel. She listened quietly as we went about
our work of preparing mixtures for the ailing sisters. After
some minutes of my monologue, I said, "But forgive me,
Sor Ana, for speaking of such things that are closed to you
because of your sacred vows."

"Not at all," she replied. "I find your discourse
interesting, as always, Doctor Cardero, and the pleasures
of travel would not be forbidden me if I someday decided
to forsake my home here. I have not yet felt Our Lord call
me to my final vows."

At hearing this news, I behaved like a silly boy and

dropped the flask that I was holding, spilling its contents onto the tile floor. Sor Ana helped me clean it, after which we attended to our patients.

January 1643

I must give answer to those who have offered me the ship's physician post. I have led them to believe that I intend to accept, but I find that I cannot leave without discovering whether there is a chance that Sor Ana would forsake the convent for me. Has my interpretation of our recent encounters been but wishful thinking on my part, or can it be possible that she might feel for me some small part of the growing love I have for her?

If I were to go to America, once there I would not return for many years. If Ana could find it in her heart to accept me, I could not drag her to a new land so soon after tearing her from the womb of the convent she has known so many years. Yet perhaps she would not find it a hardship—indeed, I dare hope she might delight in accompanying me next year. If this is my wish, it is all the more reason not to wait any longer in my negative response to the ship's captain. I do not wish to appear capricious to those of whom I would request that they postpone their offer for a year.

At thirty-four years of age, I find it strange to contemplate marriage. As the years have passed and I have seen my brother and sister married, I had come to suppose that I could fill the part of favored uncle. I have known other intriguing women, but none with whom I have wished to share my life. I believe that my proposal, if handled delicately, will not be an insult to Ana. I am only six years her senior. From what I understand, we are of equally gentle birth. Although my financial circumstances are less exalted than those of her late father or her brother, a prestigious *arbitrista*, I can give to her a comfortable, an honorable, life, in which she will know love.

February 1643

I asked her today. I will record my proposal here, so that I shall never forget the particulars.

"Sor Ana, may I speak to you on a personal matter?" I could hear the timid sound of my voice but could do nothing to strengthen it, now that I was so close to discovering whether my hopes would be fulfilled or denied.

"Of course, Doctor Cardero. I know that you will say nothing to offend. I am always happy to attend you."

"You have mentioned to me that you have not taken your final vows," I said.

"That is correct. Although some of my sisters who have been here much less time than I have taken that step, I have not felt a strong enough calling to do so."

"I hope that I do not transgress the boundaries of propriety in asking this, but I wonder whether you have ever considered abandoning the convent."

Ana looked into my eyes, paused a moment, then responded, "I have at times thought of this, but did not know what kind of life might await me outside these walls."

"Would you have any particular disinclination to the married life?"

"Married life is sanctioned by God and Holy Mother Church. If a thoughtful and kindhearted man were to truly see me as a desirable wife, I believe that I could find great happiness in that state."

"Ana," I finally dared to say, "I do see you as a wife with whom I could joyfully share my life—if you could deem me an acceptable husband. Indeed, I have come to hold you most dear." I held my breath as Ana paused before responding. If I was not the kind of man that she could accept, I knew that I would never see her again, that I could not bear to see her, knowing that I would never take her into my embrace.

"Doctor Cardero, I would be most honored to be your wife. I should blush to say it, but it is something that I have come to wish for most ardently."

Although I had dreamed of this response, I was not prepared for the elation that I felt to know that Ana would be mine. All other desires of my life seemed as nothing next to this.

February 1643

I awoke this morning with a feeling of great exultation. Ana accepted me yesterday. She will speak to the abbess about leaving the convent. I shall have a wife who has already shown to me goodness of character and curiosity of mind, and I do believe that she will cherish me, as I will cherish her.

I shall be blessed to have her as my partner. I have even thought to times ahead when we might add a child to our happy home. Though she is not as young as many new brides, there is no reason that we might not be blessed with children. Of course, we have not yet spoken of such things, but I am sure a woman of her heart would wish for such a gift from God.

I saw my life in shrunken circumstance. My vision of myself, my profession, my interests, even my dream of the New World, did not include what most men desire. Now she expands it all for me—wife, true home, hope of children—and I see how barren my existence truly was.

March 1643

We are to marry in two weeks' time. Ana made an agreement with the Madre Superior that she will accompany and assist me in my visits to the convent. I believe this greatly mollified the good sisters, as they will sorely miss my Ana.

ANA

The recollection of her joy at Emilio's proposal now mingled with guilt and sorrow. Seeing his record of their conversations, she wondered how she had forgotten his early reference to travel, and her seeming implication that she would be open to it. She saw now that throughout their lives together, she had not understood him as well as she had believed. Though her ignorance of his great desire to go to the New World had been innocent, she mourned as lost the better love she might have given had she seen his dream. Her lack of comprehension seemed to her a sign of her imperfect love for him, while her husband's concealment revealed a purer love. More than this, she knew that he forgave for that which she had unknowingly but irrevocably taken from him.

The burden of this new comprehension, along with the day's events, would continue to rob Ana of sleep, and so she allowed herself to continue, to see whether Emilio's further reflections would bring her solace.

14

Emilio

October 1643

My life is full as a married man. We have settled into a comfortable routine. Ana assists me not only at the convent but also in my preparations and in visits with other patients when it is seemly. She appears to derive great satisfaction from this work, and we usually spend quiet evenings together, conversing and reading, with occasional visits to the theater or the homes of family and friends.

Though others might not credit it, I find myself lucky not to have married a much younger woman, for I understand that they can be petulant and overly demanding of one's attention. Ana has maturity and enough of her own interests that, even with my work, I still have time to study, read, and reflect. I do not have as much time as previously, of course, and I have quite neglected my readings on the New World. I must take up my task again, with an eye to practical understanding. I still hope we shall sail next summer, though I have been reluctant to broach the subject with Ana. This is unworthy of me, for if we are to go, the preparations must begin shortly after the new year.

Though we have been united in hope, Ana is not yet with child. We know that it is far too soon to worry, but I see the monthly disappointment in her face. I must admit that now I have come to worry that she will come with child, for how could she withstand a long sea voyage in that condition?

January 1644

I had not yet told Ana, as I wished to delay until the last possible moment, to see whether she would conceive a child, but I had been offered and tentatively accepted a post as a ship's physician, to leave for New Spain in May. I had hoped that Ana would accompany me on the trip. Now, however, it seems that once again my place has been usurped by another, this time a cousin of the captain, who nevertheless assures me that next year he will hold a place for me.

October 1644

Ana's sister-in-law, Margarita, has had a child, a beautiful girl who has been christened Juliana. To see their joy is a grace, and my Ana loves the child most dearly, but I perceive the pain she tries to hide when she holds the child of another.

January 1645

Ana is with child, and I must confess that my feelings are somewhat mixed, though I show only my joy to her. She is having a hard enough time with the pregnancy, and I would not add to her worries. Still, I cannot help but feel some disappointment, for though I had not yet secured a position, I had held on to the hope that someone might need a ship's physician. Now there is no question of our sailing for the Indies. The voyage would be much too

difficult for her in this condition. It now seems fortuitous
that I delayed in telling Ana of my wish. She would be
sorry to let me down. I tell myself that a journey is a
small matter compared with the birth of a child, but it is
a dream I have held close these many years. Perhaps next
year we will travel to the New World with our son.

February 1645

A most incredible tragedy has struck the home of Ana's
brother! I cannot fathom how it could be true. It is but
another scene in the sad play our beloved country seems
destined to enact.

March 1645

Sebastián's wife is no more, and, though much of Madrid
speaks of it, he will not utter her name or allow it to be
spoken in his household. Her portrait has been removed,
and a servant whispered to me that Sebastián has had it
destroyed. It is as though life has turned to nightmare. I
will not try to write of it here, for doing so would seem to
place it in the realm of the comprehensible.

April 1645

Ana miscarried three weeks ago. Her grief was palpable
and sharp, mixed with the lingering horror at her sister-in-
law's death. I do wonder whether that malign event did
not contribute to the loss of our child. Now my beloved
wife is simply quiet, and only two or three times a day do
her eyes fill with tears. We know that our suffering is
slight relative to what others have had to endure, but
weighing sorrows does not lessen pain.

I have seen other women miscarry, and I have always been shocked by their level of grief for a child unseen. Still, that the mother would develop a loving bond with the child beneath her heart should not surprise. What I did not notice, but which I now do not doubt was there, was the sorrow of the fathers. Surely if I had looked into their eyes, I would have seen the torment I now feel. But society does not expect this from a man. Yet just as his wife has done, surely a father has held his child in his mind's eye, has seen him laugh and play and cry, has seen his son come to him for comfort from life's pangs, has seen him grown into a man, married and with children, and cradling his own father in his arms when he is old and dying. What can he now imagine?

July 1645

Ana is much improved in mind and body, though I cannot seem to shed my sorrow. Perhaps that is because she now looks forward with hope to another child, and I have not had the heart to discourage her in this. Sometimes I wish that I were not a physician, because then I would not know that the strain that Ana's body has already suffered reduces her chance of conceiving and bringing a baby to full term.

ANA

Ana awoke to a confusing tangle of memory, made fresh by her reading of the night before and magnified in discordant dreams: the joy of her wedding day, the terror of Margarita's death, but most of all the grief of her own childlessness, and what she now realized was her blindness to the depth of Emilio's suffering. There had been not only the heartbreak of her miscarriage, but the misery of seeing each month's hopes destroyed, only to be built up again, then end again in sorrow.

Although for many years Ana had told herself that she had accepted God's will in not gracing Emilio and her with children, that did not mean that melancholy never overtook her. Every few months, she found herself thinking about how old their child would have been. When she was walking through the city streets, she looked for children, and in more recent years those bordering on adulthood, to see what their child might have become at this age, to imagine what moments of delight Emilio and she might have had. She did not deny that there would also have been difficulties to bear. Still, it seemed to her that any struggles would have been made lighter by the offsetting joys.

And what of Emilio's dream? Where before she had felt guilt, she now felt betrayed that he had felt joy, but some disappointment, too, when he had learned that she was with child. Her recollection of his happiness was marred by what she had just learned of his ambivalent feelings.

Now, though, the events of the previous day flooded in with renewed force, perhaps because of her dreams' reminder that misfortune and catastrophe are possible, though the mind gropes for benign explanations.

It could be that Sebastián had gone to Sevilla on business. She knew that her brother invested in ships that carried goods to the Indies and returned with payment in silver, and that such ventures had become increasingly risky as the power of Spain to dominate the seas had waned. The constant shifting of alliances and hostilities had exposed the Spanish fleets to attack by Dutch, English, and French ships. There were also the reduced payments sanctioned by some of the colonies' viceroys, and the increasing tendency of His Majesty's government to confiscate a portion of a returning ship's cargo as an impromptu tax. Could it be that some such crisis in his interests had prompted Sebastián's hasty departure?

Perhaps he was traveling in his role as *arbitrista*. Most of these ideamongers to the king were content to stay within the shadow of the court, but Sebastián's honor demanded that he see the peoples and regions his designs would affect. Though he had not ventured from the peninsula to Spain's holdings in Naples or the Indies, he had traversed all the provinces of Spain. His enthusiasm for his projects had more than once impelled him to precipitate excursions, but he had always left the particulars of his plans for Ana, and he had never taken Juliana.

If Sebastián had gone off with his daughter, that could explain his lack of communication. After all, details of his journey were usually only an excuse for his notes to her, to charge his sister with overseeing Juliana's well-being in his absence. If she were traveling with her father, there would be no need for those instructions.

What, then, of Fernando's frantic visit and Constanza's tears? Ana was back where she had started and could not believe her own conjectures. They offered only empty consolation, as with the heretic whose confession has saved him from the stake but bought for him the noose.

Leaning her head back and closing her eyes, Ana saw played there again the vision of herself walking through her niece's devastated room and Silvia's barren one. A hasty departure could have caused chaos in Juliana's chambers, but there seemed a savage edge to it. Silvia's tidy nature could account for the order of her room, but not its complete evacuation. Ana opened her eyes and prayed that today a simple explanation would be revealed.

By evening, no such elucidation had presented itself. Her apprehension, more than her day of ministrations to the ill, had taken its toll on Ana's strength. She fell asleep in a chair, her head upon her desk, cushioned by Emilio's unopened journal.

The next morning Ana awoke with the dawn. Somewhere in her restless night, she had decided that she must leave immediately to search for Sebastián and Juliana. Guilt suggested that perhaps she had delayed the needed journey because of her own aversion to travel. She must be the capable woman whom Emilio had described in his journal. She must not let her fears mock his words of faith in her. She pulled out her writing paper, ink, and quill.

Esteemed Señor Monsalve,

I know that it has been a long time since we have been in touch, but my dire circumstances lead me to beg a

73

*favor of you. I understand that, from time to time, you
send a carriage to Sevilla to deliver papers and other
articles of importance to your business partners there.
Further, I have been told that it is sometimes possible
for persons to book a seat in this carriage, to the
advantage of both parties.*

*I was very much hoping that you might have such a
conveyance leaving shortly, as I find that I must make
my way to Sevilla. It would be exceedingly kind of you
to let me know as soon as possible whether, by chance,
this is a possibility. If it is not, I shall seek other
means. Believe me when I tell you that I would not
impose upon your gallantry if it were not from the
most urgent necessity.*

Sincerely,
Ana Torres López
Widow of Emilio Cardero Díaz

She called Manuel and asked him to deliver the note
immediately, giving him directions to the house. Though
she was averse to it, Ana had from time to time since
Emilio's death found that she had need of calling upon
some acquaintance of her husband to help her with some
problem. Her husband's kindness had left her the heiress of
many persons' gratitude. She had usually relied upon Sebastián, but some cases seemed better handled by others,
and she did not like to depend on him in all things. A
choice of benefactors was a paltry independence but sometimes all that a woman was granted.

The answer came more swiftly than she had dared to
hope, arriving by early afternoon.

Honrada Señora Torres Lopez,

I am very grateful that I can be of service to you. Your honored husband is held in my memory with affection and respect, and any assistance I can give you is insignificant compared with the great debt I feel I owe.

As it happens, there is a carriage leaving for Sevilla tomorrow. The man who brings you this note, Señor Rojas, will be in charge of the carriage and all of the arrangements. In light of what I perceive as the sudden nature of your travel, if you have not made provision for a place to stay, I can suggest a room in the house of a Señora Nelleda. Business associates whom I have referred to the home have found it to be comfortable and practical, and Señora Nelleda to be honorable, pleasant, and a good cook. You need only inform Señor Rojas if you desire to accept my recommendation, and he will take you there.

You do not reveal the reason for your journey, but if you are in further need of aid once you have reached Sevilla, please allow me to refer you to my partner there, Señor De Ovando, who I believe was also acquainted with Don Emilio. Señor Rojas will be able to direct you there as well, should you find you wish to avail yourself of his services.

I wish you a pleasant journey.
I am Your Most Humble Servant,
Bartolomé Monsalve

Ana looked up from the note to the short, sturdy man before her.

"Señor Rojas, I am happy to meet you. I am afraid that Señor Monsalve has forgotten to mention the fare that I should pay you for the trip to Sevilla."

"For you, there is no fare, señora. The carriage was scheduled to leave anyway, and there are already two other passengers, a priest and a young girl. I hope that you do not find it too uncomfortable to have to share the carriage."

"On the contrary, I am most grateful that I shall be able to travel with you so soon."

Having given Ana the particulars of when the carriage would leave and what she should bring for her comfort, Señor Rojas bid Ana farewell until the morrow. Closing the door behind him, Ana asked Clara, who was wiping imaginary dust from the large chest near the entranceway, to accompany her to her room. Ana was well aware that Clara would be curious about the activities of the day, but she had purposely kept her plans from Clara until they were set. She knew that Clara would find many objections to Ana's traveling alone to Sevilla, with no real reason for supposing that there she would find Sebastián and Juliana.

Having reached her room, Ana told Clara of her intention, and of the arrangements she had already made. Her predictions as to Clara's reaction had been justified, for no sooner had Ana revealed her purpose than Clara's protests commenced. Ana half listened while beginning to lay out the things that she would need for the journey. As she offered no rejoinders to Clara's remonstrations, the housekeeper would have been justified in assuming that this argument would follow the course of so many others, and that she had a tolerable chance of wearing down her mistress's resistance through her own unrelenting persistence.

Here she would be proven wrong, however, for finally Ana paused in her preparations, looked into the other woman's eyes, and said, in a voice low but firm, "I shall not be deterred in this, Clara. I feel that something is wrong. I have concluded this to my own satisfaction, and my own satisfaction is all that I am inclined to consult in this matter, that it is reasonable to believe that Sevilla is the destination to which my brother and niece are bound, and so must I be also." Ana's gaze remained fixed on Clara for some moments, and the housekeeper, so unused to this tone or manner from her mistress, yielded. She did not do so with goodwill, however, and the very formality of her reply was itself a rebuke.

"Very well, señora. Please be good enough to inform me what you would like me to do in preparation for your departure."

Ana hid both her surprise at Clara's acquiescence and the hurt she felt at the cold response. She had endeavored to appear certain in her resolve but was far from believing that her undertaking was completely rational. She knew only that she would find no peace waiting at home for word from her brother. Her journey might not afford her peace of mind, but she had reluctantly learned in her life, in part from Clara herself, that activity could calm the mind, or at least distract it, and even dull the pangs of a grieving heart.

When Ana had written to Señor Monsalve only that morning, she had not believed that her plans would take shape so quickly. Many of Clara's objections had been her own just the previous evening. Wishing to find justification for her actions, she set out for Sebastián's home without her usual afternoon rest, in the hope of finding something that pointed to Sevilla.

Usually she enjoyed the walk to her brother's house just north of the Plaza Mayor. Today, however, she was insensible of any of her usual pleasures. As she approached her brother's home with its stone facade, of which he was so proud, it took on an ominous air. She walked to the door, opened it, and stepped into the dark hallway. The cold of the flagstone floor chilled her, and she wished that she had thought to bring Manuel, or at least Constanza, with her. The dark *armario*, taller than she, loomed in the corner, its carved panels not reflecting but absorbing any light. She opened the paneled doors. Two of her brother's coats hung neatly, but his sword was missing, and it was always kept in here when not in use. Still, this was hardly to be remarked upon, for, although Sebastián did not wear his sword at all times, as some gentlemen saw fit to do, he would certainly have taken it with him on a journey away from the city.

The other rooms of the ground floor revealed nothing unusual, and Ana proceeded up the stairs to the suite of drawing rooms. As was to be expected in the home of a man of her brother's station, there were several salons. Everything seemed as ordered as Sebastián always demanded the reception rooms be kept, and Ana walked quickly through them, the religious figures looking at her from the paintings on the wall, apostles and martyrs giving mute testament to the silent space.

The door to her brother's study, adjacent to the last, least formal salon, stood ajar. Ana opened it farther and entered. She had never been in this room, for, as much as his bedroom, Sebastián considered this his private domain. Here he pored over reports on the deteriorating conditions of his country: depopulation; abandonment of the countryside; decreasing production in the areas of agriculture, textiles, metallurgy, and shipbuilding; unstable money supply; deteriorating trade; millions spent on armies struggling to keep control of the far-flung empire. And what the reports did not say: the rich living from the labor of the poor; the king spending money on the upkeep of the Buen Retiro, his second residence, and the lavish entertainments held there while the peasants starved. Here Sebastián struggled to devise plans to help his country out of this morass. To analyze and see what should be done was the easiest part of the task. To create a plan that could get past city *cortes*, royal councils, ministers, powerful families, and the king was the nearly insurmountable difficulty.

So much information to absorb, yet the room seemed barren. The massive writing table was completely cleared of any article. No writing instruments, no books, no papers, nothing to suggest that a lifetime's work was in this room. It was as though Sebastián hoped to counter the deluge of his country's problems with his own order, as though his will could check the world's collapse.

One could not search here, for to do so would have meant to remove each book and paper from its shelf. There was no hint of the occupant's latest thought or emotion, no place to start. It was too daunting.

Across from the door through which Ana had entered was the threshold to Sebastián's bedroom, and she crossed it. The order in the room was less complete than in the study. A clean collar on the floor, a single boot, an overturned candlestick betrayed some haste. The open door to the *armario* revealed the remaining clothes all pushed to one side, as though rejected. Nothing whispered the cause or destination of a flight.

Ana opened the massive chest, which she recognized as having once occupied their father's room. Its contents were undisturbed, and the articles had the scent of things long stored. On top was a lovely lace mantilla, the most delicate that Ana had ever seen, and which she remembered Margarita, Juliana's mother, having worn on her wedding day. Ana was shocked that Sebastián had preserved this treasure from his wife, she whose memory he had sought so desperately to banish. Ana smoothed the mantilla, and an intense sorrow flooded her, but it was an old torment and she dare not sink into its embrace. The mantilla covered a baby's dress, made of the finest silk: Juliana's christening gown. Storing such sentimental treasures was normally a woman's domain, and Ana felt a pang of sorrow for her brother's lonely life, his need always so well hidden.

Cushioning the veil and dress was a small, yellowed pillow, embroidered with simple flowers, and Ana's eyes filled as she caressed the gift that she had made for her brother's fifteenth birthday when she was only six years old. Their father had been displeased with the offering, saying that it was fit for a woman, not a young man, and he had told the servant to take it from the room. Ana had never seen it again and had not dared to ask its fate.

The rest of the chest's contents seemed to be old clothing of Sebastián's, too worn to be of use but kept against some unexpected future extremity. As she returned the other items to the chest, Ana heard a sound, as of paper, and reached beneath the clothes to find a package wrapped and tied. As soon as she had opened the chest, she had realized that it would cast no light on her current dilemma, and she had been loath to probe her brother's private world, but the beloved items had led her on, and the hope to see another impelled her to remove the ribbon and lay aside the folds of paper.

A woman looked at her from a gilt frame—not a beautiful face, but a happy, strong one. The face looked familiar, and as she studied it, she saw reflected her own jaw and brow. Though a lovely portrait of their mother smiled on all who entered Sebastián's salon, this one seemed more intimate somehow, and Ana again felt the desolation of a child who never knew her mother, gone in childbirth. Ana came back to herself and wrapped the portrait, ashamed at the thought that her brother might discover she had riffled through his things.

She stood to go and saw something protruding from under the bed. She retrieved the book *La Celestina*, the familiar story, written at the end of the fifteenth century, of two young lovers brought together by a go-between. The young girl, Melibea, kills herself upon seeing her beloved die. The book was lying open toward the last pages, the lament of the father at his daughter's death:

"But, what forced my daughter to die, but the strong force of love? So, flattering world, what remedy do you give to my fatigued old age? How do you command me to remain here, knowing your falsehoods, your snares, your chains and nets, with which you trap our weak wills? Where have you put my daughter? Who will keep me company in my lonely sojourn? Who will turn my waning years to gifts?"

Ana read the words. Here, before he fell asleep, her brother must give himself a short reprieve from the reports that could only enumerate his country's failing grandeur. A strange relief, this, to journey in his mind from a real sorrow to an imagined one.

Ana left this room but passed by Juliana's, knowing that it would take the longest, and advanced to Silvia's room. The starkness of the empty chamber mocked her efforts, as though saying, *Here you will find nothing of aid or solace*, and Ana quickly quit the room. She hoped to find the chaos of her niece's room more welcoming, the discarded clothing and broken jars at least implying that once there had been life here.

Vaguely aware that she had hurried through so many rooms that might have held some secret, Ana disciplined herself and began to methodically examine her niece's belongings. She picked up and shook each piece of clothing, though she could not imagine what she expected would fall

from them. She walked carefully around the remnants of
the jar of cream and began to examine the contents of the
delicate chest of drawers, with its mother-of-pearl inlay.
Most of the drawers were empty, though some held remnants of clothing that her niece had outgrown.

The *vargueño* was the last thing to be searched. More of
a writing cabinet than a table suitable for a young girl, it
was another of Sebastián's indulgences. Ana had thought it
excessive but could understand her niece's delight in the
abundance of intricately detailed drawers. As she opened
each one and perused the contents, she remembered the first
time she had seen the desk. Juliana had been only thirteen
years old, brimming with excitement as she showed her aunt
her new treasure. Ana had smiled at how enthusiastic the
usually serious girl was over a piece of furniture at which
her father expected her to spend many hours of study. She
had insisted on opening each of the four tiers of drawers,
each level's drawers deeper than the ones above it. At the
third tier, she had leaned close to her aunt and whispered,
"Look, Tía, this is a secret compartment, which I discovered
quite by accident. When you drop something behind the
drawer, it disappears into the space behind the drawers below, and when you open the drawers on the bottom row,
you do not see what has dropped behind, unless you take
the drawer out completely."

"My, that is interesting," Ana had replied, fearing that
the "secret compartment" was caused more by the cabi-
netmaker's negligence than cunning. On the top two rows,
the shelf upon which the drawers slid went all the way to
the back wall of the desk, so that one did not run the risk
of loose articles falling behind the drawer. But on the
third level, for whatever reason, this precaution had been
abandoned. Still, she would not spoil the girl's pleasure,
nor her own at the intimacy of the confidence.

By now Ana had come to the fourth row of drawers and pulled the end one out all the way. The light was getting dim in the room as the afternoon waned, and the overhanging drawers above obscured the back wall of the desk, so Ana reached her arm into the opening and felt the smooth wood of the desk. The examination of the second drawer produced the same result. Upon removing the third drawer, she noticed that a hint more light was reflected, a paler color at the back of the slot. Upon extending her arm into it, Ana felt something softer than wood. Only her fingertips touched it, but when she stood and bent her body forward, she was able to reach somewhat farther and to grasp what was held against the wooden back of the desk. She pulled out a book, a tooled-leather journal, whose pattern was geometric yet somehow suggested leaves. She rubbed her hand over the beautiful design. Opening it, she recognized the shape of her niece's handwriting, but in the dim light she could not discern the words.

Any illumination in the room came from the one window and the balcony door. Stepping over the jumble of discarded objects, Ana made her way to the door, opened it, and stepped out onto the small balcony. The chaos of the room seemed even to extend out here, where the flowering vines on the railing appeared to have been disturbed. Ana opened the book to the first page:

Madrid

30 September, Year of Our Lord 1660

Journal of Juliana Torres Coloma

Daughter of the illustrious Don Sebastián Torres López, and of his beloved wife, Doña Margarita Coloma Girón, taken to Our Lord in the year 1644, giving birth to her first child

As she closed the book resolutely, the simple words chilled Ana, in part because of the mention of her young sister-in-law, dead of an injustice, not the travails of childbirth, gone now these many years, the slightest allusion to her forbidden by Sebastián. Indeed, she wondered at Juliana's mention of her mother's name. She had not even known that Juliana knew her full name. Silvia must have revealed this to her in those close moments when she filled in for loving mother.

Ana was reluctant to learn the secrets of another's heart, but she put the book into a small pocket sewn within her skirt. Then she abandoned her brother's house.

Upon reaching her own home, she went to her room, dismissing Clara's inquiries more brusquely than she knew she should. She closed the door, deposited Juliana's journal atop the trunk that Clara had packed, and escaped to Emilio's writings.

16

Emilio

September 1645

I had not realized how much I had come to rely on Ana's
assistance. When she came with child, she quit
accompanying me, and since the loss she has had little
heart to return. I shall try to convince her to start again. I
believe it would be good for her, and I would greatly
benefit from her aid and her companionship. I do not
doubt that if I ask her she will take up her work again, for
she is a most obliging wife.

April 1646

Ana takes great comfort in her niece, Juliana, and the
affection seems mutual, as much as one can ascertain the
opinions of a child not yet two years old. Of course,
Juliana has no memory of her mother, and she retains the
delightful openness of any child her age. It is as though
Ana is trying to place herself into a familial line. She
naturally nurtures her niece but also appears to seek to
resurrect her own mother, enacting a role cut short when
Ana was but a newborn babe.

Indeed, lately Ana seems to visit Sebastián's home
ever more frequently, and I am left to occupy myself. I
know that I am always welcome, but there remains a pall
upon the household, which no denial can crush or banish.

Still, Sebastián and I have had many stimulating discussions, on topics from the theater to his views on how to make a better Spain. But while he may feverishly seek to occupy his thoughts concocting grand schemes to cure the land, I must plod along and treat the sick one by one. By day's end I am weary and often seek a restful evening.

November 1646

I still pray each day that Ana will conceive, though we rarely speak of this. I barely know what she thinks or feels, though I believe that she still most ardently desires to give me a son. I still have not spoken to her of the hopes I had of going to the Indies. We could not plan such a journey when there is still hope for a child, for I would have to commit to the ship months in advance, and I am certain that Ana could not endure the trip if she were with child.

December 1647

I see that I have not visited these pages for over a year. I have not had the heart. I have never spoken to Ana of my fond desire to see that New World. Neither do we speak of children anymore. I do not know which gives more grief: the sudden dashing of a dream, or to see one's hopes die slowly, day by day.

We have our work together, and it saves us from the quiet moments. What fills the silence of those who have no such endeavor?

May 1649

I will not go to America. I have known this for a long time now, but there is a relief in the finality of writing it here.

Though I am not old, neither am I young, and a sea voyage would not be as easy as it once would have been. What would I have done there? Even remaining for a year or two would not afford me the time to answer my questions, yet I could hardly stay longer. It would be difficult to begin in life again, to start a new practice, build a home, make new friends.

Even more, I cannot think that Ana would wish to forsake all that she has known, and I will not ask it of her. She sees Juliana as a daughter, and to tear her away would be to force upon her a second childlessness.

February 1650

I had believed my dream to understand the Indies was denied me, but it is not so. I had hoped to comprehend the New World for itself, and for its import to the Old, and through my studies I know more than I'd have known had I never dreamed. In my questioning, I have already glimpsed an answer. I know that we can never understand all that those lands are. As for us, the answer is the dream itself, and how each man greets it. Embrace it or reject it, a new possibility presents itself to us. How we answer as a man, and as a kingdom, will forever haunt or bless us. Perhaps the hand of God showed Colón the way, not for conquest, but for redemption.

January 1657

I had not thought about this journal for years, but I came across it yesterday, and I have just finished reading through it. Here I see my days reflected: my marriage to Ana came to replace my dream of the New World. I now do not regret it, though I confess that there were times when I resented her. Some would say that to let a woman

87

supplant a man's desire is to sacrifice his very manliness, but it is not so. My love of Ana has not blocked my life but opened it, and brought me to places I did not know my heart could go.

In life we do not end with the same questions with which we started. It is not because we have found the answers to them, but because the life that we have led has reshaped the very things we ask. That this is so does not make the questions less honorable or the truths we find less worthy. Who is to say that the truth found in the secret chambers of our hearts is less than the truth found in a new world?

17

ANA

Ana knew that she should rise, for Señor Rojas would soon be there with the carriage for the days-long ride to Sevilla, but her thoughts lingered on the final entries of Emilio's journal. Though she felt Emilio's sorrow at having sacrificed his dream to see the Indies, she would never have wished to accompany him, nor to be without his company for the years such an exploration would require. Ana was comforted that Emilio had said that his life with her had taught him truths he otherwise would not have known, but she wondered whether she had trespassed when she had read her husband's words.

Clara entered the room with a breakfast tray and announced that the carriage had arrived early. In the necessary haste to help Ana with her preparations, there was no time for further discussion of the trip, but as they approached the waiting transport, Clara began her arguments anew.

"I cannot believe that you intend to make this journey alone! This is insanity. What can you hope to accomplish? Even if you are correct and they have gone to Sevilla, how will you find them there? A woman traveling alone invites disrespect, at the least, and very likely danger." Since their discourse the previous day, the housekeeper seemed to have repented her submission. It was as though Clara feared that she would bear the guilt for any hazards Ana might encounter, for they might have been averted if only she had been unwavering in her objections.

"Do not upset yourself so, Clara. I have good reason to believe that my brother has gone to Sevilla, for he spoke only recently of going there to take care of some business concerns, and to study the latest effect on trade of the king's new policies. I go under the protection of Señor Rojas, trusted retainer of Señor Monsalve, and once I arrive I will refer myself to Señor de Ovando, partner of Señor Monsalve and acquaintance of my Emilio. So you see, I can hardly be accused of striking out on my own." Ana hoped that her voice did not betray her own misgivings. She had found nothing at her brother's house to support her present course. "I wish that I could bring you along, but there is no room in the carriage. Besides, it is hardly likely that a widow of my age and demeanor will be called upon to defend her honor." They both smiled at these words, but Clara was not easily dissuaded.

"Why must you go at all? I cannot understand. What could possibly justify this trip? If your brother has gone to Sevilla on business, which theory you use to justify choosing that as a destination, then what reason can you possibly have for following him there? You are playing the fool."

Ana could not deny the logic of the argument—it had nagged at her as well. "I hope that you are right. I hope that when I get to Sevilla and find Sebastián and Juliana, they will heartily laugh at my ridiculous fears. But fears they are, Clara, and I can no longer sit idly and wait."

"But what fears are they? I have yet to hear you state them. You are reacting only to the ravings of that old simpleton Fernando."

Ana paused, before responding in a thoughtful tone, "Did you not find Constanza's manner odd?"

"What has her manner to do with this, and how am I to judge? I know nothing of that girl. For all we know, she's been odd since the day of her birth. And what of your precious patients? What are they to do while you are gone?"

Ana knew that Clara was exhausting her objections if she had resorted to this, but worry tempered her relief. "They are not my patients, Clara. As I have repeated many times, I have no license as physician, surgeon, or even barber-bloodletter. Please do not refer to them as my patients, or you could cause me great trouble. They are simply people whom I try to help."

"As though any of them could afford a physician. There are few like Dr. Emilio, bless him, who would treat the poor."

"You don't often admit that you care what happens to the people who come to me, Clara."

"I never said I did not care about them. I simply feel that sometimes they make a nuisance of themselves."

Ana smiled at this apparent lack of charity, which she knew to be based upon Clara's love for her mistress.

"Whether I care is not the point. You claim to, so where are they to turn?"

"They must seek help elsewhere." Stopping, Ana turned to the other woman. "Clara, I am at a loss as to how to name my worries, and yet I cannot shake this dread. I know only that I cannot stay here. You know how much I dislike travel. Surely the very fact that I undertake this journey must convince you of the depth of my anxiety."

"I shall pray to Our Lady to keep you safe." Clara turned and went into the house, without waiting for the carriage to pull away.

c/o

Ana should have slept, for the short and fitful hours of rest of the past few nights had left her drained, but exhaustion was not an adequate sedative. The sway of the carriage was far from rhythmic, the wheels seeking out each pothole and bump in the road. Neither could her thoughts calm her, though her fatigue thwarted any logical pondering of the situation. The abrupt departure of her brother and niece defied explanation, and for this reason her mind would not relent. It drifted from one theory to the next, and just as an interpretation seemed to elucidate the events, a fissure appeared and widened, swallowing the possibility.

The crowded feeling of the carriage at least provided some small defense against the pervading chill. Ana's fellow passengers seemed as lost in thought as she, and exchanged only occasional pleasantries. The thin priest with the kind face was Father Del Valle. He mentioned that he had been seeking a way to make this journey for several days, and that he had been quite delighted the previous day, when Señor Monsalve had informed him that the carriage would be leaving the following day. Other than this, he had not much to say. Ana thought his look even more distracted than hers must be, and she wondered what would be the troubles of a priest.

The other passenger was a girl named Andrea, somewhat younger than Juliana. She had told Ana that she had been employed in the household of Señor Monsalve, but that he had recommended her for a position as a lady's maid for the wife of one of his acquaintances in Sevilla. Señor Monsalve had also instructed her to be of whatever service she could to Ana on their journey, and Ana had been at great pains to convince the girl, without crushing her eagerness, that she preferred to be left on her own. So much for Señor Monsalve's explanation of his gallantry of asking for no payment from her. Clearly, Andrea, his own servant, had not paid, and Ana doubted that the generous Monsalve had required fare from the priest.

The day passed slowly, and Ana found that still she could not answer its tedium with sleep. They stopped shortly after midday and ate the food that Señor Rojas had instructed each to bring, but there was nothing else to break the journey.

The three passengers seemed to have made a pact to maintain their silence. Each appeared lost in the anticipation of what would greet them at journey's end. Ana tried to keep her agitation at bay, having realized earlier in the day that a studied calmness was her only defense against the waves of nausea brought on by the incessant rocking of the carriage.

She gazed out at the barren landscape. An occasional cork tree relieved the starkness of the arid terrain, but there were few signs of people. Ana remembered Sebastián's having said that part of Castile's—indeed, all of Spain's—problems was a decline in rural population.

As a child, Ana had occasionally made excursions to the countryside with her father and brother, and she had been fascinated by the point where land meets sky, as though one could simply walk to God. If the land were the top of a hill, how much stronger the illusion. Even after her father had explained to her that one could never walk to the end because the earth was round, she had been unable to dispel the notion.

Now horizon did not beckon, and her knowledge that the earth would never reach the sky, that she could journey on and on and never make an end, was dizzying and appalling. In the approaching darkness, she missed the security of the capital, where the black shadows cast by buildings seemed, by contrast, to illuminate the unshaded regions.

So it was not only the ache in Ana's head and bones that caused her to welcome the sight of the inn where they would stop for the night. The abject appearance of the buildings and the forlorn features of the courtyard seemed the inspiration for the inn at which Cervantes's Don Quixote had found his Dulcinea, and Ana smiled, hoping her giants were mere windmills.

Señor Rojas had brought food for the passengers' dinner, as inns rarely had provisions for guests, because of taxes imposed on all food and drink. They had arrived late, and the innkeeper explained that his wife had already gone to bed, so he himself set to preparing the food they had brought. As Señor Rojas and Ana's fellow passengers settled down to their jugs of wine, Ana approached the innkeeper.

"May I help you, señor?"

"I could use some help, señora, for my wife is not feeling well, but this is hardly fit work for a lady such as you."

"Not at all, my friend. I have performed tasks much humbler than this." This was true, for in the convent, in her search for union with Our Lord, Ana had shunned no task, though she would have been excused from the most objectionable chores. Her father had, after all, paid a large fee when she had entered, a dowry to the Lord.

The man accepted her help and prepared the rabbit they had bought from a hunter, while Ana cut the vegetables.

"I am sorry that your wife is not well. I hope that it is nothing serious."

"Oh, no, señora. It is just that she is expecting our sixth, and she usually rises very early, to see our guests off and begin the day's work."

"*Gracias a Dios*, a child is such a blessing!*"

"Oh, yes, and all of our children are living and are a grace upon our household, helping their mother and me, even the small ones, as much as they can."

As always, Ana felt pain at the thought of a newborn babe. Surely it must be difficult for the innkeeper to support all of these children. Truly, another child would be a burden. Why did the Lord give in surfeit to these people and deny Emilio and her? But she must banish these thoughts. All of that was long past change, and it was not for her to question the ways of the Lord.

"Your inn is quite well kept, and you do a service not only to your guests, but to God and country as well, in raising such a fine family." Already Ana had noticed that this inn, while humble, was much cleaner than others she had seen in her limited travels, and she had great hope that there would be no fleas to disturb the night's rest.

"You might wonder why I have decided to brave the roads," Ana remarked aloud.

"I would not presume to wonder, señora."

Ana hesitated but continued, hoping that sharing a confidence with him would cause the innkeeper to answer more thoroughly the questions she would then put to him. "I travel to Sevilla to see my mother. She is very ill, and we fear that death may call for her any day." Ana was not by nature prone to lying, but at least, she consoled herself, her lie could bring down no retribution on a mother so long gone.

"Now it is I who am sorry to hear of your loved one's illness. May Our Lady grant her recovery. I am sure that your presence will be a great comfort to her."

"Thank you. I hope that it will. My brother and his daughter are also on their way to see my mother. They left Madrid three days before I did." Ana tried to purge her voice of the nervousness she felt. "I imagine they would have taken this route, and if they were as lucky as we are, they would have stopped at your comfortable lodge. Do you remember talking to them—a man and his daughter, a girl about sixteen, and her *dueña*, an older woman?"

"Let me see, three days ago. I do not recall. . . . Oh, that night I went to get some provisions, and I was delayed. I did not return until quite late."

"Perhaps the next morning?"

"As I said, señora, my wife is the one who rises early with the guests, and, as I was late in my arrival the night before, she was forced also to see to their needs until my return, my poor Josefa. I will tell you, señora, it is hard for me to watch my dear wife toil so. For myself, I do not envy the rich. They have their problems. But I would like to give Josefa an easier life. She was very beautiful when we married. We were both young then, and worked here when it was still my father's inn—may he rest in peace with Our Lord and all the saints. Yes, she was beautiful, but now . . . well, the hard work has made its mark upon her."

Ana was regarding him peculiarly.

"Do not misunderstand me, señora. I love my wife deeply, more than when she was young. It is just that it saddens me, for her sake, and I know it grieves her, to see herself so changed."

"I know you love her, señor. I can tell by your voice." Ana found it hard to conceal the note of envy at this man's appreciation of his wife's lost beauty.

They worked in silence for a while, the innkeeper perhaps remembering the beauty of the young girl he had taken in marriage, Ana remembering the love Emilio had given her. She wondered again if he could have cared for her more had she brought him loveliness.

"So, it is possible that your wife might have seen my brother and niece?"

"You can ask her in the morning, señora."

After dinner, Ana went to the one separate guest room available at the inn. Though it was extremely simple, she appreciated the privacy after the long day in the carriage with the other two passengers. From what Señor Rojas had hinted, this would probably be one of the more luxurious accommodations they would patronize on their journey. Though her body ached from the constant jostling and the confined space, Ana knew that sleep would elude her, and she lit the candle on the small table by the bed.

She felt the shape and texture of Juliana's diary, and she extracted it from her bag. She did not wish to pry into the private meditations of her niece. She understood that when loved ones speak to us, what they choose to tell and how they tell it are shaped by their love, for love may struggle to survive with all raw thoughts laid open to the world. Still, reading Emilio's journal had taught Ana that eavesdropping on the reflections of another could offer insight.

Ana's fears for Juliana were hard to suppress, and it was partly in the hope of finding some hint of where she had gone that Ana would read the book, but that was not its only pull. She also wished to feel Juliana's presence through her words. Though she was hesitant to intrude upon yet another loved one, surely Juliana's journal would lay no grave fault at Ana's feet.

18

Juliana

My father has given me this wonderful book as a gift for
the celebration of my sixteenth birthday! I shall value it
highly, as much for the beauty and value of the book itself
as for the gratification it gives to me to think that he
believes me capable of making worthy use of it. He said
that I might use its pages to record my thoughts on my
studies, and this I intend to do.

Perhaps I might also use it to record the minor day-to-
day happenings of my life, so that when I am older, I shall
be reminded of tales of my youth to tell my children and
grandchildren.

11 October

I have been somewhat nervous about recording my
observations here, but now I have begun to study some
works of drama that father has given me. He said that now
that I have completed some rudimentary learning in the
classics, he would like me to study some of the great
writers of our own time. He went to some trouble to obtain
printed copies of a number of plays, for he says that they
will be a good way to start my course of more independent

study, as I should be able to discern more easily the meanings in these contemporary works. To this end, he has given me copies of some plays by the dramatists Tirso de Molina and Pedro Calderón de la Barca. Although I do have a passing familiarity with some of their works, Father wishes me to make a more systematic study of them. I am to read them and refine my thoughts on them, and then we will discuss them together. I shall record in this book my notes on our discussions.

Though Father has always shown a keen interest in my studies, and has from time to time been so generous as to take upon himself the role of tutor, I now enter a new phase of my education. Father has said that it is no longer his desire to lecture me on the meanings of works that I have read, but that he wishes instead to discover the fruit of these recent years of my study through conversations with me. We will discuss themes, even as I have heard him in friendly intellectual arguments with his friends, many of them university educated. I must work hard so that I will be worthy of the confidence he has placed in me!

This morning at Holy Mass, I noticed Antonio, son of my father's friend Don Baltasar, staring at me for long periods. I must admit that I smiled at him a few times when I looked up and caught his eye. He is quite handsome, tall and slender of leg, with rich black hair and classic features. The servants tell me that many young girls would be happy to be matched with him, but that as yet he has shown no interest in any.

17 October

I have read one of the plays by Don Tirso de Molina, *The Trickster of Sevilla*. I have also had my first discussion with Father about it, and I fear that I have disappointed him. The play deals with a rogue, Don Juan Tenorio, who seduces several young women of various classes by means of trickery and false promises. His sole delight is in dishonoring as many young women as he can, even the fiancée of his friend. In the event of discovery, he depends upon his father's high position to save him from temporal punishment. When some remind him that his actions also break the laws of God, he declares that he is young and will have time to repent before his death. In the act of escaping the room of one of the señoritas, he is discovered by her father, whom Don Juan kills. At the end of the play, Don Juan is punished, burning in everlasting fires. The girls are free to be married.

In discussing the play with my father, I chose to emphasize the dishonorable and highly immoral behavior of Don Juan, and the just punishment he received. I concluded that the end to which he was brought was well deserved, and that the play served to show that one should act honorably and well, both for honor's sake and for fear of a just punishment.

"I am afraid that you have missed the points that I most particularly wished you to see, my daughter" was my father's slow reply. "What of the conduct of the maidens who allowed themselves to be dishonored?"

"In each case they were deceived by Don Juan, who either came disguised or promised marriage, only to abandon them."

"And why did they allow themselves to be so deceived? It was a grave defect in their own characters that allowed their downfall, and this is what I wished you to discern. A woman's first duty is to guard her honor, for it is the most precious gift she gives to her father, then to her husband. Without it, she can be nothing to either man."

Although his words disturbed me, not only in their

reference to the play's interpretation, but also in his own pronouncement, I ventured to offer further proof of my understanding of the play.

"But, Father, it is Don Juan who is punished in the end. Although the girls have been deceived and made to suffer, each in the end will marry, restoring her honor. I believe that this would indicate that it is Don Juan who is to be most blamed."

"And this is the defect of the play!" Father answered. "I would have you disregard this false ending and keep in mind that each girl brought on her own shame because she did not guard her honor carefully enough. To my mind, each deserved a fate far worse than that which she received."

"Yes, Father. I am sorry that I have not understood the play as you had wished."

Father quickly relented. "Do not worry, my daughter. I believe that as you continue in the works I have given you, you will begin to find in them the lessons proper for a young woman. Good night, now."

I wonder at my father's emphasis in his interpretation. It seems that I have much to learn.

25 October

Again at Mass it seemed to me that Antonio sought out my glance in a most interested manner. Yet I wonder whether this might be the work of my desiring imagination. When he has so many young, honorable, and well-born girls to choose from, I do not know why he might single me out. I do not even know if I am pretty. My father has told me so from time to time, but might not this be merely a father's love? I have inherited my father's tallish stature, perhaps too much so for a girl, although

Antonio is yet again a full head taller than I. My hair is
brown, with somewhat of a curl to it, which my nurse,
Silvia, tells me I inherited from my mother. My hair is
perhaps my best feature. When I look into my mirror, I
think that perhaps my face is somewhat pleasing. But then
it could be only that I wish it to be so.

4 November

Once again, I have failed to understand the elements of a
play as my father had wished. I am trying not to be
discouraged, but I am afraid that he will lose his
confidence in my ability to discuss my studies with him,
and I so hoped that I could make him proud of me.

19

ANA

The next morning, Ana pondered the strictness of her brother, though she knew that he loved his daughter most deeply. She herself felt some satisfaction that she had indeed read a little of her niece's heart, in supposing that she had been interested in a young man. Relief that Ana had found nothing so far for which to reprove herself mingled with hurt that she had not been worth a mention in her niece's reflections. She knew these thoughts to be unworthy of her and of Juliana, but it was hard to push them away.

After leaving her room, Ana spied the innkeeper's wife, Josefa, and began to help her in her tasks, the better to have the chance to speak with her in private.

"Señora, I was speaking to your husband last night, and he told me that, as this morning, you are the one who sees the guests on their way each day."

"That is so, señora," the woman replied, pleasantly enough, but without pausing from her duties, which, Ana could see, had taken their toll on the woman's beauty, as her husband had lamented.

"He also mentioned that he was late in returning to the inn three evenings ago."

"The days all run together here, but if that is what my husband says, I'm sure it must be so. Why do you ask, señora?"

"As I told your husband, I am on my way to Sevilla, to my sick mother's bedside, and I wondered whether my brother and niece, who left three days before I did, had stopped here. My niece's *dueña* would also have been with them. Do you remember any such party?"

"Three nights ago . . . Now I recall. There was a group from a caravan who stopped that night, but there was no gentleman or girl among them."

"You are quite certain? There was no one else here at all?"

"No, señora. There was no other group here that night."

Ana hoped that her face did not betray her distress. Perhaps they had not traveled this way after all. Perhaps Sevilla was not even their destination.

"There are other places one could stop, señora," Josefa pointed out. "I am sure that must be the case, and that all is well with them."

"Of course you are right. Thank you for your help."

A half hour later, Ana climbed back into Señor Monsalve's carriage, along with her companions. It was certainly possible that Sebastián and Juliana had stopped elsewhere, but there were not a great number of inns along the way, and this was generally recognized as by far the best route to Sevilla. Still, they might have found another inn, or even gone another way. Even if she were to concede that they might not be destined for Sevilla at all, there was little she could do to change her plans now. Traveling alone, she could not leave the protection of Señor Monsalve's carriage. She had taken the initial step to embark and, having done so, must follow her decision to its end.

The knowledge gave her little comfort, and after most of the morning had passed in silence, Ana decided to en-

deavor to make the time pass through conversation with
her fellow passengers. Father Del Valle had successfully
nodded off, but Andrea seemed more disposed to conversation today. The monotonous journey must be difficult for
the girl, and though there was nothing in her looks or
manner that resembled Juliana, her youth alone reminded
Ana of her niece.

"How did you find the inn, Andrea?"

"Oh, it was very nice, señora," and the answer held all
the enthusiasm of one whose opinion is not often solicited.
Ana wondered how much comfort the inn had afforded the
girl, for she knew herself to have occupied the only private
room. Still, Andrea was hardly likely to have ever had the
luxury of her own room, and her innocence might easily
have invited slumber.

"Did you rest well after our long day's journey?"

"Oh, yes, although I must admit I did lose some sleep
worrying about my ability to please my new employers. It
was so kind of Señor Monsalve to recommend me for the
position, and even allow me to travel in his carriage. Did
you sleep well?" Andrea ventured to ask, and then stopped
abruptly, as though she were afraid that this was too personal a question to ask of a lady. She seemed relieved at
Ana's easy response.

"I am afraid that I do not sleep very well in general."

Perhaps mystified as to why a fine lady would be unable to sleep, Andrea changed the subject. "I was able to
help Josefa with the smaller children this morning. I love
children, but at the house of Señor Monsalve, only the
dueña was allowed to play with them."

"You had other duties, I expect."

"Yes, but still, in the evening, I would have been glad
of the opportunity to help with the children."

Ana smiled at the girl, so young herself but already

years in service. She hoped that Juliana was properly grateful for the life she led.

"I hope that in my new position in Sevilla, there will be children. Do you think that I will be able to play with the children there, since I will be in a higher position than I was at Señor Monsalve's house?"

"You will have to wait and see, I suppose," replied Ana, unwilling to squelch the girl's simple hopes by replying that a lady's maid would hardly have occasion to take care of the children, being required more for the comfort of the lady than for the care of her offspring.

A loud, pounding rain started to beat upon the roof of the carriage, and they fell into silence for some time after this, each absorbed in her own thoughts. Ana realized that, in some ways, this girl's immediate future was more certain than her own. At least Andrea knew for certain why Sevilla should be her destination, where she would go, and what she would do when she arrived there.

The inn at which they stayed that night barely deserved the name, but Ana didn't dwell on that. She decided that in questioning Josefa that morning, she had been too specific about the day on which Sebastián and Juliana might have arrived. She would not repeat her error.

Shortly after their arrival, Ana made her inquiry, asking whether there had been a gentleman traveling with his daughter and the girl's *dueña*.

"No, señora."

"Over any of the past few nights?"

"No" came the curt reply of the innkeeper, whose level of friendliness seemed perfectly matched to the surroundings. His unwillingness to converse prevented Ana from indulging in the fabrication of the evening before. She would not oblige this man with a lie to explain her curiosity.

"Please, think. It is quite important."

"It is hardly likely that I would forget a gentleman and his daughter. Most men would not subject their daughter to the hazards of the open road," the man replied, eyeing Ana with suspicion, as though she shared the culpability in such a father's lax behavior.

Ana would not be put off. She had spent much of the day in the carriage belittling herself for not having been more persistent in her questioning of Josefa. "No one came in at all?"

"Only some members of a caravan one evening, with its merchants. Even the muleteers paid to stay here, which was unusual, since they usually sleep in the open. Still, occasionally they stop here, for the conveniences we offer."

Ana wondered what conveniences those might be, having already surveyed the filth about her.

"No one traveled with them?"

"Only a boy, who must have paid to allow him to travel in the safety of their company, though he looked like he could not have afforded to pay much. There was also an old woman, who waited on the others. That can't be much of a life."

Ana was surprised at the man's sudden magnanimity in worrying about the life of another. "Indeed, it could not." Surely she had exhausted every line of questioning. The results of it increased her anxiety, but she would have nothing for which to reproach herself during the next day's long hours.

There was no private room that night, and Ana spread her blankets on one of a group of pallets in a corner, next to Andrea and within a protective square that Señor Rojas and Father Del Valle attempted to create through the placement of their pallets. It was evident that they were both quite disturbed at the necessity of Ana's sleeping in a common room, so, to ease their concern, she had attempted to appear not in the least distressed by the indignity. Her apparent natural acceptance of the situation was a pretense, for she did find it extremely difficult to relax in such an atmosphere. One by one, the other guests' breathing calmed to a slow rhythm, and finally she judged that all must be asleep. She carefully reached into her bag and found Juliana's journal, then rose and went to the fireplace, which afforded the only light in the room. If anyone did awaken, she hoped they would think that, unable to sleep, she had risen to read her prayers.

20

Juliana

10 November

Much as I have always enjoyed my studies and found a
deep gratification from them, I lately find it difficult to
concentrate. There is a matter much concerning me of late.
I have begun to wonder why my father has done nothing
to find a husband for me. I am already sixteen, past the
time when many girls are already wed. Yet yesterday,
when I ventured to speak to Father on this subject, he
reacted strangely.

When I asked him about it, he simply answered softly,
"Are you so anxious to leave me, daughter? Marriage does
not always bring happiness, you know."

"I know that to be the case, sir," I replied, "yet I
believe that you and Silvia have taught me well, and that I
could make a good and conscientious wife. I have faith
that you would find me a husband who would love and
honor me."

At this he only looked at me oddly and said, "We do
not always have control over the demands of honor."

I do not know what to think of this reply. Surely it is
every father's desire to see his daughter married and
settled, so that she may bring him grandchildren to
comfort his old age. Why does he doubt that marriage will
make me happy? It is the desire of most of the young girls

of my acquaintance. Although my education has been more broad than that of most of my friends, I am one with them in my desire to be a wife and mother. Of what use can a young girl's knowledge be but to converse with her husband when he so desires, and to oversee her children's training?

I had hoped this discussion might have gone better. In my imagination, I had even dreamed that perhaps Father might have asked me if there was any young man in particular to whose father I might wish him to speak. Then I had been prepared to be so bold as to name Antonio, for I am convinced that, for his part, at least, the idea would not be altogether unacceptable. And, after all, his father and mine have been fast friends these many years. What more fitting, happy match?

25 November

I have had somewhat better success in my discussions with my father, though I feel little satisfaction. This evening I nervously approached him and informed him that I had finished another work that he had given me to study, *The Mayor of Zalamea*, by Don Calderón de la Barca. The play presents a prosperous peasant, Pedro Crespo; his son, Juan; and his daughter, Isabel. The king's army is traveling through the town of Zalamea, and a captain of the army abducts Isabel and violates her. At first she runs from her brother, for fear that he will kill her, as the symbol of the family's dishonor. She comes upon her father, however, and offers herself to him: "And men will say that in your daughter's blood/ You have your own dead honor now revived." But Crespo does not kill her and later stops his son from redeeming their honor with her death.

Crespo tries to convince the captain to marry Isabel, offering him all of his family's wealth, but the captain disdains the offer. Then, in his capacity as mayor, Crespo has the captain arrested and executed. The king deems the judgment just, for, as Crespo says, a man's honor is his patrimony. Isabel will enter a convent.

In my presentation to my father of my understanding of the play, I pointed out the overriding importance of Pedro Crespo's honor, and that his actions were justified because they were done to restore that honor. Father seemed pleased with the points that I made, and I was emboldened to express my feeling of sadness that the character of Isabel would have to enter a convent. For, although for many this is a happy and a holy choice, it did not seem that this is one that Isabel would have embraced had she been untainted. My father pointed out that her father and her brother had spared her.

"And who would marry such a girl? Where could a father find a husband, once her shame was known? Honor is satisfied by her entrance into the convent."

I persisted: "It is unjust for her to be sent away from the father she loves."

Father frowned and seemed to gaze into a distance I could not see.

"She had been dishonored."

"But through no fault of her own!" I protested.

"In Spain we live by a very strict code. Sometimes we fall victim to it, but it is still our definition of ourselves. Without it, we would be lost. Go to bed now, daughter, and do not trouble yourself any longer with the fate of a character in a play."

Yet I ponder it still. Father was the one who wished me to gain understanding from these plays, and I cannot help but question the cruel message that they teach.

19 December

Six days ago, I again approached my father on the subject of marriage, and I still shake when I think of it, so unexpected was his reaction.

"Have you been conversing with some young man without my knowledge?" he demanded quickly.

"Of course not, Father," I replied meekly, stunned by his accusation though feeling somehow guilty for the quick looks and smiles I had stolen with Antonio in public. "It is just that it is a girl's duty, if she is not to be consecrated as a bride of Christ in the convent, to become wife and mother, or so the Church tells us. I am already of an age —"

"Silence! How dare you quote to me Holy Mother Church's teachings to conceal your own immodest behavior! I can see that I have been too lenient with you."

When I tried to protest my innocence, he left the room. Perhaps most peculiar of all is that he has not returned to the subject again, though I have lived in fear of another such episode these several days. Nor has his demeanor toward me changed from what it was before this scene. He is once again the kind, loving, and indulgent father I have always known and cared for.

Yet I cannot let the subject go. It seems I am obsessed with the question of what is to become of me. I will not deny that I have thought overly much of some of the young men I have seen, particularly of Antonio. Is it possible that my father has noticed my attention to him? But how wrong can my feelings be? Though I am but a maiden, I shall soon be a woman, and I look to have only what all ladies want: husband and household of my own, children to love and who will love me in return.

I told Silvia of my discussions with my father. Though

I was somewhat embarrassed, my perplexity and desire for her insight overcame this sentiment, and she has ever been my confidant. I cannot understand her response any more than I do that of my father. She urges me to let go of these desires and allow my father to lead me in all things. She seemed saddened as she said this, and I cannot help but feel she is concealing some knowledge that is beyond my understanding.

6 January 1661

We have passed a holy and a happy Epiphany this day, and Father told me of a wonderful surprise he has in store for me. He recognizes that I have been working diligently on my studies, and he believes that a trip to the theater will aid my understanding of the dramas. He has already booked places for us, he with the gentlemen and I with the ladies. Although some of my friends have been to the theater, Father usually prefers the quiet of his study. When he has attended the theater in the past, his friends have always accompanied him and I have never been invited. I am anxiously awaiting the day!

My father has still not returned to the subject of finding me a husband, and I am now afraid to mention it. His anger was so sudden, and so unlooked for, that I dare not try again.

21

ANA

The room was chilly, and even the embers from the night before had gone cold. Her pallet had afforded Ana only a fitful night of sleep. The phrase *happy match* had come to her each time she half woke, but she could not discern the meaning of it. As she came to full consciousness, she remembered Juliana's confusion and desire. There was a reason why Sebastián would be reluctant to endeavor to find Juliana a husband, though Juliana might never be told that.

Ana was anxious to leave the inn. It had afforded little comfort and no new information, unless one could term it information that her brother and niece had apparently *not* stopped at this particular place. She could find no consolation in this thought, however, and as the carriage pulled away, she had to acknowledge that their stop had served only to increase her anxiety over the course that she had chosen to follow.

After they had traveled for almost an hour, Father Del Valle had already fallen into sleep, and, should he follow the pattern he had already established, there was little that could awaken him. Ana wondered at his limitless ability to slumber, and whether its cause was some long-endured exhaustion or something more akin to the many days of sleep through which she had sought to escape her grief upon Emilio's death.

Indistinguishable days followed, one after the other. Andrea's conversation had long since been depleted, and, after a few brief exchanges, Ana and Father Del Valle had said all that each wished to share. In reality, the creaking of the coach, the sound of the horses' hooves, and the wheels crunching along the road did not lend themselves to easy discourse.

Olive trees, sheep, barren land, fields with meager crops of grain, all passed by Ana's window in no particular pattern. Some days she tried to find a kind of loveliness in the starkness of the landscape. At times she succeeded, marveling that beauty could reside amidst hopelessness and suffering, just as she had perceived the dignity and grace in a painting of Christ Crucified.

Trying to temper her despair, Ana prayed her rosary, but always she soon found that while one part of her mind repeated the prescribed prayers, her thoughts reviewed what she had heard the night before. After her failure at the first two inns, each night Ana had made sure that she had asked about all of the possibilities, since she did not know whether Sebastián traveled with Juliana and Silvia, whether Silvia traveled with Juliana alone, or even if Sebastián accompanied Juliana and Silvia had disappeared elsewhere. Always the story was the same, however. No gentleman with his daughter and her *dueña*. No *dueña* with her charge. No girl with her father. With each negative response, it seemed less likely that Sevilla was her loved ones' destination. Since there was nothing else she could do now, she would continue and, when she arrived in Sevilla, proceed as though she had not met with negative replies at every stop.

Even Juliana's journal did not beckon Ana. In truth,

she had come to both fear and long for an answer there. Now, at night, the exhaustion produced by her days-long journey overwhelmed her anxiety, and her body sought the refuge not allowed her in daylight hours: a deep, though troubled, sleep.

As they approached their last overnight stop before arriving in Sevilla, Señor Rojas informed Ana that they would be staying in the town of Carmona, and that his cousin was in the convent of Santa Clara there. He suggested she might like to spend the night with the sisters, and Ana gratefully accepted this promise of a brief but peaceful respite. The sisters welcomed her with calm and graciously invited her to join them in evening prayers in the church.

The church and the soft hum of the nuns' prayers soothed Ana, and her own prayers asked for guidance and strength for whatever was to come. As though it were a physical blessing, Ana found solace in the graceful Mudéjar architecture, which reminded her of the similar Moorish influence on the architecture of Toledo, whose streets she had walked with Emilio on a short visit there.

When she returned to the tiny room the kind sisters had provided for her, Ana again ventured into Juliana's diary.

22

Juliana

My first trip to the theater was today! Along with my father and his friend and colleague Don Lorenzo Pizarro de Robledo, we saw a play by Don Calderón de la Barca, *Life Is a Dream*. The play was most interesting, and I shall describe here the action and themes, to aid in future recollections of this wonderful day.

The heroine, Rosaura, has gone to Poland to restore her honor, stolen by a man who made her promises and then abandoned her. She chances upon an imprisoned man, Segismundo, who was put there by his father, King Basilio, the king having read in the stars that the son would be a tyrant. Now Basilio has decided to test Segismundo and has had him brought to the castle in a deep sleep. Segismundo awakens, responding to his new freedom and power with the cruelty his father foretold. The king had sought to coerce fate, but by those very actions, which imprisoned his son and made a beast of him, Basilio ensured the very destiny he had wished to avoid.

A sleeping Segismundo is returned to his prison and, upon awakening, is told that all was a dream. He has little choice but to believe this, declaring, "All of life is a dream, and dreams are but dreams."

Basilio plans to put his nephew, Astolfo, on the throne, but the army rebels against this idea and releases Segismundo. Basilio's forces are vanquished, but Segismundo shows his father mercy. Only in kneeling, of his own will, before his father, can Segismundo hope to tame his nature through his own humility and moderation.

Segismundo pledges Astolfo to Rosaura in marriage, as Astolfo was he who stole her honor. All applaud Segismundo's wisdom, and he ends the play explaining that he still may awaken from this dream, but that all human happiness passes thus, and that he will act righteously and enjoy it fully while he may.

After the performance, my father invited Don Lorenzo to our home for a light repast, and they discussed the play at length, arguing its subtler points. In his discussions of the qualities of dream and reality, and of the fleeting nature of this life, if I may be so bold as to pass judgment on them, my father's comments were most astute. Even Don Lorenzo, who has attended the university and is himself most learned, conceded that my father had pointed out aspects of the play that had previously eluded him.

When they began to speak of the question of honor, however, my father became most unreasoning, his discussion straying from the subject of the play. His voice began to rise, and he declared that whatever is done in the name of honor is justified, that the pernicious nature of honor is such that, though we may be blameless in its loss, we are duty-bound to restore it. At one point, my father was so agitated that he began to scream.

"Whatever the cost! Whatever the cost!"

Don Lorenzo, quite taken aback by the vehemence of my father's outburst, attempted to assuage him. "Of course, Don Sebastián, honor is of paramount importance in the life of any man."

"And of any woman!" my father shouted.

"And of any woman," Don Lorenzo agreed quickly. "But man is the guardian of the honor of any woman under his protection, and thus it can be said that he is doubly burdened."

"It is no burden to guard one's honor. Without it, what is life?"

"Indeed, Don Sebastián. But it is getting late, and I must make my way home. Thank you so much for your hospitality. It has been a pleasure, Don Sebastián, to have the honor of accompanying you and your lovely daughter to the theater. Good evening, Juliana." Don Lorenzo then looked at me in a way that made me feel uncomfortable. Perhaps I held his gaze too long, for as I responded, "Good night, Don Lorenzo," my father cast a stormy look at me.

Don Lorenzo left, and I turned to my father, bewildered by his sudden disapproval. "Thank you for allowing me to go to the theater, Father. I enjoyed it very much."

"See that you remember its lesson!" he replied roughly, then abruptly left the room.

I do not know what I could have done to offend my father, nor to which lesson he referred. Though my *dueña* tells me that I can be headstrong, I have always obeyed and honored him in all things. I must assume that my father referred to the question of the restoration of Rosaura's honor as the lesson that he wished me to hold close. She held it above all else, and its loss cost her dearly. Still, I must admit that I was more intrigued by the questions of dream and reality, of fate and free will, that were presented in the play. How can we be sure of what is real? How large a part does fate play in the drama of our lives?

23

ANA

As Ana rode in the coach the next morning, she wondered whether she had found in the latest entry from Juliana's diary an explanation for why her niece had been so agitated the morning when they had met for Mass. Her father had been inexplicably sharp with her, and she knew that Juliana was very sensitive to even his slightest rebuke. Still, Juliana had concluded her entry with philosophical musings about reality and fate, not further anxious comments about her father's behavior.

Once again, Juliana's account of Sebastián's attitude worried Ana. She had known him to be intractable, and all those years ago, tragedy had been the result. But Ana tried to put that out of her mind, for always she had observed a gentleness in Sebastián in dealings with his daughter. Could it be that Juliana's emotions had caused her to exaggerate the virulence of her father's comments? Could a sixteen-year-old girl be a faithful chronicler of her father's words?

Ana put aside these disturbing reflections, as she needed to refine the story that she had mentally prepared for her meeting with Señor de Ovando, partner to Señor Monsalve, and acquaintance of Emilio. She had decided that she would go to see de Ovando as soon as she was settled into the home of Señora Nelleda, the woman Monsalve had recommended.

⌒⁄⌐

Anticipation vied with anxiety in Ana's mind as she approached the house of Señor de Ovando. She had met him, but only on a few occasions, and then had spoken to him only briefly. She knocked on the door of the house, which spoke of respectability and affluence, if not great wealth. The servant who answered the door went in to announce her to his master, and she was soon asked to wait in a study that succeeded at looking both serious and comfortable. Señor de Ovando had taken care to show an inherent respect for his guests and visiting business associates by providing them with a chair as fine as his own. Both had wide arms and a slightly cushioned seat covered in tooled leather. The writing table was quite impressive for the modesty of the home in general, being of mahogany from the colonies, rather than from walnut, as was most common. Even Sebastián had not allowed himself such a luxury.

Her observations proceeded no further, as her host entered the room. "Ah, señora, it is delightful to see you. It has been such a long time, but I seldom get to Madrid anymore. What is the point? Things are in such chaos there that I might as well stay here and try to keep my business interests from dwindling any further."

Immediately Ana recognized the long, thin face, with the turned-down nose and prominent lower jaw, which she had previously associated with images she had seen of the Habsburg kings. As the unusually tall man walked toward her, she saw that his gait was hampered by a slight limp, which she did not recall having noticed in the past.

"It is very kind of you to see me, Señor de Ovando, and you are right. We have not met since before my husband's death."

"I was gravely saddened when I heard of Don Emilio's

121

death. How can I stand here, complaining of petty business matters, when you have suffered so much?"

"Your letter of condolence was a great kindness. I do hope that your wife and family are enjoying good health."

"Oh, yes, and our eldest daughter, who married last year, is soon to give us a grandchild." Señor de Ovando relaxed again, happy to be speaking of his own family.

"Wonderful news indeed!" Ana replied, as she felt the familiar pang. It did not matter if her mind wandered, for Señor de Ovando was contentedly cataloging the current accomplishments of his family.

"But I must stop boring you with such details."

"On the contrary, it is always a pleasure to hear of the good fortune of those with whom one has shared experiences. I do find that this is especially so with those who knew my husband before I met him. Somehow, conversing with you or other of Emilio's old friends makes me feel as if a part of him carries on still, independent of my own memories of him.

"I have heard some women say they feel jealous of anyone who knows something of their husbands of which they themselves are ignorant. I might add that I have met men with similar sentiments about their wives. This is foreign to me, for I have learned, though it has not been an easy lesson, that what my husband was outside my comprehension makes him even more than I knew him to be. I now try to love that unknown part of him, as I always loved that part that was familiar. Realizing that there were complexities in his heart that I did not fathom adds to my grief in some ways but also gives me more to cherish in memory."

Ana looked up to see Señor de Ovando fumbling with the papers on his desk, and she blushed to realize she had wandered into such personal musings with a man whom, niceties aside, she did not know well.

"But you must forgive me for my somber ruminations. I confess I am becoming overly pensive."

"Not at all," Señor de Ovando replied, still obviously uncomfortable. "May I have some tea brought for you?"

"You are very kind, though I fear I am already taking too much of your valuable day." Having uttered the prescribed phrase to show that she was aware that she was imposing, Ana paused, hoping he would ask the reason for her visit.

"What brings you to Sevilla, Doña Ana? As I recall, Don Emilio once told me you do not care for travel."

"That is so," Ana said, and briefly wondered if Emilio had ever confided in Señor de Ovando regarding his dream of the Indies. "However, I am here for a most specific reason, and, as your kind letter of condolence offered help if ever I should need it, I have presumed to come to ask a favor of you."

Señor de Ovando stiffened slightly but replied, "I am at your service, señora."

"These circumstances may sound very strange to you, but please believe that my mission is urgent and there was no other to perform this duty. My brother, Sebastián Torres López, is in Sevilla on business, and I have come to seek him on a critical family matter. I felt that I needed to come myself, to convey to him the gravity of the situation, and to persuade him to return with me to Madrid immediately."

"And of what help can I be, señora?" Señor de Ovando asked, his curiosity piqued and his manner more relaxed, now that he sensed that no very great sacrifice was to be required of him.

"Unfortunately, I do not know who my brother was planning to see here, and though I asked his secretary, even he was unable to apprise me of the details."

"That is odd, is it not?"

"I thought so, but I can hardly worry about that now. What I have come to ask of you, Señor de Ovando, is your help in locating my brother. I hoped that if you could possibly contact other businessmen of your acquaintance, someone might have knowledge of him."

"But, Doña Ana, surely you must realize that Sevilla is a large city, a very busy port. Visitors here are not noted, as men of business constantly come and go. I could make inquiries, but I can hold out to you very little hope of success."

"Your effort is all that I ask, Señor de Ovando, and believe that I accept your offer with most heartfelt thanks, even should your endeavors prove fruitless." Señor de Ovando had not actually offered his help, but Ana could not afford to allow him to talk himself out of making some effort on her behalf.

"Then of course I shall do what I can." Señor de Ovando smiled at Ana, accepting that he had been tricked but wishing Ana to know that he was aware of what she had done. "Tell me, is your brother traveling alone?"

Though Ana realized instantly that she should have anticipated this question, she had not. She could not hesitate in answering, as it would seem most odd were she not to have this information.

"My sixteen-year-old niece, Juliana, is accompanying him," Ana responded, wondering whether she had erred in her decision.

"He brought his daughter with him on a business trip?" Señor de Ovando asked, raising his brows. "Is that his usual custom?"

"Naturally not, but the girl has been somewhat melancholy of late, and I believe my brother wished to offer her new sites, to restore her usual cheerful demeanor."

"I have never heard of indulgence as a cure for childish melancholia. In fact, I believe discipline to be the more appropriate course. None of my family has ever suffered from this malady."

"You are fortunate indeed," Ana interjected quickly, desirous of avoiding any further listing of the virtues of her host's family. "I'm afraid that my brother is at times not as firm with my niece as he might be, but I assure you that the source of this fault is more a surplus of affection than a lack of duty. The necessity of raising Juliana alone has perhaps caused my brother to cosset my niece more than might be wise. Thankfully, my niece has a *dueña*, who is able to provide some balance. She also escorted my niece on this trip.

"Now that I think of it, perhaps it was my brother's haste to relieve his daughter of her lugubrious mood that caused him to neglect to give the details of his visit to his secretary. It could also be that a major purpose of the trip was pleasure, rather than business, and for this reason the secretary would have little knowledge of my brother's plans."

"In that case, it will be even less likely that I shall meet with success in helping you find him. Many come to Sevilla for pleasure, but they rarely consult with my business acquaintances in pursuit of it."

"Just so," Ana replied, feeling that she had put off Señor de Ovando with her portrait of a lax father bringing his daughter on a pleasure trip. "Yet I do assure you that the reason for my search is of the utmost gravity, and I have few resources here in Sevilla to call upon."

"I will do what I can, señora. Where might I get in touch with you to inform you of any progress, or lack of it, that I might make?"

Ana told him where she was staying, and as he accompanied her to the door, Señor de Ovando stopped a moment.

"Doña Ana, is not your brother an *arbitrista*?"

"Yes, he is. You have heard of him?"

"I have, and though I have admired many of his ideas, I must admit that some of his proposals have not always been popular with the business community here. We sometimes feel we are expected to forgo the fruits of our labor, to those who have not seen fit to commit themselves to hard work."

Ana knew that he referred not only to *arbitristas*, but also to the nobility, who often scorned work, and to the poor. Ana had seen for herself, however, in her work with the poor, that they could not better their situations no matter how diligently they applied themselves. She doubted, however, that Señor de Ovando shared this opinion.

"Though my understanding of such things is limited," she ventured, "I am sure there are men who, caught up in the enthusiasm of their own ideas, fail to take into account the needs of others."

"Indeed," Señor de Ovando responded, and Ana hoped that he assumed that she was in agreement with him but that, out of respect for Sebastián, she was refraining from criticizing her brother to others. A man such as he would admire such loyalty.

"Well, I shall certainly see what I can do, though I must warn you that this adds to the difficulty of the situation. Some of my business colleagues are not as open-minded as I, and they are loath simply to hear the names of those who ply His Majesty's ministers with their reforming schemes."

Ana bristled inwardly at the use of the term *schemes* in reference to her brother, though the *arbitristas'* ideas were often referred to as such. Ana knew that many of Sebastián's concepts aimed to help the poorest in the country, and that someone would have to pay for such changes. It followed that those who had more wealth would feel threatened. Still, men such as Señor de Ovando were far from the richest or most powerful in the land. The general economic problems of the country must adversely affect him. The financial factors that had led to repeated devaluations of the currency, and the foreign policies that contributed to the king's rationalization for confiscating much of the silver from the returning trade fleets, must have been a legitimate grievance of the businessmen of Sevilla. Still, some of those with even a relatively small advantage in society would always prefer to maintain the status quo over risking a change, even though all might ultimately benefit from it.

"There is a great variety of plans put forth by men such as my brother. I trust that a man like you must coldly analyze all of the ramifications of any given proposal. I would hope that you would not find all my brother's ideas detrimental to you and your fellow businessmen."

Afraid that she had become too argumentative and that she risked losing the pose she must maintain of a woman in need of help from a gallant caballero, she continued, "But why do I rattle on so? I know so little of such things. I am most deeply in your debt."

Señor de Ovando bowed indulgently. "For your gracious self, and for the memory of Don Emilio, I will do all in my power."

Ana smiled, nodded, and escaped before Señor de Ovando could think to ask who was escorting her about the great city. He might have offered her the services of one of his own servants as a suitable escort, while Ana wished to preserve as much anonymity in her search as possible.

Ana supposed that the interview had gone as well as could be expected, yet Juliana's disappearance consumed her thoughts. She was angry with herself for not having foreseen Señor de Ovando's question of whether Sebastián was traveling alone. No matter what she said, there were certain pitfalls. In the moments available to her to consider, Ana had reasoned that making inquiries about two people, rather than one, would increase the chances that someone would come forth with some useful information. Though she had asked only that Señor de Ovando make inquiries of his acquaintances, she had felt fairly certain that his honor, and perhaps a sense of curiosity, would persuade him to employ whatever measures were available to him.

Now, however, she questioned whether this had been the wisest course. If Juliana was not with Sebastián, then searching for a man traveling with a daughter and her *dueña* could delay or inhibit success. More important, if Sebastián were in some sort of danger—and, in light of his strange behavior, this possibility must be considered—then perhaps Ana had done wrong in going to de Ovando at all. Furthermore, perhaps the lack of information that was available on her journey suggested that they were all traveling separately, and this might well support the theory of some danger to Sebastián. For what other reason could there be for her brother to abandon his daughter to the perils of the road, if not to protect her from some greater threat? If such were the case, then she had unwittingly foiled her brother's plan to protect Juliana, by revealing her niece's presence in the city.

Yet even as she came to these conclusions, her mind rebelled. With what sinister cause could Señor de Ovando be connected? His only real fault seemed to be his excessive pride in his family. Surely violence could not be awaiting Ana's loved ones from that quarter. Still, what feeling and suspicion had impelled her to this blind pursuit? She told herself that she had allowed her imagination to run unfettered in search of an explanation for her brother's and her niece's disappearance.

Craving a respite from these thoughts, Ana shifted her attention to her surroundings. She was coming upon yet another church, La Iglesia de Santa Catalina. She remembered that Emilio had told her that many of the buildings in this city of the Andalucían region showed the influence of the Moors, who now had not ruled the city for centuries. The Alcázar was, of course, of Moorish and Mudéjar design. Some of the churches had been built on the ruins of mosques, retaining still some features of the former style.

As Ana slowed and stopped in front of Santa Catalina, she thought she could discern such influence here. In spite of her own current quandary, she wondered what happens to a people when another tries to wipe them away. What do they leave behind of their spirits, and what do the newcomers unwittingly take unto themselves? What did today's Sevillanos have of those who called the city Ishbiliya and the region Al Andalus? Indeed, what did she carry within her of an unknown past?

A movement on the periphery of her vision caused her to turn her head: a young woman, the size and age of Juliana. Of course it was not she. Ridiculous to let herself hope for such an encounter in a city the size of Sevilla. Still, that was precisely the reason she was roaming the streets. The young woman smiled at her. It was an easy smile, and Ana envied her that ease.

Even knowing that her wandering could hardly bear the fruit she so desired, Ana continued on, trying to get a better sense of the city. The houses were more ostentatious than those in Madrid, she realized, and as she looked at those passing her, she noticed that their clothes were also more extravagant. Chastising herself for these frivolous thoughts, Ana continued on the quest she understood was probably hopeless, but imperative.

Frustration as much as physical fatigue had led Ana to return to the house of Señora Nelleda after a futile afternoon of walking the streets of the city. She had quickly succumbed to sleep, but a knock awakened her, and as she opened the door, the servant girl informed her that a Señor de Ovando was in the parlor, wondering if she might be available.

"Please tell Señor de Ovando that I shall be down in a few moments," Ana replied, as she began to straighten her hair and gown. She told herself that he must have come simply to acquire further details to aid him in his search. Still, as she entered the room to greet him, she could not help but hope that he had already met with success.

"Señor de Ovando, how kind of you to call!"

"Doña Ana, I hope that my appearance has not given you false hope. Though I have begun to put the wheels in motion, I have no news as yet."

Ana tried to hide her disappointment. "Of course. It is most kind of you to accept this undertaking. May I offer you some refreshment?"

"No, thank you. I do not wish to impose. I merely came to ask if there is anything else I might do to make your stay in Sevilla more comfortable."

"That is very considerate, Señor de Ovando, but I am quite comfortable, and I do not anticipate that my stay in your city will be of any great duration."

"I should disabuse you of that notion, señora, for with

only the most incredible luck would we find your brother very quickly."

"Perhaps my prayers will speed the process."

"I, too, am a man of faith, señora, but in many things God expects us to rely upon our own devices."

"Nevertheless, I am quite comfortable. Thank you for your concern. You are already performing such a service for me that I will be forever in your debt."

"I do not know that you will owe me much if I disappoint, señora."

"I do not believe that we will fail. Besides, even Our Lord demands only that we endeavor, not that we always triumph."

"I do not like to fail, señora."

"A quality that I am sure has served you well."

"There was one other thing, señora: I wondered if you'd heard the latest news from Madrid."

"Madrid?"

"A Don Lorenzo Pizarro de Robledo was found some days ago very early in the morning, murdered in his own courtyard. Apparently, even the servants saw nothing."

Ana concealed her recognition of the name from Juliana's diary. "These are desperate times for many, señor. Surely even here in Sevilla you have such occurrences."

"You misunderstand me, señora. This was no chance murder by a discovered thief. Nothing was missing or disturbed, and Señor Pizarro was not bludgeoned. One single sword thrust to his heart killed him. One might almost guess it was the work of some wronged gentleman."

"But a gentleman would surely choose a more public manner in which to answer an insult."

"I must agree with you. Nevertheless, the speculation is that it is in the salons, and not the alleyways, that the culprit is being sought." Ana did not respond.

"Señor Pizarro, I believe, like your brother, offered grand solutions to the government for the improvement of the nation. Were they by any chance associates?"

"They may have known each other. My brother is acquainted with many important men in the capital, at court, and elsewhere. Naturally, I am not overly familiar with these aspects of my brother's life, but I do not recall that he mentioned a gentleman by that name."

"Of course. As is Sevilla, Madrid is a very large place, and there are hundreds of men who are involved with the workings of His Majesty's government. Well, I will take no more of your time. I hope that when next we meet, I will be the bearer of happier tidings."

"I shall pray for that. Thank you for your visit, Señor de Ovando."

As she climbed the stairs back to her room, Ana's thoughts raced. Had Señor de Ovando believed that she did not know of Pizarro? She wasn't even certain why she had denied any connection. What difference could it make to Señor de Ovando whether Sebastián had known Pizarro? Did he suspect that there was some sinister explanation for Sebastián's disappearance?

Ana could hardly credit that the murder and her brother's flight could be related. Still, Sebastián and the dead man had been allies in many political maneuverings. As the country's problems worsened, those with influence had become ever less willing to compromise, for fear of losing their dwindling assets. Could someone have finally decided that rivals must be killed? Had the weapons of financial ruin or ostracism now become too weak, accusation and imprisonment too slow a way to rid oneself of one's enemies?

Late that night, in the last pages of Juliana's diary, Ana found her answer.

24

Juliana

10 February

I am wretched, defiled by that false friend of my father's,
Don Lorenzo! Last night, I heard a noise outside my
window, and as I approached the iron grill to peer outside,
the balcony door gave way. I was seized by the arm, a hand
placed over my mouth. Don Lorenzo told me that I would
not be hurt if I would but keep still. Although I could not
imagine what honorable intention he could have to come
upon me thus in my own room, in my innocence neither did
I suspect his true purpose. I nodded that I would keep still,
and he slowly released me. At first, he tried to speak to me
with words of love, and I was both amazed and frightened
that he should find this manner to proclaim it. But his real
desires soon became evident. What he wished was my
surrender, and when I indignantly refused, he grabbed me
all the more tightly and covered my mouth so that I could
barely breathe. Although I struggled all I could, his brute
force overcame my resistance. After he had finished his vile
act, he departed my room the same way he had come and
left me with my pain.

I must have fainted into sleep until this morning, when
Silvia came into my room. At once my misery was evident
to her, and as I haltingly told her of its cause, her outrage

turned to despair. Her words repeat endlessly in my thoughts.

"You must keep this quiet" was her short response when I had finished my laments.

"While I do not wish to have my situation made public, neither will I tolerate the villain being left unpunished. My father must avenge that which I have lost!"

"The loss of your honor could be a great danger to you," she said.

"Danger! What can be worse than that which I have this night endured? I am faultless! I have been violated, and I demand vengeance! How can you counsel secrecy? When my father knows—"

"It is precisely that your father must not know!" She looked at me with terror in her eyes and continued. "You know that I love you as a daughter, and I tell you this in the fullness of my love."

"A curse on love that would have me live thus, feeding my shame and my dishonor! I demand that you go and tell my father. He will heal his honor and my own!"

"Listen to me, my child. I have known your father for far longer than you have trodden this earth. If he learns of this, he will see you as a symbol of his dishonor. To him, the satisfaction to be extracted will be his, and he will destroy as he sees fit."

"And in this will lie the restoration of my honor."

"Do you not understand that the only remedy can lie in marriage or in death? This will avenge his honor, but what of you? Is this the price you wish to pay for one night's unhappiness? Be careful that it is not you who answers for another's sin."

"I will listen to this no more! I demand that you tell my father! If you do not, I will go myself!"

"No! I will do as you command," she said, and she gave me a look of inconsolable sorrow, as from an older grief. "Grant me only this, I beg of you: let me delay telling your father until tonight. This will give us both time to further think this through."

I did not know how pondering my plight could change its facts, but I conceded to Silvia's plea.

Soon I must meet Tía Ana for Mass, and I will also seek the confessional, to see if there is any penance that can cleanse this stain.

10 February (evening)

I do not know why I did not wish to confide in Tía Ana, but that Silvia had convinced me to hide my sorry state from her. I have sadly continued my deception, writing to my *tía* not to return to my home to check on me.

Tomorrow Silvia will inform my father, but now her warning plays as a constant refrain in my mind. I sent Silvia to my father, that he might avenge my honor. Only now, in the stillness of my room, do I begin to wonder what form that vengeance will take. Silvia said that to remedy the violation, my father would demand that Don Lorenzo marry me. I knew this to be true, and yet the full horror of it strikes me only now. My satisfaction must come from submitting myself to the man who saw me as a thing to defile and abuse. How can this alleviate my grief? My lord and husband will be he who has so brutally destroyed my maidenhood. My father would reward him with my hand. Gone are any hopes I might have had that Antonio will one day be my husband.

Despair overpowers me, and I pray to the Virgin Mary to help me in my time of need and torment.

I write these final words in haste as Silvia prepares for our flight. She came to my room a short while ago.

"Ay, Juliana, my child, all is lost! We must flee, for I do not wish to live to see you die!"

"What has happened?" I asked, confused and frightened by her words.

"Early this morning, I went to see your father. I have learned that Don Sebastián then went to see Don Lorenzo and demand that he marry you, but Don Lorenzo refused—"

"Refused? But why?"

Ignoring my question, Silvia continued. "He refused, and your father became enraged. Drawing his sword, he ran Don Lorenzo through, then ran off, to we know not where."

"What? How do you know this?"

"My nephew, Pablo, is servant to Don Lorenzo, and he has just come to relate the news to me. He was the only witness, and I told him to tell no one and to leave the city. Oh, my Juliana, you must run away!"

"Why? I don't understand. What my father has done, he has done for me. I will not abandon him now that he needs me."

"No, my child. Your father's anger is not spent. Pablo heard Don Sebastián say that one of two of the stains to his dishonor has been destroyed. He will cleanse the other, though it be to shed his life's blood. Your father means to kill you!"

"No! You must be wrong. My father loves me! Why would he punish me in my innocence?"

"Because his honor is above all other things to him. I had hoped that the years had healed this in him, but they have not. I have before known him to be so unjust."

I do not know what these last words meant, but even as I protested, I knew that she was right. I knew that now he would be blinded to a daughter's love and would sacrifice all for his rapacious honor.

I will place this book in its hiding place. Perhaps some girl in future times will come across it and learn from my sorrows.

NEW WORLD

RACHEL

St. Louis, Missouri, 1992

I pushed through the stolen sleep, my mind registering the blinking light as an ambulance. I leaped to help, to inform the drivers, but I fell onto a cold, hard floor. My legs prickled, and my arms were numb. The lights were from the monitors, tracking my mother's life. They droned on. No change for six days.

I shuffled back toward the straight chair and dropped into it. In my dream, my mother held my hand. She was bent low, her hand cupped close to my ear as though to tell me a secret, but I didn't feel her breath tickling me. "We have to let Daddy rest now. Everything will be all right. Mama's here."

I had never called my mother Mama, and she had never referred to herself that way. I called her Mom, or even Helen. I shifted in the chair. The door squeaked, and my eyes rebelled at the light.

"Honey, try to lie down and rest. I'll sit up with Helen." The meaning of Ned's words drifted into my consciousness.

"I'm fine. I'll just stay a little longer."

Ned pulled the other chair close and sat down.

"I was just dreaming about my dad. Helen kept saying it would be all right."

When I woke up again, I was lying in the bed next to my mother's, sunlight streaking through the gaps in the blinds. Ned must have coaxed me into the bed before he left. There was bustling outside the room. The nurse would be invading again. She was only doing her job, but all the disturbances had accomplished nothing. The door cracked open, and I turned toward it, preparing my vexation, but Gabe stuck his head into the room.

"Hi, Mom. How's Grandma today?"

"About the same." Always the same.

Gabe came closer, and I groaned a protest as a rare hug pinned my upper arms against my body. He was tall enough that I had to look up at him though he was just starting high school. I worried about his reluctance to show his feelings. So like Helen, but they understood each other.

Gabe glanced at his grandmother, his voice remaining steady, with only a slight tremor around his mouth.

"Dad said he'd come by at lunchtime. He had to go round on some patients this morning."

"How are you getting to school?" I grasped at the mundane, with its easy, identifiable answer.

"Tom's mom said she'd swing by and pick me up when it's time. She's been bringing all kinds of food to the house. She says we need to keep our strength up."

"That's nice of her. She's a nice lady." I said this mechanically, and I heard myself and wondered what it mattered.

"Yeah, I guess so, but she's not a very good cook. Mom, you don't look too good."

"Gabe, I'm your mother, not one of your friends. You're not supposed to insult me, remember?" I tried a laugh but failed. I welcomed the look of concern on my boy's face.

"Well, you're in here early this morning," the nurse said to Gabe as she came into the room. Then turning to me, she added, "And you're in here late. You do need to get some rest. There's no telling how long your mother will be like this."

I recognized her concern for me, but her words seemed callous. She needed to do her job, and she couldn't if she became involved with each patient. I knew that from Ned, though he seldom talked about his work.

"I did sleep some last night. Gabe, could you sit by Grandma while I run down to the cafeteria and grab a bite to eat? I'll be back before you have to go." I made my way to the door, abandoning my mother to the care of my son.

"Has there been any change?" Ned asked, as he entered the room.

I turned from where I'd been standing next to my mother's bed. "Please stop asking me that every time you come in. If there's any change, I'll tell you."

Ned walked over and put his arm around my shoulders. "I'm sorry, Rachel."

I buried my face in his shoulder, vaguely wondering why he loved me. It certainly had nothing to do with my looks. I'm plain: brown hair, brown eyes, irregular features. I looked up at Ned and brushed my lips against his. I suppose he accepted my occasional short temper as the other side of my enthusiasm, my ready changes a counterbalance to the evenness for which I loved him.

"Do you think she'll be all right?" I asked him again.

"I don't know."

"I didn't even get to tell her about the baby."

"Rachel, you've got to get some rest. You don't want to endanger the pregnancy."

"I know. It's taken us so long. It's just that when I'm away from her bed, I'm afraid. I keep thinking about how I wasn't there when my dad died."

Ned nodded at the familiar grievance.

"Rachel, we don't know what's going to happen. This could drag on for weeks. When I come back after work, you go home and have dinner and get a good night's rest. Please do that for me. Tom's mom brings food over every day."

I hesitated but then relented. "I know you're right. But do I have to eat Tom's mom's food? Gabe didn't exactly give it rave reviews."

"Oh, yes. Let us not doubt Gabe's culinary expertise!" He kissed my forehead and went off to his own floor.

I absently rubbed the slight bulge at my middle. We hadn't wanted to tell anyone until I was further along and we felt more sure that everything would be all right. The day of Helen's accident, I had been on my way to her house to give her the hopeful news. It was the girl that she had been wanting for so long.

When I was young, I told my mother everything. The telling made excitement more real, or unpleasantness less harsh. If the effect came from the telling, and not the attitude of the listener, I was too young to notice the difference. After Dad died, my mother and I had only each other, but Helen was always so reserved. In time, I, too, became less forthcoming.

As I approached college age, there was one particularly strained subject between us. Helen began to talk about marriage, how critical it was to find a good husband at an early age. When I later announced my intention to go to graduate school, she saw this as a further postponement of my finding a husband. I didn't tell her that I'd already found the man I hoped to marry. It was small and selfish of me, but I didn't want to give her the satisfaction of thinking that her prompting had influenced me.

After dating Ned for several months, I did tell Helen about him and proudly introduced him to her. When we later became engaged, she immediately began to press us to set a date. I was in grad school by then, and Ned was in medical school. Despite a lingering rebelliousness against doing my mother's bidding, Ned and I did decide that we would be happier being together while we finished our studies, and that, though it would be difficult, we could do it.

When we married, I thought I would have my mother's full approval, but then her complaints began to center on our not having children right away. A child would have been very difficult with both of us in school, and she knew it. Still she persisted, but never when Ned was around. She was very fond of him, and I think that she felt comfortable with him, but she never talked about children when he was around. At first I was glad that Ned didn't have this extra annoyance, but as time passed, I resented the fact that I was bearing this alone, serving as a buffer between Ned and my mother. Now that I had lived with Ned for so many years, I realized that I could easily have discussed it with him. He would have been supportive of me, without condemning my mother. But back then, I was still insecure, afraid of letting anything spoil our life together, so the anger simmered and my resentment against my mother grew.

I had other married friends whose parents would now and then teasingly ask them when they would have a grandchild, but with Helen it seemed an urgent, personal need. As her only child, I was her sole hope for grandchildren, but I got tired of reassuring her that Ned and I wanted children.

"How long do you have to put it off? I'll never live to see my grandchildren." I'd remind her that she was still young and that even if Ned and I delayed children for a few years, there was no need to worry that she would not one day have succeeding generations gathered around her. I believed this. When we're young, we believe that we're spontaneous, that we revel in change, all the while denying the irrevocable and unexpected change of death. For even the most doubting young people, the future will be as they envision it.

While Ned was finishing his first year of residency and I was still working on my dissertation, we had our first child, but Helen was oddly disturbed that it was a boy. Only a few days after Gabe was born, she asked whether we would soon try to have a little girl. The old badgering made me angry, and I was hurt at the slight to my sweet newborn.

"How can you start on that already? Why is Gabe not enough for you? Please be happy with me! I thought this was what you wanted!"

"It's just that it's such a joy for a woman to have a daughter," she stammered. "You can share so much with her. . . . Besides, then Gabe can have someone to play with." It seemed to me that she added this last sentence only to placate me.

"You and Dad had only one child! Don't you think that I would have liked to have someone to play with?"

As soon as the words were out, I regretted them. My mother recoiled.

"We tried, but we weren't blessed with another child" was all she said.

"I'm sorry, Mom." I knew that it had cost her to tell

me even this. Dad used to joke that he had told Helen every thought he'd ever had and that he didn't know anything about her life before the day he met her. She would just laugh and not deny it.

"And I'm sorry about starting on you again. It's just that it's so important to me."

"Why is it so important to you?"

"We won't talk about it anymore." And we didn't. We never again talked about my having another child. I didn't share with her my miscarriages, or that Ned and I had even quit hoping.

The afternoon at the hospital passed with no change, and when Ned came that evening, I did leave for a while. On my way out I stopped by the cafeteria, unwilling to abandon my days-old vigil. The lights suspended from the ceiling were inadequate for the large space and lent the room a perpetual twilight. I got a cup of coffee and found a secluded spot in a corner, near a large yucca plant whose swordlike leaves stabbed my back whenever I shifted. I sipped the bitter coffee, put some creamer and sugar in it, then tasted it again. Then I remembered the baby and pushed the cup away. I got up and walked out the door.

I hadn't been able to get much sleep, and after dropping Gabe off at school the next morning, I drove to the hospital to relieve Ned.

"Has there been any change?" I asked, then remembered how I'd snapped at him for that question. Before he could answer, Helen's voice said, "Hi, honey."

I felt a sudden rush as I walked over to the bed. "How are you feeling?" But she didn't answer.

"She's been going in and out for about the last hour," Ned said. "I tried to call you, but I guess you'd already left with Gabe."

"This means she's going to be all right, doesn't it?"

"I don't know, Rachel." Once again, I found Ned's unwillingness to tell me what I wanted to hear frustrating. The downside of being married to a doctor is that they can't speak from the easy hope of ignorance.

"You look terrible yourself."

"Yeah, I guess I'll go up to the call room and shower and shave before I go on rounds."

I leaned over my mother and began to whisper.

"I have something to tell you. I'm pregnant, and we already know it's a little girl. That'll make you happy, won't it? Now you're going to get all better, and we'll spoil the baby together."

I searched her still face. I pulled up the chair, rested my arms on the bed, and waited. Finally, there was a slight motion. I looked into my mother's gray eyes.

"Too late," she mouthed. "I am like Ana. I have failed Juliana." Then she was gone.

26

RACHEL

Those next few days are a blur. I think I concentrated on trying to figure out what my mother had meant as a buffer between myself and grief. I interrogated the doctors, but all they said was that sometimes when older people are in great physical distress, they hallucinate or have strange dreams whose reality they insist upon. That was the only explanation offered for why my mother had mentioned two names that I had never heard, but Ned said there had been no other signs of confusion in those intermittent moments of consciousness.

My mother's death was hard on Gabe, and I worried about him. They had been good friends. I knew what it was to lose someone you love at a young age. I was just Gabe's age when my father passed away. He had a heart attack and died two days later in the hospital. I saw myself sitting at the kitchen table, smearing my tears on my shirtsleeve.

"Why didn't you come get me?" I asked my mother.

"I didn't want you to have to be there when . . . when the end came."

"You had no right! You knew I wanted to be there, but you didn't come get me!"

"I'm sorry. I just thought . . ."

"You wanted Daddy all to yourself! You knew he'd

want me there, too, but you didn't want to share him with anybody."

"Rachel, that's not true! I thought it was for the best."

"You thought! I told you I wanted to be there when, if . . ." But I couldn't finish. My mother's face looked so tired, but I felt no pity for her.

"Oh, Rachel, I'm so sorry if I did the wrong thing, but I did it from love for you. I know what it is to see death as a young woman, to carry that moment with you, to make promises that will bind you all your life. I wanted to spare you." She stopped abruptly, as though she had just revealed too much.

"Did Daddy have something he wanted me to promise?" I snatched at the hope that there would be something I could still do for him.

"No. He just said to remember he'll always love you."

The fall quarter at the university didn't start until late September, and I was looking forward to school starting again to at least sometimes take my mind off the loss of my mother. I was assigned to teach a beginning Spanish class, a three-hundred-level class, in which students started to read some literature but were still working on their language skills, and a class on Latin American drama, which was my area of expertise.

Even with the pressure of publish or perish, I enjoyed my chosen profession and knew that I was luckier than most. I was paid a comfortable amount of money, without needing to make any life-or-death decisions. At times it felt like plodding, but a new insight into some novel or play was still exciting, and I loved that moment when I saw a spark of discovery in a student's eyes.

I believed that working in another language gave me

an alternative way to think, and now it somehow felt like a connection to my mother, even though she had only spoken English. From the time I had entered high school she had encouraged me to study Spanish. Even when I decided to major in Spanish language and literature, she hadn't tried to dissuade me from choosing what many parents would have viewed as an impractical major: "Maybe when you have children, you can teach them to speak Spanish, too."

It had been a week since I'd told Ned that I would go over to my mother's house and start to sort through her things. He offered to help, but it would have been hard for him to get away from the hospital. Besides, I wanted to be alone in my mother's house. Somewhere in me was the hope that I would find something that would help me understand her. Although I doubted there would really be any revelation, as long as I didn't go over there, I could hold on to that possibility.

I spent a long time that day looking out the window of my second-story office, which shared one large window with the first floor, where the window was near the ceiling. Here the only natural light emanated from the bottom three feet of the room, and all of a sudden it felt like everything was upside down. I stared out at the students on the quad, whose activity seemed so pointless.

I wondered what I would tell Ned. I'd shunned my mother's house again.

I hadn't expected to find solace there. I pulled up to the simple brick house, parked the car, and unloaded the boxes I'd picked up from the grocery store. I started with the sewing room, really just a closet. By starting with the smallest space, I hoped to make more measurable progress.

The stacks of cloth were neatly folded, and the box of bobbin threads radiated colors, not knowing that more somber shades were now in order. My mother would sit at the sewing machine, stitching a side seam in a new dress for me. Rushing in through the back door, I'd wrap my arms around her. "I love you."

"I love you, too." She'd reply automatically, concentrating on her work, and I would further delay my play by observing the mysterious process by which a dress is made. When Dad came in, she'd look up in surprise and remark that he was early, even when he wasn't.

"Yeah, I finished all my service calls," he would answer, then come over to give us each a kiss, pushing aside the colorful scraps. "I missed my girls today. I'm going to change my clothes." The words of love flowed easily from him, and he neither expected nor received a like response from Helen. I don't know how he felt about that. Maybe, even after all their years together, he still found her reticence intriguing. There was something always held back, a hint of what he hadn't won but could perhaps someday secure.

"All right" was all she answered, standing to gather the unfinished dress and tools into her sewing basket. "I'll start supper."

After Dad died, I provided whatever overt show of love there was between us. As I matured, I would try to penetrate my mother's gossamer shelter. No matter what circuitous route I chose, we always arrived at the same place.

"Mom, Aunt Sandy isn't so reserved."

"We've had different experiences."

"Like what?" But she never answered.

"It's just that it's kind of hard sometimes. I always feel like there's something you're hiding."

"Hiding? You know I love you. Don't I show it by the way I act, by everything I do for you?"

"All right, Mom, all right."

RACHEL

I returned to the present and finished gathering up the loose fabrics, placing them in one of the cardboard boxes. Next I explored the contents of my mother's sewing box, trying on the thimble, surprised to find that it fit me perfectly, the tiny decorative ribbon encircling the bottom frayed and faded. I had intended to give away everything from this room. I'd never learned to sew, and now I regretted having never asked my mother to teach me. I'd keep the thimble and the pair of embroidery scissors shaped like a pelican.

I was somewhat at a loss for which room to go through next. I didn't want to do my mother's bedroom yet. Instead, I dragged a stack of empty boxes to the kitchen. There were a few crumbs on the floor, and I quickly swept them up. In the last few years, things had slipped a little. Now and then I'd noticed small lapses in my mother's housekeeping. It was nothing that I wouldn't have found perfectly acceptable in my own home, but I knew that the stains on the sink or the dust on the mantel were due only to my mother's refusal to wear her new glasses unless she was driving, and not to some newfound rebellion on her part. If she had known of the omissions, she would have been mortified. Saddened for her, I would clean the accusing blemish when she wasn't looking.

As I finished sweeping, I pushed the maple colonial-style chairs neatly under the table, pulled back the curtains, and opened the windows. The sunlight revealed the chipped paint spots on the white cupboards. I'd never noticed them before and tried to pretend that they were the shadows of small leaves on a tree that stood immobile against the wind.

I wrapped up some dishes to give away, then started packing up the china that Helen had from her grandmother. I would keep that. I'd always thought it was pretty, but she wouldn't use it very often, afraid that something would break and she'd leave me an incomplete set. I pictured her holding up the large, box-shaped sugar bowl, explaining that these had been customary when her grandmother was young. Wrapping each piece of china, I wished that she had used it more often, instilling it with memories. As I reached for the final piece, I lost my balance and knocked the creamer to the floor. Only pieces, after all those years of self-denial. I stared at them a moment, then got the broom and swept them up.

I shifted to the baking cupboard. Cookie sheets and cake pans wouldn't be so vulnerable to a shaking hand. Most of these I would give away. I reached into the dark recesses of the cabinet and pulled out an old, chipped measuring cup. I could see my mother standing at the table, precisely measuring out the ingredients she would need for her current project. She never stinted on the ingredients, but neither did she put in any extra. Every week, Helen would bake something for us and present it like a gift. I didn't bake for my family. Gabe had asked me once why I didn't. "I don't need to," I'd said. "Grandma always bakes for us."

I walked over to the window above the sink and held

the cup up to the streaming light, making out the faded red markings. I turned away and leaned against the sink, and as I clutched the cup, I slowly slid onto the floor. My eyes stopped focusing. I ran my fingers over the raised lines of measurement and let the loneliness swallow me, crushing me into someone new, someone with no sheltering generation to protect me from life's hardness. I was the front line, and I knew myself unequal to the task.

I felt my wet blouse. My mind hinted that it was milk that had leaked from my breasts. I felt the ache in them, and the longing to relieve the pain by taking my baby to my breast. But I wasn't nursing, only pregnant. It wasn't mother's milk at all.

I had never imagined myself sorting through my mother's things. I had imagined a protracted old age, and I had prayed that I would have the strength and patience to care for her. Would I have the love to see beyond an illness that might make me a stranger to her, and make her love for me even more remote? I had imagined trying to be a mother to my mother. But I had not imagined this.

I had heard other people talk about the painful process of sorting through the leftovers of the life of a loved one. But their experience had always been tempered by the fact that the person had been ill for a long time, or had been very old. And by the fact that it was not my mother. The belongings of their loved ones did not taunt me. I registered their stories as complaints about the enormity or the tedium of the task. But now it was my turn, and the task was many things, but it was not tedious.

28

RACHEL

I had to wait several days before I could go back, but it was a shame to leave the house empty, no one getting any use from it. This time I planned it so that I would have a limited amount of time, hopefully forcing me to be disciplined and productive.

I started with the linen closet, and when I took the first sheet from the shelf, I could almost hear the snap as my mother unfolded it with one deft movement, allowing it to float onto the bed, straight as could be. It was one of those skills that fascinates little kids, things their mothers seem to be able to do so easily and that seem impossible for us ever to achieve. But those household skills come with age and practice, and we unthinkingly perform them before our own wondering children, forgetting how once we had wished for such grace.

As I pulled out more sheets, a package wrapped in brown paper and tied with string fell to the floor. My immediate guess was that Helen had wrapped up some embroidered pillowcases, too old and threadbare to be of any use but with too much sentimental value to throw away. Maybe it was something I had embroidered when I was ten or eleven. I had kept us more than well supplied with fancy pillowcases. Once, I had embroidered pictures of baskets onto some hand towels, peach and black on a white ground.

The technique was called huck-toweling, and the project was my fifth and final piece for a Girl Scout badge, each of the five with a different type of embroidery.

I put the package aside and told myself that opening it would be my reward when I'd gone through the rest of the closet. Maybe the package didn't hold any old projects of mine at all. Maybe there were some old quilts, or crocheted doilies that my grandmother or great-grandmother had made. Helen had hated the doilies, which required starching and painstaking care to achieve the intended look of crisp waves all around the central flat portion, onto which a lamp or vase was placed. She liked old quilts but had never let us use them, for fear that they would become faded or frayed, spoiling the precious yield of so many hours' work. I knew that she had some quilts, but I hadn't found any yet. I was already planning how I'd display them to preserve their beauty and to proudly show their art, traditionally so undervalued, the invention of women. One of my friends hated old quilts, because they seemed to her the product of enforced domesticity, the pitiable offering of the only creative outlet open to our foremothers. But I had always believed that works of art endured, and that their creators would not want to see them scorned, even from a wish that they had led a freer life.

Finally, I finished packing up all the items from the linen closet except for the brown parcel, and I allowed myself to open it. It was the sunbonnet quilt that my great-grandmother had made. I recognized it even from the back, from the yellow triangle points sewn around the edge. I carefully laid back the corner to reveal two of the girls appliquéd on the quilt. I knew from memory that each one had a sunbonnet and dress in a different fabric, but no hair, eye, or skin color depicted. As a child, I had wondered what each girl would look like were her sunbonnet pushed back to unveil her true identity.

But there was a bulk and weight to the package that couldn't be accounted for by the quilt alone. I continued to unfold it and found another package nestled inside. Taped to the outside I saw, in a cursive that was unmistakably my mother's, a note: "To be opened only by my granddaughter, in the requisite faith and urgent hope that she will one day exist and embrace what I here entrust to her. Read this book and papers in the order in which I have placed them here, so that you will learn your history as you were meant to do, and to pass it on as others have done before you."

Curiosity and sorrow and anger seemed to compete for the upper hand. My heart raced and my hands shook, and I noted these with some wonder, as though my inner literary critic were observing. How many times had I scoffed at such reactions in a story, as not only unconvincing but clichéd?

I opened the package, my mother dead such a short time, and I already betraying her, and perhaps my unborn daughter. A lovely leather antique book lay on the top. The book's pages were in Spanish, but a Spanish from long past, and in a handwriting filled with flourishes. I was the only one in my family who spoke Spanish. Tucked inside the book were extra pages in English, but the handwriting was not my mother's, nor that of the book's author. Under the book other types of papers were stacked, some curling or yellowed with age, some sewn together, some glued in an odd fashion on the edge, all with a variety of handwriting. Having found it on the top, and obeying this, at least, of my mother's instructions, I picked up the small book and began to read.

29

Juliana

12 February 1661

I write by the dim firelight of a poor room at an inn. I have fled my lifelong home, not knowing what awaits me. To remain was to die at the hands of my own father, seeking to regain his honor by putting to death his only child. I was the innocent victim of Don Lorenzo's most vile lust, and my father has sent him to his everlasting punishment.

I must write to put my thoughts in order. Though I had to leave much behind, I have brought this blank book, given to me by my beloved Tía Ana, whom I doubt I shall ever see again. She said that it was beautiful, as I am beautiful. She spoke from love, but what did any beauty I may possess buy me but violence and betrayal? Remembering her words, I find that the charm of the book now taunts, rather than consoles, and so it is a fitting symbol of my life, an apt receptacle of my thoughts. The incidents of these last two days seem unreal, and yet my circumstances assure me they are not.

Silvia and I have no destination yet. We travel to the south.

13 February

We depart for Sevilla, as that is the destination of the caravan that has allowed us to become a part of their group. I am disguised as a boy, my place purchased with money from Silvia's lifelong savings. It is unusual, for any boy would normally work to pay for his journey by helping with the animals and provisions. Silvia travels with us also, but she does work to pay her way, helping with the cooking, cleaning, mending, and any other tasks she is assigned. Although he looked at us askance, as though he knew there was more to our story, Silvia convinced the caravan master, Señor Suárez, that I am her sickly grandson, traveling home to Sevilla after a pilgrimage to Ávila to ask Santa Teresa to come to my aid and give me health.

Silvia brought my mother's jewels, my only dowry, used now not to go to a husband but to escape a father's wrath.

14 February

We are in Toledo. I snuck away from the caravan and put on one of the dresses I had brought. I found a buyer for some of my mother's jewels, though I have no knowledge of their value. They were probably worth more than what I was offered, but I had no choice. I felt that I should sell the jewels only a few at a time, so as not to arouse suspicion, for why would a girl have these things to sell?

My father spent some time here at the university, and it seems as though I feel his presence. I know it is my foolishness, but I shall be glad when we quit this place upon the morrow.

15 February

I must enter a convent, using my mother's jewels to secure my place as a gentlewoman and to pay my way. Although I would wish to avoid the conclusion, it is inevitable. Where else can a woman such as I go? Don Lorenzo in one night denied me the future of which I had always dreamed. I must run to the enfolding walls, where I will hide my shame and sorrow till I die. My only bridegroom shall be Christ. I pray He gives me strength to accept Him as my all.

I am no longer Juliana Torres Coloma. In this caravan I travel as a boy, and when I go to the convent, I shall use Silvia's name. Silvia said she could not find my mother's purity-of-blood papers, but I will need them to enter the convent. Silvia has brought her own papers, which she will give to me. This, also, will aid in my disguise. I shall be hers in name, as well as love.

16 February

Each day proceeds, no different from the one before. The chill reaches my bones almost as soon as we depart our shelter, then warms a bit at midday, only to become colder as the day wears on. Riding on and on and on. When I at last gain a place to lay my head, I fall into a sleep. But tonight, though I am exhausted, I cannot find the peace of slumber. Each time I close my eyes, I see Don Lorenzo's face and I begin to shake. When at last I succeed in banishing this dark vision, my present danger leaps to mind and I cannot rest. I have found a place where the moon provides a feeble light, and I write here in my diary, the repository of the truth of this unfamiliar life.

The tenuous nature of my plans has begun to weigh heavily upon me. In my haste to escape my father's vengeance, my course was uncharted. I knew only that flee

I must, or die as punishment for a sin that was not mine. To a convent, yes, but where? I shall have to be careful in my choice and cunning in the lies I must invent.

They tell me that in two days we shall reach Ciudad Real, but now all places are the same to me.

19 February

Though we travel toward Sevilla, that is not my final goal. I have made a momentous and frightening decision, but I know that it is right. I would forsake this, my homeland, which condones a daughter's murder. I shall discover for myself the New World, yet from within the limits of the convent walls, where I shall bury all the hopes I once held dear.

20 February

The journey is most tiresome, yet I am glad of my disguise, for as a boy I ride astride a mule, as do the merchants. Though it is most uncomfortable and my body aches from this unaccustomed means of travel, I prefer it to traveling in a litter fastened between and carried by two mules, constantly swaying and suffocating me within. The cold, my pain, and an ever-present nausea afflict me.

The inns that we have stopped at have hardly been reprieve from the days' travails. The filth evident everywhere is enough to make one sick, and I have many fleabites on my body. The inns do not offer sustenance, and we are required to provide our own, which we purchase along the way. Mostly we buy bread and eggs, though two or three times we have happened on hunters who have sold us partridges or rabbits. Silvia at first tried to procure things for me especially, but we soon learned that the entire caravan shares all provisions.

From other travelers I have learned I must be careful
of my belongings, for many of the innkeepers' servants are
not to be trusted. It is rare that Silvia and I have even the
meanest room to ourselves, so we have slept with our
meager possessions every night. In most of these wretched
places, all travelers pass the night in a common room.
Some nights we go to our rest on piles of straw. If the
straw is fresh, this is preferable to a bed, which might be
infested with bedbugs. Our only consolation is that the
price is modest, at two reales, as the rates are fixed by
royal decree.

22 February

Tonight we have reached Andújar. I am told that we have
completed more than half of our journey from Madrid to
Sevilla. I am relieved, as there has been little to occupy
my mind beyond my bitter memories, and at times I think
I shall go mad. We try to shelter ourselves from the cold
and rain as we ride, but with little effect. Though many of
the areas we pass through are stark, with little of beauty
to recommend them, I have come to welcome a view not
obscured by foul weather.

I am growing ever more anxious about what precisely I
shall do once we have reached Sevilla.

23 February

A most frightening scene occurred today. One of the
muleteers, having relinquished his reins to another on the
pretext of hunting some rabbit for our dinner, dropped from
his place in the line and approached me. From the first, he
has looked at me in a way I did not understand, and, riding
beside me, he began to murmur vague threats. At first the

mad thought went through my head that he might know my identity and my plight, but the more he spoke, the more it became clear that his meaning referred to a depravity I did not know existed.

I loudly repulsed him, and as he reached to grab my arm, I felt a deadly fear and could not think how I would resist him. Then the leader of the caravan, Señor Suárez, came to my defense. He struck the young man hard on the back with the flat of his sword and uttered in a fury words I could not hear. The young man retreated angrily, and Señor Suárez approached me.

"I am sorry that you have been subjected to this. I am ashamed that this has happened in my train. I vow upon my honor that it shall not occur again."

I could not even answer, and I began to tremble. He looked at me thoughtfully and said slowly, "I think that you have had your share of troubles. We shall not add to them."

To this I have been reduced, to seeking a father's protection from a stranger whose close scrutiny could present a danger of its own.

25 February

We stop in Córdoba tonight. I am too tired to write very much, for I have slept little these past two nights, fearing what might happen if the muleteer decided to defy his master. But now I must depend upon the guard of Señor Suárez, for I cannot keep my vigil yet again.

I did not tell Silvia what happened, for she seems unwell and beyond fatigue. I cannot heap another burden upon her. How I wish that my Tía Ana were here to hold me in her arms, to offer me comfort and guidance! I cannot think that I shall ever see her again, and this adds another weight to my sorrows.

26 February

Try as I will to build up a wall of bitterness and hatred toward my father, I have not succeeded. I tell myself that I am the most wronged of creatures, and that, even above the treachery of Don Lorenzo, lies the betrayal of one who should have defended me. Yet I find myself protesting that he does care about me. How could it not be so? He who has shown me all my life a loving kindness could not wish me harm.

But it is so, and this is the most difficult of all. I forsake a father who has loved me, but who holds his honor higher. I must try to harden my heart against him, or the pain will break me.

28 February

Now our journey's end is in sight. We are to reach Sevilla in two days. I feel some apprehension at leaving the caravan, though it has held dangers of its own. There is a comfort to rising in the morning and knowing how you will occupy your time. I have grown accustomed to my role as a sickly boy traveling home with his grandmother. Would that it were true. But I have only started my inventions.

30

RACHEL

The fading daylight, obscuring the lines of writing, returned me to the present. The world had gone silent, filled only with what I'd just read and my mother's final words: "I am like Ana. I have failed Juliana." Here was a Tía Ana, and the writer, who said that she would change her name from Juliana Torres Coloma.

I sat immobile, staring into a past over three hundred years old. I don't know how long I sat there. How could this be genuine, sequestered here in my mother's home? Yet surely she wouldn't perpetrate such a cruel hoax, even to her last moments.

As I read the first few pages of the diary, how could I not feel the genuine desperation? Still, as a teacher of literature, how many times had I admired the creation of whole worlds that never existed? How many times had I ached for the tragedies of its inhabitants?

I told myself that I would rely on my professional knowledge and detachment. The writing did seem genuine, and similar to other seventeenth-century Spanish texts that I had read, like reading Shakespeare, but not in your first language. I reminded myself that I knew from my studies of Golden Age theater that nothing was more precious than honor, which was to be defended at all costs. But then I faltered. Could a flesh-and-blood father follow such a monstrous course? But maybe this very question showed that I, too, was hampered by the perspective of my own time and place.

I gathered the papers and placed them in the quilt, then put it all in one of the grocery store boxes. Even as I doubted their authenticity, I felt guilty at handling precious original sources so unceremoniously.

I shouldn't have driven in my state, but I needed to get home. Ned and Gabe would be wondering where I was. I'd manage to act normal enough. After all, they'd seen me in a lot of different moods over the last weeks.

On the way home, I decided that I wouldn't tell anybody what I'd found. Not only was I unsure of what it was, but the note from my mother, saying that the papers were for her granddaughter, pulled me to secrecy. I wouldn't let the papers overwhelm reality. I'd allow myself to read only a few pages a day. Maybe if I took more time, things would make more sense, I told myself, but I knew I was reluctant to unmask a truth that could be painful.

And still I had my mother's death to mourn. I struggled to maintain my equilibrium. My colleagues seemed to think my strained manner was attributable solely to my mother's passing, though I tried to appear cheerful. I was reminded of that old show tune about whistling to hide your fear and in the end defeating it. But I had never been able to whistle. When I was a child, I would pucker my lips and try desperately to make a sound, dreading a stalking terror that would find me unprepared.

"Some days are easier than others." That's how I responded whenever anyone asked me how I was doing, their simple question a code for other questions, too raw to ask. *How are you accepting your mother's death? Are you get-*

ting back to the normal, comfortable friend we miss? I
knew that this was what they meant, because it was what
I'd meant when I'd asked the question of friends after
some sorrow or trouble disturbed the predictable rhythm
of their lives. So I knew that they cared. They just didn't
know what to do. But how could they not see the tumult
within me? I shored up a resentment that I knew to be
unjust, isolating myself within my secret heart.

Even with Ned and Gabe, things couldn't be normal.
Each of them had grieved in his own way. Ned had really
cared about Helen and had done everything he could for
her when she was alive. I sometimes kiddingly complained
that my mother found in him her ideal son-in-law, that I
was being overshadowed. Of course, it wasn't really true,
and I had been glad that we could be a sufficiently close-
knit group, my mother, my husband, and my son. Still, for
Ned grief was something that he had learned to conquer,
or at least not to let it conquer him. He often saw people
die, but he had to get beyond the loss. Sorrow wouldn't
help the next patient. He had become used to doing all he
could for people while they were alive, and then letting
them rest in peace. He mourned my mother's death and
was shocked at the suddenness of it. But he knew that his
attentions gave her joy when she was alive, and he allowed
that to console him. Unlike with my inertia, he seemed to
push himself harder at work. It probably wasn't a conscious
decision, but it seemed that helping the living would be
his memorial to Helen. I knew that it was difficult for him
to see me as I was, apparently still lost in grief, but I held
myself and my secret apart, and he had no way to reach
that part of me.

Gabe seemed to be coping better now. Though he was
getting to be a young man, his sorrow was that of a child,
overt and deep but not irreparable. He brooded for a few

weeks but then seemed to have put his sadness behind him, or at least not to take it out so often to look at it.

So I hoarded my secret and my grief, glad not to have to share them with anyone. If that required some deception, then I forgave myself. What happy family doesn't have some dissembling? Without a private self, what depth is there to anything we give?

I was becoming ever more caught up in Juliana's diary, searching sincerely for a meaning behind the avalanche of words. I quelled my skepticism about the pages' origins. While I had conscientiously avoided reading prematurely the other papers enclosed with the diary, as Helen had directed, I couldn't help but notice that among the papers in English were some that seemed to be a translation of the diary.

I treated the pages as a precious new piece of literature. The joy of reading it for the first time could never be relived, so I didn't allow myself to look ahead to solve the mystery. I was well practiced in suspension of disbelief.

Every moment that I spent reading the papers now bound my mother to me, but it was a two-edged connection. I didn't want to come to the end of the papers and lose this new bond. At the same time, though, I was afraid that there might be some revelation that I would regret learning. Worse, what if the papers didn't reveal my mother's secret at all, and I would be pushed even further from her? And so I only slowly allowed the papers to divulge their truth, in the hope that I would build up my strength for whatever was to come.

While restricting my reading, I allowed myself to search for other clues that might shed some light. I spent time in the university library, reading about antique papers and inks. I knew that there were extant manuscripts at least as old as what I'd found, but I needed more confirmation that a seventeenth-century diary could have survived intact. I spoke to the university's archivist librarian, and she told me that yes, it was certainly possible for a document from that period to have survived, that paper in that period was usually made from cotton and linen rags and in fact was sturdier than most paper made today. She was quite intrigued by my question and told me that if I had such a document, she would be very happy to look at it. I avoided answering her.

At times I told myself that if the letters had no real connection to me, it wouldn't matter. If they were genuine, they could be of great use to me professionally. My married female colleagues and I joked about the great discovery we would make, which would advance our careers, guarantee us tenure, and ensure the respect of our male counterparts. Our sarcasm masked our recognition that we had made other commitments, precluding the freedom to spend summers abroad, discovering trifles about some author.

A particularly obnoxious member of the French department used to leave his wife and three children every summer to study in Paris. The year before, he had published two articles on an intriguing new aspect that he had discovered about the life of a nineteenth-century novelist. He had spoken at a conference and was working on a book, for which he already had a publisher. We told ourselves that we didn't care, that his information wasn't crucial, that works of literature should speak for themselves and not require the revelation of some obscure aspect of the author's life. But we were envious. It wasn't easy to gain recognition in our field, and none of us would shy away from such an opportunity. Perhaps this manuscript was my chance.

31

Juliana

2 March

We rest tonight in a home for visitors to Sevilla. My relief is tempered by Silvia's illness, brought on by the rigors of our travels and her duties in the caravan. I believe that the size of the city, even larger than Madrid, assures our anonymity, but Silvia disagrees and says that my father knows that we have fled together, and that separating will make it less likely that any inquiries he makes will lead him to me.

3 March

Silvia will go to stay with some distant cousins who live outside the city. Although she did not wish it, I pressed upon her some of the money from the sale of my mother's jewels. I also paid for a messenger to send word to her cousins that she is in need of their aid. They will arrange transport for her to their home.

I tried to set up a means for us to communicate, but Silvia said that it would be dangerous for us. I cannot see how this could be, but, as she became ever more agitated, I agreed to her demands. She left with me her papers that I will use to enter the convent, in case we do not meet

again. Our parting was most sorrowful, and I feel that yet
another stone has been placed upon my heart.

I fear for my beloved *dueña*, who has been a mother to
me. I do not know whether rest will answer her needs. I do
not know whether I shall ever see her again. Shall we never
stop paying for the evil in men's hearts?

4 March

Today I learned from a man of business staying here that
my only chance to travel to the New World is to go with
one of the two fleets that cross the Atlantic to bring
supplies and return with riches from our colonies there.
Although courier ships, *avisos*, leave with some frequency,
they do not usually offer passage, and would never allow
an unaccompanied woman. The treasure fleet will have
some sixty ships. Many of these are warships to protect
the cargo ships on which I hope to book passage. The next
fleet will not sail until May, bound for Vera Cruz, so I
must remain in Sevilla until then. Perhaps this delay will
mean that I shall have the chance to see Silvia again.

5 March

I have obtained a room in the home of a businessman and
his family. Señor Luis Herrera Moreno is somewhat portly,
but has an open and pleasant face. He is respectable, but
not so prosperous that he disdains the fee my room and
board will bring him. His wife, Doña Catalina, has a soft,
matronly look, and a kind, cheerful manner. My obvious
fatigue allowed me to delay giving them the particulars of
my circumstances here, but tomorrow I will need to
explain why a young woman would be traveling alone,
arriving in a city with no sheltering friends or relatives
awaiting her. I had to invent yet a new identity for myself.

I am Señora María Ramos de la Fuente. I shall have to carefully work out the particulars of my story before I attempt to present it.

But I am so tired now. I believe that I will sleep tonight, although my heart aches for my Silvia.

6 March

I presented my tale to the Herreras this afternoon. I shall write here the details of our conversation. Perhaps because of the height of my emotion during our discussion, I remember each moment.

After the modest but adequate midday meal, Doña Catalina turned to me. "How is it that a young woman of such obvious refinement finds herself alone in Sevilla, without even an acquaintance to offer her shelter and protection?"

"Ah, señora, you may think my story is somewhat strange. I confess that much has happened in the last weeks, many details of which I do not understand. Naturally, I must trust in the wisdom of my husband and try my best to do as he has instructed." Having started out with what I hoped would be an adequate excuse for any discrepancies they might discern, I went on with my narration.

"I am the wife of a young merchant, Juan Vásquez Méndez. Shortly after our marriage in Madrid last year, Juan traveled to Sevilla and sailed with one of the fleets to the New World. He had made a small investment of his own, and he managed to persuade some important businessmen to hire him to oversee their much more impressive sums." I smiled shyly, modest in my pride of my imagined husband, who was entrusted with so much by men of such influence.

"It is most unusual for investors to accompany the fleet, and even more so for powerful men to entrust large fortunes to a young man who, if you will pardon my saying so, señora, has not much experience," Señor Herrera said, frowning slightly. "He had no previous dealings with these men?"

I realized my unwitting error and hastened to correct it. "Of course, one of the men had employed my husband for some time, in the management of some of his business ventures in Madrid. It was his recommendation that helped Juan to win the appointment."

"Evidently a young man of much talent and integrity." Doña Catalina nodded and smiled.

"Once Juan arrived in Vera Cruz with the fleet, it seems that he found even greater trading opportunities than he had expected. When he returned, the investors realized a very nice profit, and they were quite pleased with his accomplishments on their behalf. Juan decided to try to convince them that by staying in Vera Cruz and working there, he would be able to effect even greater returns for them if they would undertake to hire him for that purpose. He would receive as payment a certain percentage of the profit. Although he had done well for them on the first venture, the investors said that they needed several weeks to decide the matter, so he returned to me in Madrid to await their response."

"It is possible that correspondence to France, or even farther, had to be sent and received," Señor Herrera murmured thoughtfully.

Fearing that I had already embroiled myself in another problem, and truly not understanding Señor Herrera's comment, I innocently confessed my ignorance of his meaning.

"I do not understand," I said, with more than feigned

confusion. "I believe that all of my husband's associates reside here."

"Of course, there is no reason why a young and pretty wife, unacquainted with the trade, which is our lifeblood in Sevilla, should understand my idle wondering. You see, foreigners are excluded from direct commerce with the New World. However, at times they employ local agents in Sevilla—traitors, I consider them—to represent them, to serve as a front for their trade, and thus skirt the law. These dealings rob from our city, and from the monarchy itself, valuable revenues that are ours by rights." Bitterness entered his voice as he said this last.

He mistook my blushes for embarrassment or indignation, and continued more gently. "I am not implying that your husband is knowingly employed by such men, but it is very common, and their long delay in coming to their decision aroused my suspicion."

I didn't know how to respond to him, and so he continued, apparently still concerned that he had hurt or insulted me.

"But I should not worry you about such things. These gentlemen are probably only being cautious and wish to examine the proposition from all sides."

Somewhat flustered, I went on.

"Only three weeks ago, Juan received word. They had accepted his proposal, and he was to leave as soon as possible. Within a day, he had left for Sevilla. I was to follow him in a week, after I had prepared for our journey as well as I could and bidden an anguished farewell to my beloved family, whom I shall never see again."

Doña Catalina sighed and said, "And your poor mother—how could she bear parting with such a lovely child?" I could see her picturing such a fate for herself, and her horror at the thought of forever losing her own

daughter, now a chattering girl of six. But I sensed that
she also felt sincere sympathy for me, and a pang of guilt
made me sorry for this necessary deception of these kind
people.

"My mother and I . . ." I trailed off into silence,
unable to imagine a parting from a mother I had never
known.

Doña Catalina must have taken my reticence as grief
and apologized for intruding into my pain. "Please
continue, my dear."

"I was to go to a place my husband had described to
me—the home of one of the investors. When I arrived in
Sevilla yesterday, I engaged a young boy to show me the
way. Upon arriving at the house and inquiring for the
gentleman, I encountered his wife, who was of course
curious about why a young woman, unaccompanied by
relative or *dueña*, would be asking for her husband. After I
had explained myself, she seemed to be satisfied and
instructed one of her servants to accompany me to her
husband's office, where she said he could be found.

"I reached the office and made my request to a clerk
sitting at a desk. He simply looked at me and nodded but
kept on with his writing. After waiting a good deal of
time, I again approached the clerk and asked him whether
I might be able to have a few moments of his employer's
time. He asked my name again, as he must already have
forgotten it, and reluctantly rose and slowly walked to a
closed door and knocked twice. A voice answered from
within, and he entered. He immediately came out again
and said that I might go in.

"After introducing myself to the gentleman, I
explained further. 'I am the wife of Señor Juan Vásquez
Méndez. I have just arrived from Madrid. I believe that
you have engaged my husband in some business dealings,

and he gave me your name, saying that you could put me in touch with him.'

"'Ah, yes, Señora Ramos, forgive me,' he said. 'I am afraid that you have missed your husband. So well had he convinced us of the wisdom of having a man residing in Vera Cruz, we decided that he should return there as quickly as possible. We managed to get him onto one of the *avisos*. He was extremely agitated about missing you, but he left several days ago.'

"I'm sure that I turned quite pale at this news, because he seemed alarmed and quickly approached me, adding, 'But he has left a message for you.' At this, he crossed to his desk, opened a drawer, and produced a paper. It was a letter from my husband, instructing me to follow him on the next available ship. The letter also included the name of a gentleman whose acquaintance Juan had made when he was last in New Spain. Juan wrote that if I inquire for this gentleman upon reaching Vera Cruz, I will surely be directed to his business establishment, and that he will contact Juan for me."

"How extraordinary!" exclaimed Doña Catalina. "He expects you to make your way alone, not only here in Sevilla, but across the sea and even in the wilderness of the New World?" Her astonishment at my husband's decision and her concern for my predicament got the better of her courteous duty to refrain from criticizing my husband to me.

"But he did not think that I would be alone," I began, glad for this chance to explain my plight of finding myself here without companion or protector. "My brother had expected to accompany me. However, at the last moment, he was called to return to his military post. I decided that my *dueña* and I would have to make our way alone, as I saw no other recourse. However, on the trip she was taken ill and was forced to return to Madrid. I felt that I could not retrace my steps, for it was my desire and my duty to join my husband as soon as possible."

"Of course," Doña Catalina replied, obviously relieved at having been reassured of my respectability, though still distressed by my situation. "You poor thing—you must be distraught and missing your husband terribly!"

"Yes, but I look forward to being able to join him soon," I replied calmly.

"Surely, señora," Señor Herrera began hesitantly, "you realize that only sailing with the fleet would be considered appropriate for you, and the next fleet will not sail until May. You must also understand that booking passage is not an easy matter."

Feigning ignorance of the departure delay, I replied, "I am afraid that my husband's letter failed to inform me of these details." I then whispered, "What am I to do?"

"How could your husband leave you in such straits?" Doña Catalina demanded, all attempt at courteous discretion now abandoned.

When I simply looked at her, unable to reply, her generous heart provoked her to continue, already searching for answers to my dilemma. "You may remain here with us, of course. And perhaps your husband's business acquaintance could arrange for your passage?"

"Oh, that would not be possible!" I blurted out. I had not been aware of the problem of obtaining passage, and so had not foreseen the suggestion of its solution.

"But surely he would be able to perform this small service for the wife of a business associate," Señor Herrera said, perhaps suspicious of my quick and vehement reply.

I had to think quickly, and appealing to the protective side of the gentleman seemed the best refuge. Perhaps the blush that had colored my face in my agitation served to

give credence to my story, masquerading as a symbol of
offended modesty.

"I am afraid that I could not return to see that
gentleman, let alone ask a favor of him," I said, with all
the conviction I could gather. "You see, I hesitated to
include this in my account, but he behaved in a less-than-
honorable fashion toward me." This seemed an entirely
likely explanation, for would not a woman traveling under
such circumstances easily be open to such insult? Again,
their sincere concern for me was touching, and my
response produced the effect that I had desired.

"Dear, could you not arrange for passage for Doña
María?"

Her husband was flustered by this request, especially
since it was made in my presence, where it would be even
more difficult to refuse, but his honor as a gentleman was
being tested, and he must not be found wanting. Even
more than that, it seemed that his wife's simple faith in
him softened his resistance and prompted him to respond,
"It is very difficult, but perhaps some business
acquaintances will be able to accomplish it."

I envied the look of love and confidence that Doña
Catalina gave to Don Luis, a husband who would endeavor
to do for her that which he, for himself, would not have
undertaken lightly. This man possessed a sense of honor
that shone in stark contrast with the false face offered to
society by he who had destroyed me.

Despite his words of encouragement, Señor Herrera
seemed worried about the task which he had set himself
and, making his excuses, left me in the company of his
wife.

"Doña Catalina," I began, "there is yet another matter
of which I must speak to you. I am fearful that my
resources will not cover my expenses. I was embarrassed to

speak of this before Señor Herrera, ashamed and confused that my husband should not have made better provision for me. I know that the amount that I agreed to pay you for board is more than fair, as I did make other inquiries before my lucky chance of finding you. Please tell me if it would be possible for me to do some work here around the house, and thus reduce the amount you must charge me."

At this, she looked truly distressed. "But requiring a lady of your quality to work . . ."

"It is from necessity that I ask this. I could perhaps help with the needlework for your family. It is true that up until now I have used my needle only to entertain myself, by embroidering pillows and other decorative articles for the home of my family, but I am skilled with the needle, and I am certain that I could put my abilities to more practical use."

Still she hesitated. "Would it not be better for you to get word to your family that you are in need of money? Surely they could render assistance that would make this step unnecessary."

"There is yet another complication, which I had not wished to mention, but your kindness and my necessity prompt me to be totally frank with you. My family did not altogether approve of my marriage. As you have guessed, I am of gentle birth, and my family did not desire a son-in-law who had to work at business to earn his living." At this I paused, realizing I had inadvertently insulted Señor Herrera, who likewise provided for his family through his business. Doña Catalina gave no sign of taking insult, however, either because she was too taken up with my story, or because she was so familiar with the attitude that she hardly took note of it.

"My parents tried to force me into a marriage that they deemed more proper, but I can be strong-willed, señora, and my family finally acquiesced to my marriage to Juan. So you see, I do not wish to parade before them my chagrin at having their misgivings justified even beyond what they had suspected. It is not my intention to sound disloyal to my husband in saying this. My very loyalty to him compels me to protect him, and myself, from my family's criticism."

"Perhaps, if you could be persuaded to help with the children, I could convince my husband."

I leaped at this chance. "Oh, yes! I love children! I have always enjoyed spending time with my younger cousins. I could play games with them, and read to them, and—"

"Can you read well?" she interrupted.

"Yes, my father demanded that all of his children master that skill."

"It is settled, then. If you can work with my children on simple lessons you can devise, I am sure that I can convince my husband to accept your services in lieu of any payment. He has a great desire for our young children to increase their learning."

"But I did not mean to imply that I could pay nothing!"

"No, if you are learned, we will be happy to have you teach our children."

In the household of my father, I had never considered myself learned, but to Doña Catalina, it seemed that I was, and, amid all my troubles, this gave me pleasure.

"I cannot thank you enough, señora."

"Nonsense. It is settled to our mutual satisfaction. Now, you must be very tired. Off to bed with you." And, assuming a protective attitude, she embraced me like the mother I never knew.

How easily lies come to my tongue when urged there

by necessity! As I review what I have written here, I find myself yearning to be the young woman I have invented. Oh, that my plight could be exchanged with hers! If only I had a loving husband awaiting me! If only I were leaving behind a caring though disapproving family. But I must make my way alone, my only friendly company the ghosts of families that I have dreamed.

Yet, at least for now, I have this temporary shelter for which to be grateful. Thank you, Virgin Mother, for giving me the protection of these kind people. I pray that you will guide me in my plans. Please watch over Silvia and bring her health and peace.

32

RACHEL

The ease with which the writer of the diary invented lies as she needed them reminded me that all of this could, in fact, be a deception. Still, if it were, it was a very elaborate one—one that took place within my mother's home. Lately I had begun to wonder whether my mother had herself been tricked somehow. But what would the purpose be? If the diary were not authentic, someone had gone to a great deal of trouble to obtain materials that seemed to be of the period, to write in language appropriate for the place and time, and even to affect a handwriting that seemed similar to manuscripts from the period. And then there was the narrative itself. It seemed to ring true, and I was becoming ever more involved in the story that I had found wrapped in a quilt in my mother's house.

As a literary scholar, I was trained to read with dispassionate observation, and this trend had become ever stronger in literary scholarship. Any hint of appreciation for the emotional connection of a story had come to be viewed as unsophisticated at best, unprofessional at worst. But I had never been able to repress this emotional pull, nor would I wish to, and I would have hated to see the field filled with those who saw a piece of literature merely as an interesting artifact, with no care for what the author felt or wished to say.

As I entered the Romance Languages Department office, I was thinking about the pages I'd read the night before. I was submerged in Juliana's plight, and I sadly wondered what the fate of Silvia would be. The details of Juliana's various deceptions somehow seemed fantastical, yet their level of detail added verisimilitude. I didn't think that if I'd read those details in a book, it would have strained credulity.

I was lost in these thoughts when I looked up and saw Lorraine. There she stood, sorting through her mail, and the mere sight of her comforted me. Only the day before, I'd mailed her a letter. It wouldn't reach Buenos Aires for a few more days. She had been on sabbatical, researching the writings of a local poet. As a single woman, she didn't have the somewhat self-imposed restrictions that those of us with families had. She was able to travel as freely as the men of the department, and, rather than resent her flexibility, we other women were happy that one of our number had that opportunity.

A frantic call from the department chairman, who had hurt his back playing racquetball and needed her to teach his classes, had brought me this unexpected gift of coming upon my friend. Lorraine and I had known each other ever since graduate school, and although we rarely spent time together outside school, she was my best friend. All we had in common was that we were the only two in any of the language departments who had trained at the university where we were now professors. Her colorful language and totally unpretentious manner appealed to me. Hers was a rough facade, built over caring generosity.

I had once asked Lorraine what she saw in me as a friend. "It's my mission to educate you about the realities of life." She laughed, but I knew that she was only half kidding. Though she was only two years older than I, and though I'd experienced lots of things in life she hadn't, including marriage and motherhood, Lorraine still considered me in need of guidance.

Lorraine looked up now and enfolded me in her arms, her smell of cigarette smoke somehow comforting. "How are you doing? Let's go get coffee." Though she worked harder than any of our colleagues and was one of the most insightful literary scholars I had ever known, Lorraine was always ready to take a break. She expected everyone to be as flexible as she was and would accept no excuses.

"Come on," she'd say, "the world of Hispanic letters can wait for your dramatic revelation. Live a little!"

She always won, and as we walked downstairs to the lounge, she often added some other comment about coffee sloshing around with the creative juices. We entered the glorified coffee room, which now went by the name Café Etienne. Lorraine and I had laughed over the name, which one of the French professors had supplied, based on a character in his favorite novel. The lounge had also recently become strictly nonsmoking. Lorraine sighed as we entered.

"I'm sorry I wasn't here."

"That's okay."

"Do you want to talk about it?"

"Not really. I don't know. There isn't much to say. She was hit by a car, and then she was gone. I'm having a hard time, but I'll be all right."

"You know she'll always be with you."

I looked at her for a minute and then laughed. "Come on. I thought you'd spare me the platitudes." I could be like that with her. Lorraine was relaxed and sassy, and she made me feel that way when I was with her. She was constantly cracking me up with her dating horror stories, implying how lucky and sheltered I'd been. And she occasionally reminded me of the difficulties of a black woman attaining the position she had.

She stared at me until I felt uncomfortable. "What?" I finally said, but she didn't answer.

"Oh, Lorraine, I know that she'll always be with me, in my memories, even in Gabe's smile. But let's face it. She's no more with me than the characters in the novels we teach. She exists only in our imaginations."

"You're wrong, and I'll tell you why." Lorraine settled into her chair, and I could tell she was going into her lecture mode, but with an unusually confiding manner. "I'm about to tell you something that I've never told anyone else, so feel privileged." I waited while she studied me to see the effect of this prelude. "My apartment is haunted."

At first I was shocked, then hurt. What she was saying belittled my loss. How could she joke about this?

"Lorraine . . ."

"I'm not kidding." The urgency in her voice made me realize that she was serious. Whatever she was about to say was important to her, a truth of her life.

"What are you talking about?"

"When I first moved into my apartment, back when we were grad students, I felt there was something strange about the place. In my best moments, I put it down to being homesick, and in my worst moments, I felt scared. Mostly I had a sort of anxious anticipation about whatever it was that might develop.

"Then one night, as I lay in bed, wondering for the hundredth time if I'd screwed up on some bullshit paper or other, I felt a definite presence in my room, sitting in the rocker that was in the far corner."

"Oh, Lorraine, come on!"

"Shut up now, and listen. I wouldn't play with you." But she'd strung me along many times before with her wild, complicated tales, only to draw me in, then turn around and tease me for my gullibility. It was part of her charm.

At my skeptical look, she added, "I wouldn't play with you at a time like this, now, would I?" And I had to admit that she wouldn't.

"Over the next few weeks, I found myself getting familiar with that old presence. Don't ask me how I know, but it's a woman, for sure, older, who has seen some hard things. Gradually, I moved the rocker nearer to my bed. Now she's a regular comfort to me. Well, that's it. That's what I meant. Your mom could be closer to you than you think." For once, she wore an expression devoid of all skepticism, and I didn't know how to read her.

"Lorraine, you can't seriously expect me to believe you."

"And why not? Don't tell me I confided this to you for nothing. What a waste!"

I wanted to believe, an accidental hope. "But why didn't you ever tell me?"

"At first, I didn't know anyone here that well. I was probably acting pretty weird, because I won't say all of that didn't take some getting used to, but nobody here knew me well enough to know that I wasn't always that strange. You probably all thought it was part of my mysterious and intriguing persona. After that, well, I just couldn't bring myself to share it with anybody, not even you." She paused and gave me a look I had seldom seen from her, a look of loss, or longing for an abandoned wish.

"You know," she continued, "you certainly don't tell me every private thing that happens to you. You tell me funny stories about Ned and Gabe, but you don't reveal all of the innermost aspects of your personal life to me, do you?"

I was taken aback for a moment, but I knew that I had absorbed more of my mother's reticent personality than I usually admitted. Somewhere within Lorraine's comment were feelings of hurt and accusation, but also there was just a matter-of-fact acceptance of what she and I told each other, even as close friends.

"No, and you shouldn't, either, because frankly I couldn't take it," she said, framing her newly revealed feelings in her easy, taunting manner. "Well, I wanted to have something personal, intimate, too, and since it looks like I'm not going to find it in the man department, I had my ghost. She at least was mine."

"And now mine," I said softly. "Thanks, Lorraine."

We sat quietly for a moment. "My coffee's cold," she said abruptly, and rose to go over and warm it up. Taking the few steps transformed her back into her old self. I didn't want to let go of the mood she'd created by her revelation, but I knew that she'd declared it over.

"Why the hell did you think I've hung on to that awful old apartment all these years?"

"I *did* wonder." That was an understatement, and Lorraine knew it. Her apartment had seemed borderline unlivable even when we were in graduate school and none of us had any money, but as we'd "risen through the ranks," Lorraine had never moved, always giving flimsy excuses, like not having time to look for another place.

"You know," I said, "all during childhood I heard stories of ghosts, and witches, too. Some were from my dad's mother, and then her friends after she died, swearing that she had knocked on their walls and told them to give her family a nice meal after the funeral. Others were from an older neighbor lady, who had more complicated tales. Her sister-in-law was a witch who could change into an animal and back again, always for some dark purpose. But those were all stories from the old country, and my father and mother dismissed them."

"Well, I don't have an old country as recently in my

family history, but I've always believed such things were possible. My grandmother was from New Orleans." She left it at that, and quick visions of the grave of the voodoo queen we'd seen on the National Parks tour of the cemetery on our visit to New Orleans sprang to mind.

"So, see, if you can convince yourself to believe, maybe your mom will grace you with a visit." Perhaps she thought this sounded a little cavalier, because she added, "Really, kiddo, it's something you could hope for, and after a while, as the hope dies away, maybe you'll realize you don't need it anymore."

"Even if I believe, wouldn't she have had to believe, too?"

"Now, *that* I don't know. Maybe believing after she's passed over is enough." Lorraine stood to go.

"You didn't really tell me much about your ghost, Lorraine."

"No, I didn't." She smiled her smile that said I wasn't going to get any more out of her, and turned and left.

There was something I didn't tell you, either, Lorraine. Maybe my mother was already haunting me.

It could have been the season, approaching Halloween, but I kept thinking about Lorraine's story of her ghost. The doctors had said what they often say when they have run out of things to try: that my mother's life depended on her will to live. Even though she was unconscious, maybe she was fighting to stay with us, and she did hang on for days after the accident. I had to admit that, even before Lorraine told me about her own ghost, I had caught myself looking for some sign that she would come back and explain things to me. But there was no sign, and the diary was my only link. Its pages had to be camouflaging a clue from her.

33

Juliana

I feel fairly safe here in Sevilla. I doubt my father would
think that I would be able and willing to come so far. I
have always been dependent upon him, as any young lady
relies upon her family. But now that I have cut myself
from him forever, I know that I must be capable of doing
that which I am capable of conceiving.

Even more than for my safety, I wish to flee Spain
itself. It has become for me the symbol of all that has
happened to me, all that has shattered my life. I not only
abandon Spain. I condemn her.

8 March

Today I overheard Don Luis telling Doña Catalina that he
had heard from a friend an unusual story about a business
acquaintance, a Señor de Ovando, who had received a
request to search for a girl, believed to be visiting the city
from Madrid. Don Luis's friend found the story rather
strange, and said that he had heard it from yet another
party, and that the particulars seemed to be rather
muddled. Don Luis questioned why a girl would be visiting
from Madrid without parent or dueña, and the friend said

that upon reflection, he now recalled that there was talk of the girl's father. Yes, that was it. The person was searching for a man and his daughter. Doña Catalina remarked that men were just as likely as women to gossip, and to get the facts confused upon the telling.

At first I had panicked upon hearing that someone was looking for a girl from Madrid, as I was afraid that my father might somehow have guessed at my destination. Once Don Luis had clarified that it was a father and daughter who were sought, I was greatly relieved. Still, my reaction, though short-lived, betrayed the fear that I harbor, even in the house of this benevolent family.

14 March

The Herreras continue to treat me very kindly, and I am truly fond of their four children, who range in age from four to eleven, three boys and a girl. Each seems interested and eager to learn the simple lessons that I teach. But my heart goes out especially to Floriana, who is six. On the first day, she was to be excluded from the lessons, as she is only a girl, but she cried most pitifully until her parents allowed her to participate along with her brothers.

She is curious, friendly, and unafraid. She stands up well to her two older brothers, yet I have seen her be quite tender with her younger brother. At times I look at her and pray that her fate will be to find a loving husband who will care for her and her children, that she will be lucky as her mother is lucky.

Seeing the sincere consternation on the part of Señor Herrera and Doña Catalina upon the dramatic demonstration of their daughter's desire to study has caused me to wonder about my own education in my father's home. I always vaguely realized that in this I was

not like other girls, and I was glad for and proud of the
knowledge I gained. Now I wonder why my father was so
different in this regard. I do know that my Tía Ana has
more learning than most women, and so perhaps my father
simply absorbed the attitude of his own father in this
regard. Still, I wonder whether he allowed and even
fostered my instruction because it was the best way that
he knew to connect with me. Perhaps it was because he
wished that I had been a son.

15 March

A boy named Rodrigo, acting as page, accompanies me on
my excursions from the house onto the city streets. Of the
invented tale that I presented to the Herrera family upon
my arrival, this was true, that I had hired a youth to
direct me when I had first arrived in the city, though I
instructed him to help me find a suitable place to stay,
rather than the home of my husband's business
acquaintance, as I had said. It was strange how Rodrigo
had seemed to appear from nowhere, offering to help me
with my luggage, and to offer his services to me when he
discovered that I was alone. Though I am inexperienced, I
have seen in Madrid many boys and men, and even women,
who live by their wits, and the goods they can cajole or
purloin from others. But Rodrigo seems honest enough,
and I have little choice if I am to learn more about this
city in which I find myself. I wish to see new sites and
experience what I can of the life here. Soon enough I will
travel across the sea, then close myself off from the world
forever.

Having satisfied Doña Catalina that I am not
wandering about alone, she is content to have me discover
a bit of Sevilla on my own. She and her husband were both

born here and display a particular pride in their city. I must admit that I never expected to admire it so much. Having spent my life in Madrid, in the city of the court, with all of the pride and pomp entailed therein, I had hardly expected Sevilla to outshine her in many ways. Not only is Sevilla much larger, the activity and riches one sees here are quite dazzling. The exteriors of the houses are more ornate than in Madrid. Even as we approached Sevilla, we could see the Giralda, the steeple of the cathedral, which I am told was the minaret of the Grand Mosque in the time of the Moors. There are not only many churches and chapels, but also numerous convents and monasteries. At the same time, next to the symbols of wealth and faith, there are areas of great poverty.

The ladies of Sevilla seem more free to go about than is the case in Madrid. They are usually veiled but foil any modest intent of that garment, often revealing only one eye, in a manner that seems to pique the interest of the young men. I have taken to veiling myself as well, though not in the Sevillian manner. I am forever past the innocent pleasures of trying to attract the attentions of young men. From time to time these last weeks, I have thought of Antonio, and of the girlish fantasies I entertained of our lives together as man and wife. But he is part of the past I have abandoned, and I will try to torment myself no further with thoughts of him.

16 March

Today I persuaded Rodrigo to take me down to the docks, though he was initially quite stubborn in his refusal to do so. He objected that the docks were no place for a lady, and I must admit that he was right. There were many unsavory characters to be seen, both men and women, but there were also wonders to behold. There were hundreds of barges on the river, the Guadalquivir, which connects Sevilla to the sea. Among them were those bringing products which will ultimately be taken on the next fleet to leave for the Indies. All types of goods were in evidence, from fine cloths to timber and cordage. Rodrigo says that ships from all of Europe come to Sevilla, the gateway to the Spanish Indies, by the law of Spain.

18 March

Today I shall write of another aspect of Sevillian life, one that I did not expect. It is the number of slaves. It is true that in Madrid there are some slaves, but it is rather uncommon, and as a foolish young girl I did not give it much thought. But here in Sevilla, indeed in most of Andalucía, it seems there are many slaves, most of black skin. Rodrigo tells me that many families purchase slaves, rather than hiring servants, and he showed me, as a matter of course, slaves being sold on the steps leading up to the cathedral. Even though they are but heathens, how could they be treated in this manner? Rodrigo tells me that many who have lived here for a time have even been baptized into Holy Mother Church, yet are bought and sold.

I am ashamed of the anguish I have felt for my misfortunes, for they are as nothing next to the humiliations these people have suffered. Shall not the tolerance of these violations serve to close men's eyes to cruelty in every form? And this evil is far from limited to Spain. Most of those passing through this port are on their way to the Spanish Indies, to live a life of hopelessness and outrage. This is the refuge to which I hope to escape? They and I shall share an exile from our homelands, but how much kinder mine will be.

25 March

Before my beloved Silvia left, she explained to me that I could come with child because of what Don Lorenzo had done to me, and she told me the signs. I had thought that surely God would spare me such a trial, but that is not to be.

I succumb to despair.

1 April

I have started to emerge from my despondency. I cannot tell Doña Catalina of my condition, and she has attributed my gloom to my difficult circumstances. She tries to make me focus on my husband's joy at receiving me. I know that were the Herreras to know the truth, they would insist that I remain with them until after the child is born. Even were they to relent, no captain would knowingly accept as passenger a woman in my condition.

Though for now I feel safe here in Sevilla, I fear that if I linger much longer, I may be in danger. I long to escape, to begin a new life, to relinquish memories and nightmares.

5 April

If only I had here the love and wisdom of my Tía Ana! Why did I never seek her knowledge in matters of the body? Perhaps it was in part because my father always spoke of her knowledge and charities with distaste, as though they were inappropriate for a woman, especially a lady of her class. Then, too, I did not expect to be cast adrift with no loving protector. I do not even know when my condition will start to become evident. I believe that it will not be for a while, but I am told that the journey to the New World takes two months. As we depart in mid-May, it will be mid-July when we make landfall. I will then be five months along. I believe that the fullness of the skirt of my *guardainfante* will make it possible to conceal any thickening. If not, I shall have to bind myself.

20 April

The routine of my days blurs them together in my mind. Only the ebb and flow of hope and of despair make one distinguishable from another. The loss of all that I have known, and the fear of what is to come, at times seem unbearable. The pleasure that I derive from being with the children helps me through the days, but at night in my own room, I find even this seems a bitter gall. For what of my own child? What joy will I ever have from my own babe?

24 April

I have been preparing for my journey. Little do I know what to expect. I am frightened, tired, and often sick, and I understand that sea travel makes many people ill.

It is difficult to describe what I feel for the child. I have often thought of my mother and wondered what she felt for the life growing within her. Was she happy? Did she love me? I wish that I could say that I do not resent the child for the deeds of the father, but this is not altogether so, and why should I require of myself that I love it, when I shall be compelled to give it up? But perhaps it is best to let myself feel the love for this child carried within my womb, for I shall never have this chance again. In my foolishness, I write as though one could control love.

Thus are my thoughts as I go about my daily tasks. I do not know whether writing them helps me purge them from my mind or imprints them on my memory.

30 April

Señor Herrera has shown his concern for me in many ways, not the least of which was finding a servant girl to accompany me. I expressed my aversion to the thought of purchasing a slave, and it took him several days to locate someone who was willing to set sail for New Spain. However, today he arrived home quite excited, announcing that he believed he had found the proper person.

"There is only one condition, to which I am certain you will gladly concede, Doña María," he explained.

"And what is that, Don Luis?" I asked.

"You must promise to engage her as your household servant when you reach your new home. I know from her current employers that she is a hardworking and honest girl, and that she learns quickly. I am certain that you could continue to find some use for her once you have joined your husband."

I did not wish to thwart his enthusiasm, but I tried to dissuade him from this solution. "I do not wish to appear ungrateful, señor. I know that you have been devoting much time and energy to identifying just such a girl, but are you certain that there is no possibility of finding someone who would come with no such encumbrance?"

Señor Herrera's face betrayed a hint of surprise and displeasure. "I have, as you said, devoted much time and energy to this task, and I assure you, Doña María, that this is the best possibility. I am sure this girl will serve your needs well, not only on the voyage but also in New Spain."

I recognized his tone as similar to my father's when indicating that a discussion was closed, and that his opinion would overrule any objections I might raise. What recourse had I but to accept? Once again, I would practice deception to carry out my plans, but this time I might be inflicting harm on another young woman like me.

10 May

In two days, my companion, Luisa, and I shall sail for a land that seems unreal. The hope I have nurtured of being able to see my Silvia again has not come to pass, and I have had no word from her since she left to go to her cousins. I shall see her only in my memory, like all else I leave behind. I can help her only in my prayers.

11 May

If each and every scene I have imagined should be true, the New World is indeed a strange one. I shall be sad to bid farewell to the Herrera family, more kind to me than he whose duty it was to be so. Yet I cannot help but feel some excitement, too. What awaits me, I do not know, but I feel a strength earned from what I have endured, and no remorse in leaving this sorry Spain, which would condone the tyranny of honor.

12 May
Aboard the Ship Queen Isabel

This morning, the entire Herrera family accompanied Luisa and me to the ship. It was not easy to bid them farewell. They have been so kind to me and done so much for a girl who was more desperate than ever they could have guessed. Doña Catalina wept as she embraced me, and pressed into my hands some sweets that she had prepared especially for me. Floriana clung to my skirts and refused to let go, imploring her newfound friend and teacher to stay forever. Finally, Señor Herrera had to pull her from me, and she buried her tear-stained face in his shoulder. Luisa suffered no such distress in leaving friends behind. Indeed, there was no one there to wish her well or urge her to stay. She is slightly younger than I, and I admire her courage in seeking to cross the sea to a new land. She must have even less than I to tie her to this place. For both of us, our resolve has brought us to this journey, and there is no turning back.

13 May

The departure of the ship yesterday morning was both confusing and exciting, serving to take my mind from my worries. Thousands of people gathered at the banks of the Guadalquivir River to see the ships sail. Many are gorged with goods for the Indies, destined to return loaded with even greater riches. And what a number of ships! There are several dozen in the fleet, some merchantmen, others armed galleons, to protect us against Dutch and English ships and pirates, though I am told that the greatest danger is when the fleet returns, transporting precious metal from the New World. I remarked to one of the officers that there seems to me to be booty enough to entice the most avaricious of pirates, our cargo including fine cloth and other luxury items. He reassured me that the bulk of our goods are things that are greatly wanted in New Spain but of little use to pirates. One of the items is mercury, which will be used in the Mexican mines to extract silver. The pirates would much prefer to wait and hope for the bounty of a ship laden with that precious metal.

As we awaited our turn to sail, there was something of a disturbance onboard. An official clambered onto the ship, claiming excitedly that not all of the paperwork had been properly filled out. The captain assured him that the officials of the Contratación had checked all the bills of lading against the cargo, and all had been cleared. This official and his assistants, however, were from the Inquisition and had not yet had the opportunity to ensure that there were no books aboard that the Holy Office banned. At the mere mention of the Holy Office, the captain asserted that, of course, he would never think of aiding in any way those who would foment heresy, and he nervously acquiesced to the demands to search wherever they wished, even though the incident delayed our departure. When the officials had done their duty and were satisfied that the ship was free of heresy, they departed, and we were signaled to leave the dock shortly thereafter. Now we are sailing slowly down the Guadalquivir river. Tomorrow we reach the open sea.

Were it not for the events of these past months, I would still be sitting quietly in my room in Madrid, attempting to decipher the secret message my father would have me extract from some dramatic work. I had no choice in my leaving, but I have a choice in my destination. My falsehoods and my determination have brought me here.

14 May

We have reached the point where the Guadalquivir empties into the open sea. Now it feels that our voyage truly begins, as we leave Iberia behind. Another ship, which sailed from Cádiz, has joined us, and I am told that there are important personages from His Majesty's government onboard, on their way to visit the viceroy in Mexico City.

22 May

Today we took on a few supplies and passengers at the Canaries, our final stop on this side of the Atlantic. The number of ships in the fleet continually impresses me, as well as reassures me a little. I must admit to a feeling of trepidation at the vastness of the ocean before us.

I am ever more grateful to Señor Herrera for having found Luisa for me. She is most eager to be of service. Although there is little for her to do onboard ship, she tries to get for me the best of what is available, and while there is not much choice, she has already learned what foods are most likely to sit well with me. She keeps our space tidy and is always looking for something more to bring me comfort, an extra blanket for the chill of the sea nights. When I need quiet, she grants me solitude, and she understands when conversation will be welcome.

31 May

Time weighs heavily onboard ship, one day much like another. I am frightened of what lies ahead, but my fear is outweighed by my desire to leave behind my life of the past, though I carry its most sharp reminder here within me. I shall devise a tale to offer to the curious, but I shall know that my babe is mine alone, conceived in violence. The father has thus forfeited any right or claim. My child is a reminder to me of my own strength in rejecting all that I knew, and will provide the determination to do what I must.

3 June

Today I feel my situation most keenly. I dreamed last
night of my Tía Ana. She was telling me that I should take
better care of myself. Somehow she knew of my condition.
I know that I am the one who chose to flee, but I feel
abandoned. Why did my *tía* not search for me when I went
missing from my father's home?

16 June

Luisa and I spend many hours sitting together in the tiny
cabin granted to us. We are lucky to have it, small and
suffocating as it is, for it provides a shield for us from the
ever-buffeting wind and the prying eyes of the sailors and
the male passengers.

Yesterday I told Luisa of my condition. She did not
question me about why I have kept this secret. Many
women, even in the most respectable of circumstances,
modestly choose to hide their situation from prying eyes as
long as possible.

23 June

I have felt my child! At first I did not know what the
strange sensation was, but then I realized what it must be. I
felt a quick surge of joy, soon to be dampened by the fear I
felt for what would become of my unborn babe, so ill fated.

30 June

I wanted to refrain from making this journal a mere
record of every small trial, yet to whom else can I
complain? Luisa is kind and patient, yet I feel that she,
too, has had her share of tribulations, and I would not

add to her burden by making her endure my laments.

I have from the first moment we reached open sea suffered from the cruelest seasickness. I cannot help but feel that my condition worsens it. My legs ache, and I get cramps at night, most probably because I do little more than sit. I can hardly walk about the cabin, it is so confining, and the delicacy of my situation makes me hesitant to spend much time on deck.

2 July

The sea seems calmer today than it has in many days, and I feel much revived by the fresh air I finally ventured to take this morning. The movements of the ship's passengers are extremely curtailed, and I must be most circumspect. Still, some of the other travelers have been solicitous and are concerned with my welfare, a young lady traveling with only a girl to attend her. What would their reaction be if they knew my story?

5 July

Luisa is a most able girl, and she and I are becoming friends. Although she is completely unschooled, in many ways she is more knowledgeable than I. I was never meant to have to find my own way in life, but Luisa knew from the time she was a young child that she herself would be her only source of support and defense, and she is worldly wise. I feel great guilt in knowing that I shall have to betray my word to her. I will have no home to take her to when we have reached New Spain. Yet I have thought that perhaps she could come to the convent to live with me for a time. I know that, at least in Madrid, many of the sisters bring servant girls with them to tend them in the convent. I have no reason to believe that things will be very different in New Spain in this respect. I do not know whether Luisa will accept this idea, but it would be so comforting to me to have her there, at least until I have become used to my new life.

11 July

The ship stopped today at the easternmost large island of the Antilles. I was able to disembark for a few hours, but only after pleading with the captain, who insisted that he could not be responsible for a young woman and her servant. When he began to see how desperate I was to leave the ship, even though it will be only a little over a week before we reach our landing point of Vera Cruz, he relented. Luisa and I remarked on how strange it felt to have solid ground beneath our feet after so many weeks at sea. All the hours ashore were not sufficient to relieve us from the rolling feeling that seems to have become a part of our very beings.

The docks were bustling with activity, and Luisa and I felt that we should confine ourselves to remaining close to that area. Though we could but vaguely see it in the distance, the vegetation was lush, even at this time of year, and it greatly intrigued us. It looked to be unlike anything we had seen in arid Spain. There were native workers and also black-skinned slaves from Africa working at the port. Never have I seen such a mixture of humanity, although Luisa and I saw few other European women.

This new land is so strikingly different from the home that I have always known, that now there is a new regret to prick at me. How much of this splendor and mystery will I be able to witness before I must bury myself behind the convent walls? How different can life be there, where all will be ruled by order and obedience? Nothing of the strange beauty of this land and its peoples will impinge on our existence there. Now that I have glimpsed it, I have such an appetite to taste of it! I have come to a new world, only to inter myself in the customs of the old, forever to be haunted by a reality barely touched upon.

14 July

Luisa and I grow ever closer, and her care for me is such that one would think that she and I had been together longer. Today she told me something of her past, and the cruelty she had to bear in her young life makes me care for her all the more. She never knew her mother either, but she was not so lucky as I in her upbringing. Her father left her always in the care of an older sister, who had a hard heart and a ready fist. The days she was neglected were the brightest for Luisa, for then at least she suffered no torments.

At the age of twelve, Luisa was sent by her father to a house, to help in the kitchen, and there the master's son, who was seventeen, forced her to commit vile and shameful acts. Luisa wept from anger and humiliation when she told me this, and hinted at the perversions she endured, and she just a tender child.

Shortly thereafter, the master's son left to marry, and, even in her own relief, Luisa felt a deep sorrow for the girl who was to be his bride. "For even though she would be wealthy," explained Luisa, "all of her riches would not be able to shield her from her husband's cruelty."

The family Luisa served married off a daughter some months later, and the mistress told Luisa that she would no longer require her services, as the household's needs had now lessened. She found a place as servant to a midwife, and there she stayed until she heard of someone looking for a serving girl to journey to the New World.

"So you see, Doña María, I wish to shed my old life. It has not been so kind to me that I will miss it much. I had heard that there are many more men in New Spain than there are women. Perhaps, in time, even I, who have been so ill used, can find a husband who will be willing to accept me."

She said this so simply that I could not express any doubts I might have; I would be only adding to her burdens.

"Perhaps so, Luisa" was all that I could find tongue to reply.

17 July

Since Luisa showed me such trust in revealing the horrors of her past, I have been weighed down by guilt over my continued deception that I would find a place for her when we reach our destination. Today I told her the truth about my flight to New Spain. She was shocked and saddened, but I shall be ever grateful to her that she cast no blame on me for having lied to her.

Now Luisa understands that I have no home in which to offer her a place. I told her of my plans to enter a convent when we have reached our destination. I proposed that she come there with me for a while. Even if she does not stay, she will have a place from which to look for a new position. She said that she would think on my offer.

"Perhaps, after what we both have suffered, a convent would not be such an unkind place to spend our days," I said, as she rose to go and get our dinner. She did not respond but came over to me and kissed my hand. She cried for both our fates, and in her tears I knew that she saw no gentle future awaiting us.

Her kindness and concern for me touched me keenly.

Sometimes the heart of those who have greatly suffered grows larger, as though to make room for the pain of others.

21 July

Tomorrow we are to land in Vera Cruz. Though I feel much unease, I am anxious to forsake this ship forever and taste what mercies this land may offer.

26 July
Vera Cruz

We have lingered here in Vera Cruz for a few days, to gather strength for the final leg of our journey. I had heard that the quality of the light and the transparency of the air in New Spain are something to be remarked upon, and it is true. It is difficult to explain how light and air can seem different, and yet they are, and are thereby quite pleasing. I do not know whether this will hold true in Mexico City, but I hope that it does, for I will continue my journey, to settle in that cultural and political center of New Spain. I have been told that there are many convents there, representing various orders. Even though I am not to participate in the life of the city, perhaps some of its vitality will reach inside the convent walls.

Luisa has agreed to accompany me, and I have secured for us a place with a party that will travel to the high country, where Mexico City is located. I knew that I could not continue to hide my condition, and so I have again made use of the story that I told the Herreras, that I am on my way to Mexico City to meet my husband. Only this phantasm can serve to lend me some respectability.

I have been hesitant to converse with my fellow

travelers, in view of my somewhat precarious circumstances, but a kindly priest, Father Quijada, has befriended me. We are but members on the periphery of our group, which centers on the high government official who was on the ship from Cádiz. Don Diego Pelayo de Porzuna is an emissary to the viceroy and the vicereine, and so our caravan is quite well organized and provisioned. We should make our way in a timely manner to the place that shall be my home.

1 August
Jalapa

We rest in Jalapa tonight, and I am relieved to find the solace of writing here. In many ways this is the only connection with my old life, this and my unborn child. But my babe shall be born of this new land.

It seems that the personage from His Majesty's court is even more important than I had realized. Indeed, I am told that he is being accorded many of the same honors that were shown to the viceroy on his arrival in New Spain.

7 August
Tlaxcala

We have reached Tlaxcala, where we will remain for three days. I am glad that we will have something of a rest here, as the journey is extremely taxing. I do not know how I would manage without Luisa's help. I thank Our Lady that Luisa has decided to stay with me in Mexico City, at least until after the babe comes.

Upon entering Tlaxcala, I was again grateful to be in the company of august persons. Although at various stages on our journey Señor Pelayo de Porzuna received the greetings of various native leaders, the entrance into Tlaxcala far surpassed anything we have yet witnessed.

In honor of Don Diego the town held a large procession, which included drums, flutes, and some musical instruments that I did not recognize. The Indians' clothing was most colorful and beautiful, but strange beyond imagining to us. Many of those in the procession appeared to be of high rank, and I am told that some were of the Indian nobility. Once again, I have found myself powerfully attracted to this new land. Humanity is so much more varied than I could ever have imagined, sitting so protected within my father's home.

8 August

I questioned Father Quijada about the extravagance of the Tlaxcala welcome. He explained that the people of Tlaxcala are a longtime ally of the Spanish, and that their aid was essential in Cortes's struggle against the Aztec state. Then he said something whose meaning I struggle to comprehend: "How diligently do conquerors mine the targeted terrain for gems of grievances between the native peoples, and raise the gems up to the sunlight to intensify their power. Then do they stealthily pocket the gems for their own gain." Yet the Tlaxcala do not seem to think themselves deceived. But what future have they bought for their descendants?

11 August

As Father Quijada, Luisa, and I traveled alone within our coach today, I ventured to pose another question to him about the procession we saw a few days ago in Tlaxcala. "Do not these people who look and dress so differently also not think and believe very differently than we?" I asked Father Quijada.

"Of course the native religions were many before we came, and some still persist, even here, after so many decades of effort to bring them into the fold of Holy Mother Church," he replied sadly. "They do not see even this world as we do, so how are we to convince them to conceive of the next world through our eyes? But we must maintain our faith that it can be done, and give our lives to the struggle."

This last was said with a hint of resigned desperation, so I sought to offer him some encouragement. "Yet unity of faith has been achieved in Spain, even after so many centuries of Moorish domination. Jews also were converted to the true faith, and now all live under the banner of Christ and all His saints."

Father Quijada gave me a strange look, as one gives to a child who innocently speaks of things she does not understand. "Yes, what you say is true, but those who would not convert were banished. We cannot use that method here, where we are the usurpers. Remember also, my daughter, that our unity of faith is preserved by the Holy Inquisition, which most ferociously punishes lapses in belief."

I could not deny the truth of what he was saying, yet I persisted. "Still, I have heard that many of the Indians do accept our faith and have already now for generations."

"It is correct that there are those who seem to have come to a genuine understanding and love of Christ and Holy Mother Church, yet many who are claimed as converts are not so in their hearts. Many of my fellow priests are more interested in gathering Indians to themselves for the labor that they can perform than in the saving of their immortal souls."

The candor with which Father Quijada spoke to me was astonishing. Never before had I heard of a clergyman reproaching his fellows, and the implied criticism of the Holy Office was not only unusual but also dangerous. Perhaps his despair, or the freedom inherent in the very landscape of this new continent, had loosened his tongue. Perhaps it was only that he did not think that a young girl would wholly understand the implications of all that he was saying. Indeed, I found myself quite unable to respond. All that he was telling me was so foreign to everything that I had ever learned that I was left confused and frightened.

Now that he had started on this track, he continued, almost as though to himself, "Oftentimes we resort to including some small elements of their religion into our teaching to the Indians. Oh, I'm sure that it began merely as a means of illustration, as a way of comparing the concepts of their beliefs with our own, for do not believe that their faith is not as complete and complex in itself as is ours. Slowly, however, I can see that they understand it not as illustration only, but also as comparability. The Catholic religion that will be practiced in times to come in Mexico will not be the same that is practiced in Spain, for all the efforts of the Holy Inquisition."

At his mention of the Holy Inquisition, Father Quijada seemed to become aware of what he had been saying to me, a stranger, whom he did not know if he could trust. "But you must forgive and forget these ramblings of an old priest, child. Holy Mother Church is one, here as in Spain itself, and I will give my life to keep it so." With that, he fell silent.

I have risen from my pallet to write this, though Luisa has long since fallen asleep. Father Quijada's words are haunting me, and I cannot banish them from my mind. It seems as though something that I had fast within my grip

213

has been torn from me. For all my doubts of other things, my faith in the Church still held firm, yet now I have heard a priest express doubts about the wisdom and justice of what is said and done in Her name. I wish to bury these questions deep within me, yet I hope that they do not take seed there and one day grow to smother me.

15 August

I have not felt well these past several days. We have had very warm weather, and no respite from the constant motion. Many times I would rather not eat at all. Still, I must try to take in some nourishment, for the sake of my babe. For some days I had not felt the child move, and I went about with much fear that my circumstances had caused some harm. But today I again felt the internal wrestling, and I am more at peace.

26 August
Mexico City

We have arrived in Mexico City, and I have procured for us a small room with a criollo family. I invented yet another tale for them, but I will not tell of it here. I am weary of recording my lies. This family does not seem as inclined to kindness as were the Herreras, but indifference suits my purpose.

The last part of the journey into Mexico City, in such high terrain, was particularly difficult. I am told that it takes some time for one to become accustomed to the altitude, and that until one is used to it, even the simplest tasks can be fatiguing.

The city is much larger than I had expected; I have been told that the population numbers almost eighty thousand inhabitants, about a fifth being Spaniards and criollos, the remainder Indians, mestizos, and mulattos. I have seen a number of African slaves here, as in Sevilla, and I do not know whether these numbers include those wretched souls.

3 September

Life here is not easy, and I have no heart to chronicle its hardships.

9 October

I had hoped that by now my nausea would have subsided, but still I feel no desire to eat. I fear for my child's nourishment, yet I grow bigger every day.

13 October

All of my body is so swollen that I scarce resemble myself. It is as though my head were stuck onto another's body, and even my face is quite round. The swelling in my hands is such that I cannot remove from my finger my mother's ring, which Silvia gave me on our journey, and which I have worn these last few months. At times it pains me, and Luisa brings me cool water to soak my hand, which gives me some relief.

I have seen women with child before, yet scarce do I recall their having looked thus. Luisa assures me that it is not altogether uncommon, and probably she is right. How many young girls pay close attention to women who are to bear a child, though it be their future destiny? And then, women of my acquaintance would not be seen in public at this advanced stage of their expectancy.

I am beginning to grow more anxious about how I will bear up when my time comes. Luisa has told me something of what to expect, and at times it seems that this serves only to frighten me the more. What if there is some mischance?

Virgin Mother, you who bore this pain to bring forth Our Savior, give me strength, and in your love extend your protecting hand over me.

18 October

There are moments when I am filled with terror about my lying-in, and I cannot help but recall that it was in childbirth that my own mother was taken to Our Lord. I have found a midwife in the area who says that she will attend me when it is my time, though she eyes me with suspicion, wondering why a girl who is obviously from a more prosperous background currently finds herself in meaner circumstances. Still, I have shown that I can pay her, and she has said that when Luisa goes to fetch her, she will come.

I pray that the Virgin Mary, she who also bore her child so far from home, will have pity and aid me. Dearest Virgin, do not judge me harshly for daring to think our situations similar. It is only that you are a woman and I trust to your clemency.

21 October

My babe's foot is most often pushing against me now, right below my chest. The little lump changes position when I press on it, seeking relief. Though my fear of the birthing has not lessened, the days are so difficult now that I yearn for it. It cannot be worse than this miserable waiting.

23 October

I long to see my child now, to hold it in my arms and suckle it. Though I would have sought not to feel a mother's love, knowing I cannot keep the babe, already these months I have held the child most dear.

9 November

My daughter is seven days old. I have just nursed her and laid her down to sleep. She seems strong, and the midwife says there is no doubt that she will flourish, even though she was subjected to the harshest travel while in the womb. Luisa laughs when I praise my girl as a most special babe, and says that all mothers think so when first they hold their newborn child. But my daughter is the only family left to me. I have heard of women who reject a child begotten under unwelcome circumstances, but to me her beginning is now but as a dream, and she is all that is real. I am both mother and father to her, and I shall love her doubly.

I am still quite weak. I had a difficult time delivering my child into the world. The midwife said that even for first-time mothers, never had she seen such a trying labor end in the survival of both mother and child. My pains came on slowly and built excruciatingly over the next several hours. This, I understand, is normal, and under the direction of the midwife Luisa did all she could to comfort me, wiping my forehead with water, talking soothingly to me, and allowing me to grip her arms when the pain was strongest. But after many hours of this, the character of my labor began to change. I have no recollection of this time. Luisa tells me that she became much affrighted and placed all of her hopes in Our Lady, who alone might save me. My body shook as though possessed by some demon, and I seemed to go in and out of delirium. Throughout a whole night I lay thus, drifting in and out of reality. Luisa said that the midwife warned her to prepare herself for my end. Finally, Luisa knows not how or why, I seemed to awaken from these troubles, and the tremors ceased. Then the final pains came quickly on, and it was time to push my babe into the world. As the midwife attended to what needed to be done, Luisa laid my daughter on my chest, and we studied each other. She did not cry but seemed only to look about in wonder at this strange new world. I have named her Mercedes, for the mercies shown to me by Our Lady.

34

RACHEL

I had let myself read a longer section of the diary, but the thing that most weighed on my mind was Juliana's account of her trials during childbirth. Unreasonably, it caused me to dread my own delivery. It was ridiculous of me. Juliana lived over three centuries ago and didn't have at her disposal even the expertise that would have been available had she been in Madrid, in the home of a husband of her class. Besides, I experienced a fairly easy delivery with Gabe. Still, I searched frantically for information, trying to diagnose what had happened to Juliana, and to identify what remedies would be used nowadays to prevent or relieve such a frightening and painful labor.

Did I no longer doubt Juliana's existence? The aspects of the period and place, with which I was familiar from a career spent as a Hispanist, seemed to support the diary's authenticity, but it was Juliana herself who was convincing me of her reality.

I didn't want to discuss my pregnancy with anyone other than Ned. He was thrilled about the upcoming baby, and when I was with him, I appreciated his manifest gratitude for all that I was going through. He was always patient with me, whether I was irritable or crying for no apparent reason. Even with the emotional swings, naturally aggravated by Helen's death, I'd been luckier with this pregnancy than I had been with Gabe, experiencing almost no nausea. However, I was starting to show, and I reacted in various ways when anyone other than Ned commented on my condition.

When I was carrying Gabe, I was still taking some classes for my graduate work. At the end of the quarter, the professor took me aside and confided in me that I had been the best pupil in the class. The surprise in his voice was evident. Apparently, he didn't think the mind and the body could both produce at the same time. This very professor was now one of my colleagues, and I could see that his consternation persisted.

I knew that my mother had a very difficult time carrying me, and I used to wonder how she could help hating me by the time I was born. I had already caused her so much misery. One of my aunts told me once that, even when she was a little girl, she would always give her mother a present when it was her own birthday. She felt that her mother was the real heroine of the day, having endured so much to give her life. I always thought that was a wonderful idea. But I never followed her example. Helen was not that kind of mother.

As the days and then weeks dragged on, I still didn't tell Ned about the diary, and that betrayal gnawed at me. The papers didn't relate directly to him, but I was deceiving him by keeping from him something that so dominated my consciousness. Still, I reminded myself that he hardly told me everything, and that I'd invented for myself those parts of his inner life that weren't observable. I imagined that many people in love created their partner in this way, and sometimes it was this created self that we held most dear.

35

Juliana

All fares well with Mercedes, though I am still somewhat
weak. I was worried that I might not have enough milk for
her, yet my body seems to use whatever it gets to nourish
the child, and that is how I would have it. To me she is
the fairest of babes, though Luisa has let slip that she is
to her as are most other newborns, and that her head is
still somewhat misshapen from the birthing.

Though the sight of Mercedes flooded me with
happiness from the first moment, still the suffering I
endured to bring about her birth caused a feeling almost
of wonder. It was as though I had to reconcile myself to
the idea that such pain could bring forth such joy. Many
were the times, when I was striving to learn a new lesson
or to earn some favor at my father's hand, that he would
remind me that nothing worthwhile comes at light cost.
Yet now I think that mostly do these words ring true when
coming from a woman.

30 November

My Mercedes is so helpless and so beautiful. I nurse her
and her hand touches my breast in the most innocent of

caresses, and I fancy that she looks at me with trusting eyes. I shall not abandon her totally, for I am slowly devising a plan whereby I shall be able always to be near her, though I may not acknowledge her.

18 December

At times I worry for my Mercedes. I tell myself that she is not sickly, but her legs and arms seem to me too thin. Lately she sometimes cries when I put her to my breast, and I do not know whether this is from frustration for an inadequate supply of milk, or a reluctance to drink in her mother's apprehension. At night she does not sleep well, and she often has dark circles beneath her eyes.

20 December

Today I was able to get Mercedes baptized, something that has been weighing very heavily on my mind. Father Quijada had kindly given us the information of where he would be in the city, and with some difficulty I found him and convinced him to perform the rite. I had to tell him that my husband, with whom I had been reunited, had unexpectedly been called away on business for I knew not how long.

I very much wanted Luisa to be my child's godmother, though Father Quijada thought it most unfitting. My distress at possibly endangering my child's soul by allowing her to remain unbaptized finally convinced him to perform the sacrament. One of Father Quijada's acquaintances agreed to act as godfather. He was very reluctant to do so, seeing that he would be unable to carry out his future duties as such, but I persuaded him that it would be greater sin to deny Mercedes the cleansing waters of Baptism and risk that if the Lord should take my little child, the gates of heaven would be forever closed to her. I am somewhat frightened, having spoken aloud of such a possibility. I would not wish to bring about the realization of my fears by having used this reasoning to gain Baptism for her. Dearest Savior, if I have offended You, in memory of your own dear mother, please pity and forgive a mother's love.

6 January 1662

I have passed my first Epiphany in Mexico City, with only Mercedes and Luisa for company. Mercedes has gotten over her fussiness at nursing and looks better each day. Luisa and I sometimes lay Mercedes on her stomach on my bed, then kneel beside it and watch as she holds her head up, looking like a little turtle. She now curves her mouth in a way that we tell ourselves is a smile. I feel that Mercedes shows curiosity in the way she observes her world, and she will swat at things that come close to her reach, though with so little effect that Luisa and I cannot help but laugh. Not having spent time around other women, especially not those with small babes, I do not know whether these habits are common to all children or whether they are, as they seem to me, small wonders.

I find myself thinking more than ever before about my own mother. Silvia was the only one who would ever talk about her, because my father never spoke her name, for sorrow. My nurse told me of her goodness, and of the joy that she felt when she learned she was to have a child, but I know none of the particulars of my mother's death, only that she died while giving birth to me. Did she live long enough to know that she had a daughter? Did she have a moment to feel the joy that I felt when first I held my Mercedes? I believe that even if I had known that I was gravely ill, the sorrow at leaving my newborn babe would have been tempered with the joy of seeing this life's miracle.

18 January

Everything that has happened these last several months has numbed me, and finally I am drained of my strong will. All I feel able to do is sit in our room. I can see that Luisa grows ever more anxious about my inaction, though she says nothing. I cannot even pray for resolve. I would not know what to do with it.

27 January

I have begun to feel more myself, perhaps because of prodding myself to activity. Through careful inquiries, in the form of casual questions that I have put to various people, couched amid many questions about the city, I have at last begun to ascertain some of the facts that I shall need to know. I go about this secretively, even though there is no real danger I can name. Perhaps it is only from the habit I have acquired of hiding my intentions from all men's eyes.

There are some twenty convents within the city. I know that I am not suited to going to the Carmelites, and neither could I contrive to have Mercedes there. I believe that the order of the convent of Santa Catalina de Siena, a Dominican order of nuns, will best suit my temperament and my purpose. I will be able to use the money that I got in Sevilla from the sale of my mother's gems. It should be enough to secure both Mercedes and myself a place. There is another problem, however, for which I cannot seem to find a solution. If I am to enter the convent on the level that I desire, and that is appropriate to my class and to my education, I must have an introduction from someone who will attest to my birth and breeding. I have Silvia's purity-of-blood papers, which I shall use as my own, but that is not enough. I need someone to write a letter for me, and to answer any questions as I instruct him, if that becomes necessary. At first it occurred to me that I could write such a reference from some invented person in Spain. The convent could not easily investigate its authenticity, so it might be accepted. But then how could I explain why a young girl would travel all the way to New Spain, merely to enter into a convent? No, the letter must come from someone here, someone who will bear up under scrutiny. Yet whom could I convince to perform this task? Surely I have not come so far only to be thwarted now.

4 February

The rightness of my intention to enter the convent is becoming more evident each day. The position of a young mother with no apparent protector is precarious. From the attitudes of the neighbors, and from the family with whom we are boarding, I can see that I am now a person with no standing and of questionable respectability. I cannot live like this, nor can I keep Mercedes in such an atmosphere of suspicion and disdain.

As my conviction in this matter has become stronger with each day, I have striven to find a solution to my dilemma of obtaining the reference that is so necessary for entrance into the convent. I have been cruelly taught that reputation does not always reflect a man's true character, and for my purpose, that knowledge will aid me. The man who is to guarantee my acceptability must be well respected in the community and yet also open to the suggestion that truth and goodness are not always one. I need a man who can tell himself that at times the greater good is served through illusion. A certain avarice, coupled with a certain type of honor, is necessary for my purpose. I need a man who will lie for me yet never reveal the fabrication. How can I find such a person?

17 February

I believe that I may have my man. I have not yet suggested my proposal to him, but I hope that, with the help of Our Lady, I shall soon be able to obtain the letter I need.

I spent many days going to different areas of the city, where I was not a familiar figure, frequenting markets and small places of business. I took Mercedes and Luisa with me, a servant lending respectability. Those who did not know me assumed that I was a woman whose honorable husband provided for me. Of the market vendors, I asked questions about those who had businesses in the area, sometimes pretending that my husband or I might have need of their services. At times I overheard a conversation relating to someone who was respected or reviled. Though it is a fallible source, I had to rely upon reputation. It was not difficult to find men esteemed for their honor, for most men publicly guard this. For men to call another benevolent was somewhat more difficult, as each is reluctant to name in another a virtue that he fears he himself is lacking. Though it seems a contradiction, the man I approached had to also have an element of greed, and I felt that I had to rely upon my own discoveries, for I had to be certain of this. A man who was only honorable and magnanimous would not serve my purpose. I could not risk having him relate my request to the authorities, for great is the penalty for pretending you are that which you are not.

I came up with several ideas but finally decided that the best ploy would be one that was easy to carry out. I chose a man from the list I had drawn up and studied his habits, noting at which times of the day he left his home, and where his errands usually took him. I placed several gold *escudos* into my bag and planned my own walk to coincide with his. It was difficult to risk this sum, but I knew that it was necessary to sacrifice a not-insignificant amount if my plan were to yield results. As I got closer to him, I made myself trip and fall, dropping my bag as I did so. I hurriedly arose, brushed off my skirts, as though distracted, and walked away, leaving the handbag lie. The first three times I performed my own piece of theater, the gentlemen I had sought to test retrieved my bag for me and returned it to me in a most kindly and concerned manner. Although each time this occurred I was thwarted in my plan, I was happy to know that men of such integrity could still be found.

The fourth time I repeated my charade, after I had left my bag, I glanced back once and saw him pick it up and, as he was beginning to hail me, move the hand holding my bag slightly up and down, as though weighing its contents. He quickly looked around, then put my bag beneath his coat and walked away. This is the man I shall write to tomorrow, and I must admit that I am very fearful. Each time I performed my small deception, I secretly trembled at my intent. How much more difficult will it be to talk openly to this man of what I would have him do for me? I shall be placing myself totally in his hands, relying on the balance I can achieve between his honor and his greed. Will honesty or deception best serve me?

21 February

It is accomplished. My newly discovered relative is Señor Esteban de Palma Rodriguez. Now I can only pray his honor and his reluctance to admit to his own part in this ruse will keep him silent all his days.

Three days ago, I sent a note to Señor de Palma, stating only that I was a lady in need of his aid. I did not mention the incident of the bag, for I wanted to appeal to his sense of his own generosity, not to his shame. The first note requesting a meeting was not successful. I am sure that such gentlemen frequently receive requests for help, but I hoped that mine would be unusual enough to pique his curiosity. For two hours, I waited at the spot I had designated in my note. As each hour passed, I grew more anxious and was subjected to ever bolder looks from the young caballeros passing by. That night was difficult for me, and as I lay in bed, I tried to devise another scheme to achieve my purpose, but I could come up with nothing else. So, rising from my sleepless bed, I wrote another note to Señor de Palma, this one more urgent than the last.

I do not know whether it was my persistence or the tone of my second note that prompted him to meet with me, but yesterday he came. As he walked toward me, I grew more anxious about how he might react to my proposal. I had chosen the Plaza Mayor for our meeting, hoping that the public nature of that place would somewhat lessen the ill impression he would have of a young lady so forward as to approach him in the manner in which I had done. The eyes of passersby also served to protect me from any possible dishonorable intention on his part. It was only at the moment he was about to speak that the thought flashed through my mind that he might recognize me from the incident with my handbag. This, I feared, would raise his suspicions against me, causing him to question my motives and intent. To my relief, however, I saw no light of recognition in his eyes as he came closer.

"Doña Silvia?" he asked, and I thanked the Virgin Mary for the kindness I heard in his voice. I had used Silvia's name since arriving in Mexico City, as I would need to use her papers to enter the convent. I had not used Silvia's full name in my note, unwilling to identify myself further before Señor de Palma had agreed to my plan. "I was intrigued by your mysterious notes. How may I be of service to you?"

I thanked him for coming and explained to him that I had come to know of his reputation for honor and generosity and had thus chosen him for my entreaty. Slowly I unfolded my request to him, revealing as little as possible about myself, explaining only that, because of unusual circumstances, I was presently without the means to provide my own letter of reference. It was plain to see that I am a person of quality, and I showed to him Silvia's papers proving purity of lineage. The matter of payment had to be introduced early in the conversation, to maintain his interest, but also had to be treated with great delicacy. I told him that I very much regretted the necessity to begin my religious life with a deception, but that I was certain of my vocation, and that this was the only road open to me. I illustrated my sincerity by describing my desire to atone for this falsehood by making a substantial contribution to an organization that helped the poor.

"I pray that Our Lord, who reads our hearts, will forgive me this ruse, which will enable me to enter a lifetime in His service. If I might further presume upon your chivalry, I would ask that you handle this donation for me, as I do not wish to be known."

229

He hesitated a moment and then replied, "I would be happy to be of service to you, señorita. Who am I to inhibit one with such great faith and charity?"

I am to meet him in two days, at which time he will supply me with my necessary reference, and I will entrust to him the money for the poor. I doubt that they will ever see it.

26 February

I have discovered that the order of the Dominican nuns does not typically take in abandoned infants, but I believe that if a considerable sum is left for Mercedes's upbringing, the sisters will be persuaded to shelter her. As it may appear suspicious if Mercedes and I arrive at the convent simultaneously, I have decided that I will enter first and Luisa will care for Mercedes for some months, then bring her to the convent. I initially intended to bring Mercedes to the convent first, but I decided that it would work to our benefit if I were already firmly established there when Mercedes arrived. In this way, I hope to be able to influence the good sisters to accept Mercedes if there is any reluctance on their part.

If she wishes to, Luisa will follow shortly thereafter, and I will obtain permission to employ her as my servant. I am already missing my beloved child, even as I look upon her sleeping form. I know that I shall also miss Luisa, as she has become such a friend and support to me.

25 March

Tomorrow I shall enter the convent. It has taken some weeks for my petition for entry to be accepted, but now all is prepared. I have paid the three thousand pesos the convent requires as a dowry. In addition, I was required to keep some money aside, to pay for my ceremony of profession, should I decide to take my vows. I understand that there are women who have retreated to the sanctuary of the convent without committing themselves in this manner, and I shall have much time once I have started my new life to decide whether I wish to submit so completely in heart, mind, and body.

I have entrusted to Luisa the amount to cover their needs until she brings Mercedes to the convent, wrapped within the blankets that will provide her sorry shield from a cruel world. After leaving Mercedes at the convent door, Luisa will wait for two days to present herself, lest their arrival appear connected. I have also given to Luisa a large sum for her to bring with Mercedes.

The money will serve both to lend credence to the story of Mercedes's birth to a well-placed gentleman and to soften the hearts of the sisters at the prospect of harboring the foundling for many years.

What would my mother have thought if she had known that her jewels would be put to such use? From what Silvia has told me, she was so good that surely she already resides with Our Lord and all of his saints. In these last several months, in my loneliness, I have come to think of her as looking down on me in love, suffering over what has befallen me, and even interceding for me when I am in need. I do not think that she would judge me harshly.

I cannot bear the thought of leaving Mercedes for so long, and I wonder how she will be changed when next I see her. I held her much of the day today, even though at times she seemed anxious to be free of me. I have noticed that she seems most content to lie unencumbered on a blanket and look out at the world. Even though she is but a few months old, I fear that she bears me some grudge for having had to wean her at such a tender age. Luisa and I agreed that finding a wet nurse would require explanations we were not prepared to give. For now, Luisa gives her bread soaked in goat's milk, and she says that she has also heard of giving babies grains soaked in broth. Any guilt I feel must be offset by the knowledge that I am doing the best I can for Mercedes, given the circumstances of our lives.

I have written the note for Luisa to put with Mercedes when she brings her to the convent. I tried to mimic a masculine handwriting. The note reads thus:

"For the love of Our Lord, who loved all children, please care for this baby. Her lineage from me is noble, but, to my everlasting sorrow, her mother lies in an early grave, having sacrificed herself to give this child life. I cannot bear the grief that it causes me to look upon her face and see my beloved wife. I shall leave this land, which has been so unkind, and return to Spain, though my family there will not welcome me. I can only pray that in dedicating my child to the religious life, in some small part I will atone for my guilt at thus abandoning her.

Raise her with the love of a hundred mothers. May the Lord bless you for the patience you will need and the joys you will know! In loving mercy, raise this child, my beloved daughter, Mercedes, away from the world and its anguish."

36

RACHEL

I was relieved when Juliana and Luisa finally arrived at their destination. I rejoiced when Mercedes was born and grieved at the harsh circumstances she would encounter. I marveled at the inventiveness of Juliana's scheme to get a letter of recommendation for the convent. I worried that her plans to have Mercedes join her there would somehow go awry, though all of this happened three centuries ago. Although our lives corresponded in no way, other than in the elemental fact of being women, I found myself comparing our experiences as daughters, as well as mothers.

Juliana wondered what her mother would think of her, because she never really knew her. I had my mother till my middle age, but what did I really understand about her? These papers seemed an impossibility, even as I held them in my hand. My mother now appeared to be someone I knew even less than I had thought.

I continued to ration out the pages, allowing myself only a set amount at a time, neither skipping ahead in the journal nor looking at the other papers, which might reasonably have been expected to quickly solve the mystery of their origin. At times I saw a glimmer of my professional curiosity. What of this Father Quijada, who dared to question the wisdom of the Inquisition? How common was it for ordinary people to speak or even feel such doubts?

But such concerns were secondary. These papers seemed to be an unbelievable treasure, but I could think of nothing that would pardon my mother's deception.

There was another "distinguished" professor in town, and everyone in the department was expected to attend his lecture at four o'clock. The talk was on a medieval work, *La Celestina*, or *The Go-Between*. I usually had the Latin American drama class at that time, but I told my students to attend the lecture in lieu of meeting for class. Of course, the topic didn't have much to do with Latin American playwrights, but I felt justified in the substitution, since most students got little or no exposure to that period in Spanish, or any other, literature.

The professor had finished his presentation and was accepting questions from the audience. I believed that my students had at least learned something of the history of the literature they were studying, lending it context, if not nuance. It had been a somewhat outdated interpretation of the work, and if I hadn't gained any new insights, I enjoyed hearing such lectures by way of review. I believe that I have never since known, and never will again know, as much as I did when I was studying for my doctoral exams. Though at the time I thought it an excruciating exercise, I afterward looked back on that period as an orgy of self-pampering, allowing myself to spend months solely in the pursuit of a subject that I found intriguing, justified by my mentors' stamp of authority. Hearing this talk was like regaining knowledge that I had once possessed but that, through lack of use, was slipping into the realm of the forgotten, settling in some distant land with past passions and grocery lists.

Lorraine's hand went up as the professor was gathering

his papers from the lectern, providing less detailed answers to questions, signaling his desire to end the session. I could hear the chairman of the department, a great friend of the lecturer's, let out a groan. Though he was still wearing some kind of back brace from the injury that had caused him to summon Lorraine back early, and had come to the university today only to escort the visitor around, I felt sure that his complaint was not the result of any physical ailment. Lorraine was notorious for giving guest lecturers a hard time, and what the chairman found even more embarrassing was that Lorraine always made some excellent points.

"Excuse me, Professor González," Lorraine said loudly, waving her arm in the air. The professor had been looking assiduously down at his papers, trying to ignore any last, lingering questions, probably thankful that he had been able to maintain his pose of infallibility throughout the course of the presentation. Fleetingly I wondered if the chairman had warned him to avoid Lorraine's entrapments.

"Professor González, one more question here, if you please," Lorraine persisted, and I eagerly anticipated what I was sure would be a moment of watching the grand, suave professor squirm.

"Yes, señorita," he responded, the very title he gave her an attempt to put her in her place.

"Professor Marcham," Lorraine corrected. "Professor, you have said nothing about the interpretation that many scholars give to the final speech in the work, the agonizing despair of the father of the dead girl. Some have suggested that his view of the world could be explained by the theory that the author might himself have been a converso, a Jew, who, having been forced to outwardly reject his own beliefs, now found the universe one of chaos and injustice. Could you give us your thoughts on that?"

235

She'd lived up to my expectations. In preparation for his visit, the chairman had passed around some of the articles recently published by his friend, so that we could familiarize ourselves with his work. He always did this, and I always found it insulting to our professional capabilities. However, I always grudgingly read the papers. Lorraine, on the other hand, relished these assignments. "Ammunition," she called them, and the chairman never seemed to learn.

"As you may know, I do not agree with those theories," replied Professor González, "first of all because it is ridiculous to forget that this is but a character in a story, and not a real human, whose background can only be speculated upon." This might ordinarily have been seen as an insulting response, presuming to correct Lorraine for committing the distinctly undergraduate tendency to forget that characters are just that, creations with a purpose, not humans as we know them. Readers must have faith that the author has been skillful enough to tell us what we should know about the character, and we should not invent our own interpretations, which may be more pleasing, but unfounded in the work. To use characters to make assumptions about their creator is an even more egregious fault.

But Lorraine knew, as we all knew, that in this case Professor González was not attempting to insult her, but rather he had simply given his primary and only argument against the interpretation she had brought up. In his arrogance, he seemed not to have bothered to closely study the points of those whose arguments he was refuting, but simply to have rejected them out of hand and written an article, confident that one of his friends on the editorial board of some journal would see to it that it got published, as indeed it had.

I almost felt sorry for him as Lorraine read out one

quotation after another from the text, all of which gave convincing support for the converso theory. It appeared that even Professor González would have to refute his own article, but he was not one to cower before challenges, especially not one from a woman, and a mere assistant professor. One might have guessed this from his demeanor. Even so, no one was quite prepared for his response.

"Professor Marcham," he began, allowing only the slightest note of condescension to enter his voice, "it seems obvious to me that those who originally put forth that theory were in fact Jews themselves, and wished only to cast aspersions upon our glorious Spanish culture, choosing to dwell upon those moments of our history that, with the current climate of relative morality, appear to be open to criticism. Nevertheless, these scholars"—and now there was no attempt to hide the sarcasm in his voice—"have chosen to make their living by criticizing the very culture that has provided for them a pleasant profession. It is quite similar to what the Spanish Americans do when they criticize Spain for the treatment some Indians received hundreds of years ago, even though it is clear that their own Hispanic culture would not even exist if it had not been for the Spanish conquest."

It was obvious that he felt himself righteously aggrieved by this and took the stupefied silence of the audience as agreement. Even Lorraine stood mute before this tirade. But the illustrious professor needed to add one last, admonishing flourish.

"You should particularly remember this lesson, Professor Marcham. It is equally applicable to those black students who would wish to take only classes in Black Studies, while many of the writers studied in those courses would not even exist were it not for the Western civilization that has produced them."

With that remark, he strode out of the lecture hall, and for once even the chairman did not rush to congratulate his friend on his brilliant performance. The room quickly emptied, only Lorraine remaining in her place, and I along with her.

"He's a jerk, Lorraine," I said. "Even the chairman thought so."

"I've always been interested in people like that," Lorraine said, still staring ahead.

"In people like González?" I said, amazed.

"No," Lorraine's voice registered surprise, and now she looked at me. "Like the author of the *Celestina*. What happens to people, and to their descendants, when they are forced to give up who they are?" Lorraine's ability to so completely ignore the diatribe we had just witnessed to pursue her own thoughts impressed me.

"How can any of us know who we really came from? Not only blacks, but anybody. How far back can you trace your ancestors? Three, four generations?" she asked.

"If that," I replied, with a catch in my voice.

"See what I mean?" she said, and got up and left.

It had been a week, and Lorraine hadn't said much about her altercation with the visiting professor, but I wondered whether, upon reflection, she was more than annoyed. She seemed distracted, though it was not unusual for her to inexplicably withdraw at times and just as unpredictably don her old self again. But I was not as preoccupied with her mood changes as I usually would have been. I had retreated into the diary.

37

Juliana

I have now been here a week, and I am still trying to
accustom myself to the life here. As I approached my new
home, I did note that the white building had a certain
simple beauty. The windows were large, but allowed no
view of the interior, as is proper. The carved wooden
double doors seemed to be designed to keep the world out
more than the inhabitants within. I hoped that this
impression proved true, and that I would find the refuge
that I sought.

The convent includes everything that could be desired
for this life. In addition to the church, with its sacristy
and choir area, there is a courtyard, a workroom, and
areas to be used by those who must attend to the
administrative needs of the convent. I have been assigned
my own area, which is very spacious. The food that we are
served is good, though spicier than I am accustomed to.

Most of the sisters have one or two maids, but I will
wait for Luisa's arrival. For now, I cherish my solitary
moments, in which I must deceive no one. It has been so
long since I could be myself. I pray that in time I will feel
at home here, and at one with the other sisters.

Upon arriving, I relinquished the name of Silvia. I told

our abbess, Madre Mónica, that I wished to take the name
of Santa Teresa de Ávila, who also lived out her life in a
convent, though I could never aspire to her level of devotion
or erudition. Madre approved of my choice. I am Sor Teresa.

18 April

Although many of the sisters here are from families with
means, there is a diversity in our characters. Many have
come from a sincere desire to answer Christ's call to the
religious life, but there are also some who have sought the
convent as a refuge, as have I. Several have chosen the
convent over an undesirable arranged marriage. Some here
are widows, who aspire to the peace of this life after
having lived a full one abroad in the world, as faithful
wives and mothers. It seems that having had so little time
to themselves for so many years, they relish the
opportunity to pursue their own inclinations, whether
those be private devotions or other interests.

There are a few here who have chosen to maintain
silence much of the time, out of a sincere search for
holiness and communion with Our Lord, but most are such
as I, and are not capable of such self-negation. The life of
many is not so different from that of a dependent woman
in the household of a wealthy relative. They do
needlework, gossip, read, see to the management of the
servants, though here there are no nieces and nephews on
whom one might lavish a woman's love.

I sometimes look at my sisters surreptitiously and
wonder how they would judge me if they knew my reason
for being here. How many of them, like so much of society,
and even my own father, would blame me for my shame?
What would they think of my plan to bring my tainted
child here under false pretenses?

Each day I wake with a vague feeling of loss and for just a moment struggle to define its origin. Then I remember that I have left my child, and my heart begins another day of longing. At idle moments, often when it is time for prayer, I find myself wondering what she is doing or how she has changed since last I saw her, for, though three weeks is not long, as a portion of her short life it is not insignificant.

25 April

Today the abbess sent for me to take care of some final details relating to my acceptance to the convent, and to ask me how I feel I am fitting in here. As I approached her room, I caught her unawares; she had neglected to close the doors of the large cabinet that extends along one entire wall of her room, from floor to ceiling. To my astonishment, therein were contained hundreds of books! Even in the house of my father, who was considered extremely well read, there were not so many books. I could make out no titles from where I stood, but just the sight of them keenly sparked my curiosity.

I thought that all reminders of my old life would cause me such pain that I would instinctively shirk them, but I am desperate to see what works are contained in those cupboards in Madre's office. How much more resides there than a Holy Bible and accounts of the lives of the saints?

27 April

Madre Mónica's library contains so many marvelous books, more than I could have hoped for! In addition to the classics and tomes on philosophy and history, there are works in prose and poetry, and many plays, by Cervantes, Lope de Vega, and Calderón, among others. I know that I should not have done it, but I have removed two of the books and brought them to my room. What a joy reading them gives to me, unencumbered by another's expectations of my reactions. The works can speak to me, and I can answer them in my own heart, in my own way. Now I have something to keep me going while I wait for my Mercedes to arrive. Thank you for this, my dear Lord!

9 May

After prayers this morning, Madre Mónica asked me if I could come to her room. I feared that somehow she had discovered that I had taken her books, yet how could she have missed those two from among so many? Still, we had finished the last of the details pertaining to my entrance into the convent, and I could not imagine any other reason she would wish to see me.

To my surprise, she asked me to help her with some paperwork. She mentioned that she has some problems with her eyesight, not to complain, but rather to explain why she required my assistance. When I happily consented to her request, she immediately began work and pulled out a list of items that the convent had recently received. Although a friar is nominally in charge of the business of the convent, there is much administrative work that falls to our abbess. The convent strives to be as self-sufficient as possible, but as I began to peruse the list, I realized how much we rely on the outside world to complete our comforts. I found both solace and unease in this fact. I wish to feel that the convent is an isolated haven, but at the same time I do not want it to be totally separated from the outside world.

I read the lists to Madre, and she seemed to be making a mental note of what was to be done with some of the items, how they were to be distributed, how long they would last, and how they would be paid for. Some of our necessities are donated to us by the common people of the city, who wish to show their love of God by making this sacrifice for those who are dedicated to His service. For other materials, particularly those required to maintain our chapel and the precious objects entrusted to our care, we must appeal to wealthy benefactors, some within our region but some as far away as Spain herself, where the order has more influence and connections than here in New Spain.

The morning's work progressed slowly as I helped Madre Superior make her way through various tasks. It was particularly difficult to concentrate, when my mind kept turning to the cabinet, wondering about all of the treasures hidden within.

After dictating three letters to various important men in her family, requesting help or advice for the business of the convent, Madre asked me to read to her a letter from her sister-in-law, Concepción. Hearing this letter seemed to be the reward that she gave herself after the tedious work of the more formal letters. Concepción's letter contained many details about the abbess's nieces and nephews, and even a description of a play that Madre's brother and Concepción had recently seen. It was apparently quite entertaining, and was currently very popular in Madrid. To my surprise, Madre was interested in all the worldly details of the letter, and even asked me to reread sections of the description of the play that she found particularly amusing. I could not help but be reminded of my one night at the theater, which had seemed so exciting but had culminated in the shattering of my life.

16 May

I find some days more difficult than others, with a heart that is empty of all but a longing to see Mercedes. I have always been taught that prayer can offer solace in all of life's trials, and it seems that it should especially be true within my current home. But it is not so.

2 June

Since I arrived here, I have endeavored to dedicate myself to this new life. I have tried as much as I can to put aside the impatience I feel to see my child, but as the time Luisa and I set for her to bring Mercedes to the convent approaches, I find it very difficult to concentrate on anything, so great is my excitement at the thought that soon my sweet one will be here with me. I look forward to seeing Luisa, too, even more than I would have thought. I understand now how much her kind and gentle manner were a balm to ease my tribulations.

8 June

I am thankful that I have continued to assist Madre Superior with her clerical duties, and I believe that she is beginning to have more confidence in my abilities, and also in my discretion. I have come to feel that of all the sisters here, she is the one with whom I have the most in common. Although she is much older than I and holds authority over all who live within these walls, I feel a kind of kinship of spirit with her. In the last several weeks, I have realized that Madre also seems to recognize in me a like soul, and that she suspected this even before I did. It now seems evident that our abbess much exaggerated her difficulties with her eyesight, and I believe that it was her desire to better get to know me, and to test my skills and knowledge, that she first called me to her. She no longer uses the excuse of poor vision, but straightforwardly ever more frequently requires my assistance, which I am happy to give.

Madre spends much of her time reading and writing, not only in the performance of her duties as the spiritual and material head of the convent, but also from her own desire for intellectual nourishment. This is a characteristic that I have not found in most of the other sisters here, and it is no wonder. Even for a boy in sophisticated Madrid, my level of education would have been unusual. Scholarship was looked upon as an unnecessary encumbrance to a young girl's charms, and boys were not always required to study at length, since gentlemen can always find something more entertaining to do with their time. Yet Madre Mónica seems extremely learned, and from our discussions I believe that she has recognized in me a desire to expand my knowledge, though it be from within these confining walls.

13 June

Tomorrow is the day that Luisa and I agreed that she is to bring Mercedes to the convent's doorstep. I pray with all my strength that our plan will come to fruition.

21 June

It is now several days since Luisa and Mercedes have arrived at the convent. Contrary to our plan, Luisa presented herself on the same day that she left Mercedes outside the convent door, saying that she sought to work within the walls as a servant, feeling that she was not worthy of any higher calling. The nuns saw in Luisa an answer to their dilemma, for none of them quite knew

245

what to do with the infant who had been left only hours before. Luisa seemed to them to have been sent by Providence, as she proclaimed that she had cared for her younger siblings. Indeed, I heard it commented that she showed herself most efficient and loving in her handling of the new foundling child.

Although my child's presence here is now secured, I must fight a sense of despondence. I have had only a few stolen moments when I could speak to Luisa, and she filled those with her urgent explanation about why she went against my wishes and came to the convent on the same day as she brought Mercedes. She said that she feared that the nuns would not know the special foods that she had been giving to Mercedes since her weaning, and on which the babe did seem to thrive. In those brief meetings I looked upon my child, and even held her in my arms for a few precious minutes, until we heard someone approaching. Since then, I have seen Mercedes only at a distance, cradled in Luisa's arms or playing on the floor under her watchful eye. I see little chance of being able to explain an uncommon interest in the babe, and I have been assigned no duties that would cause me to be near her. Perhaps when she gets older, there will be a chance for me to work with her, and even to share with her what learning I can offer. For now I must love her from afar and feed my love with rare glimpses of her precious form.

15 July

I have seen but little of my lovely child. Today I feel deeply the bitterness of all that has happened to me. The cruelty of my father and my violator condemned me to a situation that rips from my arms the only consolation their betrayals left to me.

1 August

The abbess understands my need to educate myself
further, though she cannot suspect my deep desire to share
knowledge with my daughter. Of all those here, she and I
seem to be alone in this obsession to study. The others do
not seem interested in exercising the discipline required,
and many even seem to believe it is an aberration, though
they are slow to directly criticize the Madre Superior.

For many, the only possible reason for a woman to
study would be for her to use this knowledge to aid in the
education of her children. Since they are not to fulfill this
destiny, they see no reason to cultivate a life of the mind. A
smaller number seem to believe that humility should be the
overriding principle to be followed, and conclude that the
Lord meant for them to reject their intellect and to dwell
solely and unquestioningly on prayers and the functioning of
the convent.

At first I was greatly troubled by these sisters of mine
who believe that it is God's will that they should reject
the mind and the knowledge that He Himself has
bestowed. I spent much time trying to understand this
attitude and at times questioned whether I myself was
guilty of some hidden sin in not subduing my curious
nature. For me, three things eased my concern. First,
oddly, is the memory of my father, and although all his
knowledge did not teach him justice, he instilled in me a
love of learning. Even though he betrayed my trust in him,
I would not betray the intellectual road that he opened to
me, even if it takes me along paths that neither of us
could have foreseen.

Another source of my perseverance is the fact that I
did not choose to come to this place, at least not freely. I
do not want to embrace all of its attitudes and limitations.

Above all, I see in Madre Mónica, who I believe to be truly holy, as well as wise, a woman who is not afraid to use her mind to question, to pursue an intellectual life. I will safeguard and increase the knowledge that I obtained in my father's house. I worked for it, and it is the only legacy that I will get from him, the only one I want.

15 August

Today I was able to see Mercedes for a brief time. She seems to me so beautiful and lively. I fancy that I can see marks of intelligence in her already. Now that she is beginning to look less like a new baby and has begun to take on a look of her own, I could not help but search for any signs that she takes after her father, while all the while dreading any slight resemblance. I thank heaven that I discerned no such likeness.

1 October

Again at prime my mind began to wander. So many things intrude when I should be thinking of Our Lord: the face of my Tía Ana, memories of my childhood in Madrid and the hopes and dreams that I had then. I think about my daughter and what I would wish for her if we were free.

3 November

My duties for the abbess break up my days. She has entrusted to me the task of opening her letters, and this has become a highlight of my week. They bring news of the outside world, even though it is usually limited to instructions from Madre's superiors, or requests from wealthy families to consider their young daughter as a postulant.

20 April 1663

Days follow upon days. I rarely see Mercedes, and never alone. What claim could I have upon this child, when I am so clearly meant to help with convent business? Yet I cannot lament the role that Madre has set for me. It occupies my mind with subjects outside my own concerns. I could not forsake it, even for Mercedes.

1 August

Today Luisa left the convent. I had become complacent, assuming that she would always remain here, helping with the care of Mercedes and other tasks the sisters have set for her. But Luisa must see, as do I, that Mercedes no longer depends solely upon her, that there are others who show her kindness and even affection. There is nothing for Luisa here as time goes on but to be a servant, or perhaps to remain as a nun, but one without the comforts afforded to those of us who entered the convent with a plentiful purse.

Luisa desires what most women desire, what I desired: husband, children, home. She has suffered cruelly at the hands of men, and I pray that she will find a gentle husband who will treasure her. Since she has been here, she has sometimes ventured out of the convent to purchase things that were needed. In the past few months she has spoken of a young man whom she has come to know, and I believe that he is taken with Luisa. She told me that his dream is to leave the town and go and work the land, and she would be a great help to him. She would work hard and appreciate whatever kindness he could show her.

Since it is probable that I will never see her again, I will record here the few final words we managed to exchange. Luisa's eyes were filled with tears, and no one

questioned this, for though she left by choice, everyone felt
that she had formed attachments here and that it would
be most difficult for her to leave Mercedes, whom she had
tended so lovingly. All of us at the convent stood in a line
to bid her farewell. I did not let the tears standing in my
eyes spill over, but as she approached me, I said to her in
a low voice, "I owe my daughter's life to you, as you cared
for her when I had to forsake her. Whatever peace she and
I may find in this place is because you made it possible."

"It is you who gave me the chance for a new life," and
although no one could hear our whispered words, she
called me by the name that I have taken here. "Sor Teresa,
I hope that you find peace in this refuge, and that
Mercedes will grow to cherish this place as the only home
she has ever known."

"God go with you, Luisa. I shall pray every day for the
Lord's blessing upon you."

"As you shall remain in my prayers, always," she
replied, and though I believe that in the busy life that will
be hers, she will come to forget her promise, I was grateful
for the sentiment.

With that, she was gone. I had wondered what Luisa
thought of the life I live here. She saw only that I work
with the abbess and could have little to do with my
daughter. From her final words to me, I do not think she
judged me harshly for this.

7 January 1664

I have not felt the strength to write here for many months.
The silent time that is intrinsic to the life here is proving
an unexpected burden. Madre Mónica has noticed my
struggle and so has reduced the hours I spend helping her.
Yet, with naught to distract my mind, I dwell upon all

that I have lost, and I can find no comfort. I call to mind the kindness of Providence and strangers, which brought me safe to a new world. I am astounded at all I have accomplished when forced to the task, but it is as though the feeling were for a character in a play. At times I rebel at the circumstances that led me to my actions, but even this defiance is only fleeting, and then a cold numbness comes.

I find that I can barely make myself rise in the morning, and the last two days I have lied to my sisters. Feigning illness, I have begged to be excused from communal prayers. Yet it is not a complete untruth. Surely some real malady is causing this heaviness that I feel. My legs do not wish to bear me, nor my hands to feed or clothe me. The sisters' concerned questioning barely rouses me from my languor, and I see from their faces that at times my answers disturb them. They cannot reach down to that deep part of me to which my soul has retreated, nor can I bridge the chasm, nor do I desire to. Even the thought of my Mercedes cannot fill this emptiness.

RACHEL

Part of me lived alongside Juliana. She was a lover of books, so how could I, who had made books my life's work, not feel an affinity for her? I was glad that she could, at least to a limited degree, pursue her studies. My heart ached at her longing to see her child. I lived through her thoughts, the thoughts of a woman who died centuries ago.

Juliana wrote of her depression, though she didn't use that word. At times I'd also felt its downward pull, though my life was infinitely easier than hers. I looked through the lens of my own century and wondered briefly whether her dejection was some sort of prolonged or delayed post-partum depression. Then I mocked myself by asking whether she didn't have enough to bring her to the brink of despair.

I thought of telling Lorraine about the papers. I knew that she'd be interested on a professional level, but of course she would want to read them, and I wasn't willing to share them. I hadn't even told Ned. No, for now at least, Juliana was mine.

I bought a book on genealogy, though its possible revelations had never before interested me enough to spend any time on it. I told myself that I really had no expectation of finding anything that would help to explain the diary, that it was only that the papers had piqued my interest in my own past. Besides, what more appropriate time to think about those who have gone before than when you are about to add a new name to the family tree?

The book advised readers to start off in an organized manner, by making templates for information that would be found on each individual, as well as another template for families, and finally a large tree for several generations, filling in as information was collected. Although I had achieved a certain amount of success in academia and I knew that good research techniques were of paramount importance, when it came to personal projects I usually preferred to jump right in and go back and worry later about the details. Time and again I'd regretted this, finding myself in the middle of a project, then needing to spend twice the hours making up for the prep work I hadn't done. But I always reverted to my own inclination, forgetting past lessons, as one forgets the faults of a beloved friend.

Anyway, I soon discovered that even experts in the study of genealogy had no magic methodologies for finding information about ancestors who had lived centuries ago. Of course, I could not start with Juliana. I had to start with myself.

I was ashamed to admit how little I knew of my ancestors, but in this, I doubt that I was very different from most modern Americans. I knew my mother's maiden name, but beyond that, I had no specifics. My mother's only sibling, Sandy, had been several years older than Helen and had passed away just a year earlier. I decided to call her daughter, my cousin Carol, to see if she could help me. I would not, however, mention the papers.

On the day I went to see her, Carol opened the door and immediately hugged me. She was seven years older than I was, and though we hadn't seen each other very frequently in adulthood, growing up she had served as the big sister I longed for. I had also always really loved Aunt Sandy. She didn't look like my mother, who was tall and sturdy, while Aunt Sandy was petite, but her voice had been almost indistinguishable from my mother's, and Carol had inherited that familiar timbre. When she said, "Hi, Rachel, come on in. How are you doing?" I heard my mother's voice, but more open. Tears came to my eyes, and she hugged me again, hard. She took me by the shoulders and placed me in a chair, directing me as she had done when we were young. I was a grown woman, with a profession and a tall son of my own, but there was solace in her bossiness, blanketed with love.

"Now, now," she repeated over and over again, rubbing the middle of my back, exactly as she had done when we had shared a double bed at her house for a sleepover and I had cried because I missed my mother.

"I'm sorry, Carol." I finally managed to control my voice. "I didn't come here to cry."

She wiped the tears from her own eyes. "Well, what's wrong with crying? I miss Aunt Helen, too. She was always so good to me, and so much fun." I looked at her to check, but she seemed totally sincere, and I marveled at her impression of my mother. I had loved my mother deeply, but Carol had clearly seen her in a different light than I had.

Savoring a piece of the gooey butter coffee cake Carol had just made, we caught up on family gossip. I'd seen everyone at the funeral, but I hadn't been able to visit long with any one person. Finally, I broached the subject I'd come to discuss.

"Carol, I've decided that I'd like to go back in the

family history a little bit, and I wondered if I could pick your brain."

She gave me an odd look and said, "I understand, Rachel." I was so concerned with leading her to believe that this was only because I wanted to connect somehow with Helen that I dismissed the uncharacteristically stilted nature of her response.

"I don't really know much, though. Of course, our moms' maiden name was Jordan," she continued. "I'm not sure what Grandma Jordan's maiden name was, but I think it was Meadows, or something like that."

"I think my mom used to talk about her Grandpa John and Grandma Scottie, but I don't remember any last name for them, do you?"

"No, I don't. I never got the impression that my mom was ever very close to those grandparents."

I tried to make my voice sound casual. "You don't know whether there are any old family papers, letters, or anything, do you?"

She looked at me, then quickly away, and said, "Why do you ask?"

"No reason. I was just hoping there might be something around that I didn't know about that could give me a lead."

"I'm sorry, Rachel, but there's nothing more I can tell you."

I was about to say good-bye to her when I decided to tell Carol that I was pregnant. I hadn't been planning to do it, since, at forty-one years of age, I could have problems. I had wanted to wait longer, to feel more confident that everything would go well. Still, as I looked at my cousin, I found myself telling her.

"Ned and I really haven't told anyone else. Of course, Gabe knows, and I did tell Mom right before she . . ."

"Oh, Rach. Oh, Rach." That was all Carol could say as she drew me to her.

Things were getting busy at school, and everything took me longer because my mind kept wandering back to my own mystery. I told myself that since this distraction was causing me to be less efficient in my schoolwork, it would be better just to go ahead and try to find out what I could about my family tree. I knew that I was a part of Juliana, even if I bore no actual relationship to her, but I longed to prove the bond was blessed by blood.

I headed to the county courthouse, to see how far back I could go with minimal effort. As I quickly found out, there is no minimal effort when it comes to genealogy. I made my way through records of births, marriages, and deaths. I combed through surname indices, folio-size bound volumes called libers, and wills. I learned their language: imprimis, dower, testatrix, nuncupative, escheat. An entire language of death and property and survivors.

I discovered my great-grandmother Janet Maude Meades, née Scott, born in St. Louis, Missouri, on December 2, 1866. Her father was Gavin Scott, of Galashiels, Scotland, born 1830, and her mother was Maude Scott, née Compton, of St. Louis, born 1846. Could Janet be the Grandma Scottie I thought I remembered Mom talking about? Carol had said she thought our grandma's maiden name might have been Meadows, but it could easily have been Meades.

Over the next days, I consulted the state Department of Public Health and Welfare, the county recorder, the state and local historical societies and public libraries. I was told that I was extremely lucky to have gone back as far as I did, since records so close after the end of the Civil

War were generally very difficult to trace. Finding those before the war was purely a matter of chance. Chance did not smile. Further back I could not go.

I stayed away from Juliana's diary while I was doing my genealogical digging. I knew that I'd been ignoring Ned and Gabe, so I didn't want to take the extra time to read the papers. Still, I rationalized my time-consuming search by telling myself that the papers were mine, an accidental legacy from my mother to me. If some providence or chance had offered them, there had to be a reason.

I couldn't forsake the diary for long, however, and finally, after failing to muffle the clamor in my head, to silence Juliana's call, I decided to go back to it. Ned was on call that day, a euphemism for working at the hospital for twenty-four hours or more. When that happens, Gabe and I often had something easy for dinner. That night it was "every person for themselves," our grammatically incorrect nod to a feminist perspective. Afterward, Gabe shut himself in his room to do homework and I took out the papers.

I had noticed the last time I stopped my reading that the next entry was several years in the future from the time period Juliana had fairly closely chronicled, nor were there many pages left to her journal. I could only hope that the ending would reveal her final fate, and how it was tied to mine.

39

Juliana

15 August 1668

I came across this book today, neglected these last few years, for what have I had to record? I did take my final vows three years ago, for I saw no favorable alternative to remaining here. What would I have done, and where could I have gone? I could not leave my Mercedes, and if I revealed the truth to try to assert my rights as a mother, I doubt that the good sisters would relinquish their charge to a liar such as I.

My life here is acceptable, if only rarely happy. Who can boast of better?

2 November

I record my thoughts here today because it is Mercedes's seventh birthday. Only I know this, since her birth date was not stated in the letter that I wrote those years ago. Some of the sisters who care for Mercedes have at times given her a small token on the feast of Nuestra Señora de las Mercedes, but this is not a place for indulgent celebration.

Today I approached my daughter and asked her how she fared.

"I am well. I thank you for asking, Sor Teresa," she replied shyly, startling and pleasing me with the use of my name. I had not been sure she knew it.

"The sisters tell me that you like to hear stories."

"Only when there are no chores to be done or prayers to be said," she replied cautiously.

"Of course I know that you are an obedient child. I have heard that the sisters themselves enjoy sharing with you tales they learned in childhood, and Our Lord does not look ill upon so innocent a pleasure. Would you like for me to tell you a story that I enjoyed when I was your age?"

"No, thank you, Sor Teresa." I did not know how to reply to this unexpected rejection, and in my silence Mercedes seemed to fear that she had offended.

"The sisters tell me that you are often busy with Madre Superior, so I am sure that you have little time for such as I," she added, by way of explanation, and started to hurry away, then turned and dutifully added, "but thank you for your kind offer."

I stood bereft, deprived of even this small pleasure on my child's birthday. But what could I expect? To Mercedes, I am just one of the sisters with whom she has little contact, to whom she must show respect but no affection. Indeed, she does not seem to feel a particular attachment to any of the nuns, although I have at times seen tenderness on the part of those who care for her. Still, strong earthly connections are not especially encouraged here.

The hope that I once nurtured to be able to spend time with her, to help with her education, has not come to pass. Those who are in charge of her care have already begun to teach her letters, numbers, and, of course, her prayers. I see now that, even as she gets older, it is unlikely that any other kind of knowledge I might offer would seem to the good sisters to be needed by a young girl.

I have considered appealing to Madre on this, but I fear that even she would not understand my insistence. I have struggled with the idea of whether I should tell her our real story, but I feel that any revelation now would seem like a betrayal: that I accepted confidences about her and kept this fundamental truth about myself and Mercedes so closely guarded.

I will never know what kind of mother I might have been out in the world. Not knowing my own mother, I looked to Silvia for what a mother should be. I know that she loved me, but patience and care were also requirements for her to retain her position. I would like to think that I would have been always loving and kind, but perhaps my patience would have faltered in the challenge and sometimes tedium of raising a child.

21 January 1669

Mercedes is very ill. I am told that she has had a sore throat, and now fever and chills take their turns in tormenting her. She will eat only with great coaxing, and then often vomits what little she has consumed. Today a rash has appeared, and she lies unmoving in her bed.

Dearest Lord, please do not punish my child for any offense of mine, for the deception I have lived in this house devoted to You. Please watch over and heal her, Lord. I have borne much. Losing her, I could not bear.

24 January

My work with our abbess enabled me to take my mind from Mercedes's illness for moments at a time. I have tried

to conceal my fear for her. This morning I waited for
Madre in her room, as I had been told she would return
soon from a visit with Mercedes. I looked up as I heard
her enter, and she looked at me through tear-filled eyes. I
clutched at myself and cried out in agony, collapsing and
falling. Madre rushed to me and grasped me firmly in her
strong arms.

"My child, what is it? Are you ill? Tell me what is
wrong!"

One of the other sisters might have quickly crossed
herself and cried to the Lord for whatever demon had hold
of me to release me. But Madre Mónica was not of their
temperament. She knows that this life has enough injuries
and sorrows. It does not need to borrow any from the
next.

Finally, I was able to choke out one word: "Mercedes!"

"You are ill, my daughter? The same as our
Mercedes?"

I managed to shake my head no, still sobbing.
"Mercedes, my only child, I cannot live if you are taken
from me!"

"She is doing much better today. She even ate
something this morning. I have just come from her room."

"But your eyes were wet with tears," I sputtered.

"Yes, my child, from joy. I am sure that Mercedes has
passed the crisis." Having quickly reassured me, she
seemed to ponder what I had just said in my anguish. As
she looked into my eyes and saw the immense relief so
evident there, her expression changed, and for a moment I
saw understanding unfolding.

"I see." She breathed very softly. "Oh, my daughter."
And she cradled my head in her arms, ever so tenderly.
She was silent for several moments, then said, in an even
voice, "The merciful Lord has shown us His kindness. Our

Mercedes will soon be up and about. We must say special prayers of thanks." There was complicity in the normal tone she had adopted.

"Are you going to be all right now?" she continued. "You must not allow the others to see you in such a state over Mercedes. It would . . . worry them."

I nodded numbly, only half understanding the import of what she was saying to me. Madre lifted herself slowly from the floor, where she had knelt beside me. She is not feeble, but she is starting to show the slowness of age. I can tell that she experiences pain when she makes certain movements, especially on cold mornings or after sitting for an extended period. Despite her own discomfort, Madre bent over to help me up. It was difficult for me to rise, but I did not want her to have to bend over any longer. I pulled myself up and steadied myself on the edge of the table. Madre turned and walked deliberately toward the bookcase, extracting a book on the lives of the saints.

"I promised Mercedes that I would return and read to her, but I now remember that I must meet this morning with a family who wants their daughter to join us. I would like for you to go in my stead. She loves to hear about the saints. I believe that she is a very special child, don't you?"

"Yes, Madre," I murmured in reply to her melancholy smile.

As I entered the large room where Sor Beatriz cared for the sick, I saw Mercedes sitting up in a bed close to the window. The sun shining in emphasized the shadows around her eyes.

"Madre Mónica asked me to come and read to you. She must attend to some other things this morning."

The disappointment was evident in Mercedes's face. Even after having lived here all of her life, she was still too young to hide her innermost thoughts. It was a skill that I had just discovered had escaped me when most I needed it. Mercedes altered her expression, looked down humbly, and whispered her acceptance.

I began to read aloud from the life of St. Francis of Assisi. He had always been one of the saints I most appreciated. The way that he was always pictured with animals was what had appealed to me more than any particular manifestation of his holiness. I slowly began to notice, as we read first the life of St. Francis and then that of some of the other saints, that what appealed to Mercedes was the asceticism that was such a major thrust in so many of these stories. Although she was usually shy and quiet, she overcame her reticence and remarked, "The saints must have loved Our Lord very much to have suffered so much for Him. I hope that I will someday be able to love Our Lord that much."

For me it has always been difficult to identify the pain of intense sacrifice with love. I have found that it is rather the kindness shown to us by another that can reveal to us Our Lord's goodness and show our hearts what love can be. Such was the gift that Madre gave to me today.

29 September 1673

I have always looked to learning to answer all of my questions, but have wise men found the secret there, or do they, too, pretend? No learning could have saved me from what I suffered. God did not save me either. Is it not His duty, as Father, to care for those He has created? We condemn the human father who starts new life, only to abandon it. Can we expect less of the Eternal Father? I know these thoughts and doubts to be sin, and I would be condemned by the Inquisition if ever anyone were to read them, but in my low state, I cannot even bring myself to care. Perhaps the delusion that drives some of my sisters to punish themselves only masks the madness of not knowing, as though their sacrifice can make Him real.

18 February 1674

There are times when even the thought of my Mercedes fails to bring me joy, for if this is life, what favor have I done her? Sometimes it feels as though she were an insubstantial ghost to me, which could affect me neither one way nor the other.

5 August 1675

Over the years, when the darkness comes, I have at times thought to seek advice from my confessor. He is a kind man, but he does not comprehend the hopelessness and emptiness that at times overcome me, and he even seems a little frightened at the extreme nature of what I am describing. He gives me the rote answers, and counsels me to pray and do penance.

7 April 1678

I turn to these pages, for I feel it is the only place that I can express my fears. Madre Mónica's health seems to worsen as the weeks go by, and I find myself performing many functions for her. The need for help, which I believe she feigned so many years ago to see whether she and I were souls of a kind, has become genuine. My concern for her deepens as I see daily tasks becoming ever more difficult for her. I must also admit that it is my selfish desire not to lose her companionship that makes me lament her condition all the more.

9 August

Madre Mónica has passed on to her reward.

I am the new abbess, a position I never desired. My sisters have chosen me, I'm certain, because of my closeness to our beloved Madre Superior, and because they rightly assume that I already know the business of running the convent. If they knew how unfit I am, both because of what happened to me so long ago and because of my own sometime doubts, I would not have to accept this burden, but I, too, am subject to my vow of obedience.

30 June 1679

Some days now are filled with convent business, but even these leave time for contemplation and prayer. At times I am able to pray sincerely. More often, my prayers, the product of long habit, pass through my mind as something seen in the periphery of vision, present but of little import.

At times I cannot help but return to the past. Although Our Lord commanded forgiveness, I know that in my heart I will never be able to pardon what Don Lorenzo did to me. I tell myself that Mercedes was the gift God gave me to heal my soul, but even this motherhood has been a blighted one.

When I think of my father, who both loved and betrayed me, I realize that I have long since let go of my rancor for what he did to me, for the life I have lived because he placed his honor above all else. Now he is only a memory to me, a dream, nor yet a dream. For years each night when I have lain down to rest, I have hoped to dream of him, to once again see his face, even as but the creation of my own slumbering imagination. But this has been denied to me. If I dream of him, I do not remember.

It is only these occasional writings that I have made and kept, and the sight of my daughter, that remind me that my memories were once reality.

11 November 1680

If suffering brings us to the Lord, why do I so seldom feel that I have found Him? Should I close my mind to my thoughts and insist that I believe, insist even to myself?

Lord, I pray to You to help me, though I do not know if You are there to hear me, though I do not know if You can care.

1 December 1681

I see what I wrote here a year ago, and I feel that I should also record that at times I have been content and even happy here. I can sometimes even believe that my prayers might help others, and I find solace in this. It is some small way in which I can exist outside these walls.

I will say that it has been difficult to keep up my enthusiasm for study. Without my dear Madre Mónica to share my interest, books are at times no more than cold comfort.

30 January 1683

Although we live away from the world, as Madre Superior I do have more contact with others. As was the case with Madre Mónica, there are those who have begun to include news of the world in our correspondence about the convent's business. I have recently been told of an astonishingly learned nun, living here in Mexico City, who entered the convent so as to have no distractions from her studies.

I am delighted, and also somewhat puzzled. I must admit that I was surprised to find a woman as learned as Madre Mónica in this land that I had always, in my ignorance, considered an uncultured wilderness. So many of my father's friends spoke of New Spain only in terms of a means to gain riches. I have come to understand, though, that there are people of taste and culture here, and even women of learning, though Madre once told me that her level of education was quite unusual for a woman here in the New World, just as it was in the Old.

1 April

After my request for further information about the learned nun whom one of the patrons of the convent mentioned in a letter, I have been told that her name is Sor Juana Inés de la Cruz. A copy of some of her poems was also enclosed.

The poems are of the highest quality, comparable to much of the poetry that I read at home in Spain. But this speaks to me as a woman. I sense that it is penned by a woman's hand yet is neither sentimental nor ecstatically mystical, as is the small amount of poetry by women that I have read before, including that of my patron, Santa Teresa. Sor Juana's poetry is more refined and subtle, containing complexities of feeling that are a revelation to the soul and mind.

One poem is in the voice of a newly widowed woman, lamenting the death of her husband, questioning why she has been left behind. One marvels at the knowledge that this is nothing that the poetess has ever gone through. Yet also for me, the poem seemed to cause me to mourn a love that I will never know, a love the loss of which dims all other pain. The voice of the widow protests that heaven, jealous of her happiness, took her beloved from her. But what did I have that God so envied as to take even a hope of love from me?

Some poems speak of jealousy, the torments of love, or the sorrow of missing another, in terms so affecting, it is as if the reader can live another's life through Sor Juana's poems. How has she summoned these sentiments and committed them to paper? Perhaps it is that the passions are universal, and the creative mind need only imagine circumstances in which to place them to ignite another's soul.

15 December 1686

I have not entered my thoughts here for some years, but I have done something momentous today, and I wish to record it here. I have written to my dear Tía Ana, in the hope that she still lives, though she must be past the age of seventy, and that she will answer me. I thought of writing to my *dueña*, Silvia, also, but I do not know whether she planned ever to return to Madrid. Our farewells were so rushed when she left to go to her cousins in the countryside outside Sevilla. Then, too, she would be even more advanced in years than my *tía*.

It has now been a very long time since I could say I missed those whom I was forced to abandon. When first I came here, I yearned to see them. But even those whom we love very much tend to fade in our memories and our hearts.

In my letter I explained my story: how I had been violated by Don Lorenzo, and how I had feared that my father would take my life to restore his honor. Having never told this tale to anyone except Luisa, and that so many years ago, at first it seemed as though the memories were but a wound that had scarred over. But as more details of that time were dragged from my past, the scar was torn open and the wound made fresh again. More memories, like blood, poured forth, unbidden and undesired. Still, I had resolved to tell my story to one who had loved me so well, and whom I had abandoned without a word.

I imagine my dear Tía Ana reading my words, and I question how she will react to this news, if news it is to her, about her brother. Will my letter bring her joy to know what became of me, or sorrow, or perhaps even anger? If anger, who will suffer from her judgment: the brother who threatened or the niece who fled? If he lives, will she rush to my father with my letter, and if so, will he feel the same rancor, unfaded, even after all these years, or will he wish that he could reach back and change that moment in the past, when his rage determined all of our destinies?

I shall anxiously await the reply from my *tía*, to learn how she has fared all these years, and whether my father still lives, and what fate befell Silvia. It will take many months before I hear back. My thoughts will travel over the seas with my letter, and with their answer in return, over the route I took so many years ago.

18 October 1687

I have received my answer, and the will and missive from a man born two centuries before my birth.

40

RACHEL

I abruptly closed Juliana's diary. The reference to Sor Juana Inés de la Cruz had taken me by surprise, and for a moment I had wondered how I might add to the scholarship about the famous writer. But the next entries in the diary had quickly overshadowed that.

There were only a few pages left, but I imagined that Juliana would next comment on Ana's response, and I wanted to see whether the pages she referred to were included in the stack of loose papers I had found at my mother's, along with the journal. If they were there, I wanted to read them before I learned of Juliana's reaction to them. I wanted to read them without that filter, as clearly as a prism of centuries would allow.

I looked at the folded papers, some written on both sides, so that a jumble of half-seen words confronted me. I looked for a paper, ink, and handwriting that seemed similar to that in Juliana's diary, thinking that each age tends to have its own characteristic way of writing. I found what I thought would be Ana's letter, but as I straightened out the pages and carefully spread them out on my desk, I saw that it had been folded in such a way as to enclose several other papers, of a different handwriting, but with paper and ink that seemed similar, though the date on top said 1512. Puzzled, I put those pages aside and, with a mixture

of hope and anxiety that could have been only a pale reflection of what Juliana must have felt, began to read the
letter from Ana.

41

ANA

My dearest Juliana,

The joy to know that you are alive, that you have been alive for all these long years, my precious dear, is more than I can describe to you! And you are blessed with a daughter! Surely she has been a great source of solace to you.

My prayers have been answered, and an old woman can die in peace at last! If only you had written sooner— but you have explained your lingering apprehension. Oh, my child, you need not have feared your father's dark vengeance.

I know no kind way to tell you this, but your father, my brother, died long ago. After your disappearance, he became as a madman. He was taken away and placed with other poor wretches in his condition, but he did not linger. I believe that amid his ravings, your father grieved for you. Perhaps you will find some small comfort in this knowledge.

You also ask about Silvia, but I have never heard from her. I always hoped that she had stayed with you. I often imagined the two of you, according each other a degree of succor. I now suppose that she lived out her life in the countryside, hiding from your father's wrath.

Another blighted life, all from his injustice. I cannot imagine that she still lives.

There is something of the story that you do not know. I tried to find you and Silvia after your abrupt departure. I correctly surmised that you were journeying to Sevilla, but my basis for this guess was mistaken. I thought, I hoped, that your father had taken you on a business trip, though this required that I ignore the hasty and unannounced departure. Although I inquired of innkeepers along the way whether they had hosted travelers of your description, I did not know that your father did not accompany you, nor did I know of the precautions that you had taken. Upon my arrival in Sevilla, I asked for help from an acquaintance of my dear Emilio, but that was doomed to come to naught.

When I read the last entry in your diary and knew the explanation for your flight, I abandoned my search. I had heard of the murder of Don Lorenzo and now knew that your father had been his assassin. I no longer had any reason to believe that you might have escaped in the direction of Sevilla, and even if you had, my search for you might somehow aid your father in discovering you. Now I know that your father never went to Sevilla, but that you were still there, awaiting passage. If only I had known how to find you, my dearest, what hardship and loneliness I might have saved us both! I failed you in the moment you most needed me, just as your father failed your mother.

Although you were his victim, your father, too, was victim of his merciless honor. Try to ease any bitterness in your heart and remember him in the gentleness with which he raised you. When you dwell

273

on that, you cannot doubt he loved you, though it was not always so. After your mother's death, he thought to cast you off for what he saw as her shame. I said before that now an old woman can die in peace, and those were not mere words. I am ill, and I do not expect to last much longer, but I am content, now that I know that you are well.

You see, there is one last task I must perform before I leave this world. Your letter has made it possible for me to fulfill my vow, made to your mother long ago. You did not know her, and Sebastián would not allow her name to be spoken, although in the end, in his mad raving, he called her name again and again.

Although I knew your mother, Margarita, only two years, we were very close. She was the sister I never had. She told me her story, the cause of what she feared would be her demise, the night before they came and seized her.

Your parents' marriage had been arranged by your two grandfathers, but Sebastián and Margarita grew to care for each other. How could they not have? Each was a person of good character, noble in thought, learned and true. They loved as many married couples do not, and when your mother found she was with child, they rejoiced in this gift from God. You believe that your mother died in giving birth to you, but it is not so. It was shortly after you were born that the tragedy began to unfold.

There was a servant by the name of Mencía in your father's house, who had thought that she would be lady's maid to the new young mistress, but your mother did not care for her vulgar ways. She was a dangerous enemy to make, as we soon learned, to our *everlasting sorrow. This faithless servant looked for reason to discredit your mother with my brother, though it took her over a year to find her evil chance. One day, when you were but a few months old, she was cleaning your mother's room and began to go through her things, probably with intent to steal something. She discovered more than she hoped for, and she brought it to Margarita, to threaten and to frighten. It was a ceramic object, of a plain gold-green color, with a base about as long as my forearm. On it were eight small cups, as though to hold oil, and one larger one. Mencía claimed to have seen such a thing at a trial of the Inquisition. She said that it was something used in the Jewish faith. Now she possessed the power to punish.*

She lost no time in presenting the Jewish symbol to one of the familiars of the Inquisition, charged with reporting all suspect actions to the Holy Tribunal. She boasted of her betrayal and called it loyalty, to the Church, to the Spanish of pure blood, and to your father. When your mother heard what Mencía had done, she was apprehensive, though she hoped still that the life she had led, and the love and influence of your father, would convince the Tribunal that she was a true member of Holy Mother Church. Still, she wished to tell to me her story, and made me swear that, should she not survive, I would pass on to you the truth of her tragedy.

Her own mother, your grandmother, had given her the object, which was called a menorah, on the night before she was to wed. The tale your grandmother related was that which her own mother had told to her on the day of her marriage. For is not marriage the time for any woman to face the realities of life and live forevermore within that truth?

Your mother's family had been of the Jewish faith, living in Castile until 1492, when all were forced to choose Baptism, exile, or death. The family chose to flee to Portugal, where they and their descendants remained for many decades. Even in Portugal they did finally have to submit to Baptism but kept their Jewish faith within their hearts. In 1581, after our King Felipe II had annexed Portugal, your mother's great-grandfather moved his family back to Castile, where they hoped to find more prosperity than was then possible in Lisbon.

In Castile, they adopted a new name and were able to purchase false papers showing the family's purity of blood. This was kept a secret, and your mother's grandmother, not knowing her true name or background, and having been born here, thought herself of the purest lineage. Her parents had raised her in the teachings of Holy Mother Church, lest the family be persecuted by the Holy Inquisition. I cannot but believe that for them the Jewish faith remained ever the true one, but this sacrifice they made. They buried their faith in their own breasts, never to teach it to their children, for the danger it could bring them.

And so the secret was to pass from bride to bride, each sworn to secrecy, until her own eldest daughter's wedding day. The menorah was passed down as well, a physical reminder, so that the truth would not be lost, though it would be forever hidden.

Your mother was much distraught when she learned that she was not of purest blood, as she had always believed, but what could she do? Even had her pledge not required her to keep this knowledge secret, whom could she tell? A groom she barely knew, and who had been deceived by her family's false papers of purity?

She kept the secret locked within her heart and endeavored through her actions and feelings to love and honor your father in all things, to pay in part for this deception. I must admit that at first I was shocked to learn of your mother's heritage, but she was a true believer, and kept Christ's law within her heart.

Oh, my child, it pains me yet to think on those dark days! The authorities of the Holy Office took your mother. She was charged with apostasy. The object was enough to cause her condemnation, and no one would come forward to give testimony to her true beliefs and practices. She had expected Sebastián to come to her defense, but he did not. He forbade any of his household to testify on your mother's behalf, threatening that he would denounce any who did. He raged at the betrayal by her family and said that he would never have married her had he known she was of impure blood. He turned his back on her, and she was lost.

Nor did I come forward, and for this I have reproached myself and set myself many acts of penance, but never will I make clean my sin of cowardice. I tell myself that the Inquisition would not have accepted the assurances of a woman, especially when Margarita's own husband would not speak for her. I tell myself this, but I do not know whether I believe it.

Still, though betrayed by all she knew, your mother did not lose faith with them. Twice she rejected the chance to ease her course, because she wished to prove to your father that she was not guilty of the accusations. She could have stated her repentance and been given a much lighter sentence, but this would have been to admit guilt. Because of what was seen as her recalcitrance, she was condemned to the severest punishment, though accusations against her were light compared with those who were held for such offenses as defiling the holy crucifix.

I will never forget the horror of that day, of the auto de fe, when she was to be submitted to the fire. I saw her walking in the procession with the dozens of others, her body deformed, from what horrors only Our Lord knows. She wore the yellow sackcloth sanbenito, worn by all who were accused. But from its style, we knew she was to die. On it were fearsome and gruesome pictures of flames and devils. What holy hand had depicted these atrocities? Around her neck was a rope, which also held her arms in place. On her head was a conical hat, as though to mock her.

Each of the accused was brought before a tribunal, though in fact their fate had already been determined. We heard the charge against her, that she had practiced the Jewish faith. She insisted that she was a true daughter of Holy Mother Church, though her ancestors had been converts. Each time, the enraged Inquisitor raised the Jewish object for all to see. If she did not still harbor the Jewish poison in her heart, why did she keep such signs of the devil within her? She told him she kept it only as a family remembrance. But what were family or loved ones compared with duty to the Church?

Even at the last moment, if she had confessed and repented, she could have saved herself the agony of dying by the flame. For betraying all that she had said before, she would have been granted the favor of being strangled before she was burned. But even this she did not allow herself. Thus she wished to prove to your

*father her love, her innocence, and her defiance.
Though I myself could be sentenced to this day for
what I am writing here, I do question the justice of the
Holy Office. May God have mercy on our anguished
souls!*

*Your father was spared the customary confiscation of
his goods, as he had done valuable service to the king,
and because he so vehemently cursed your mother and
her family. Still, though no one dared mention the
horror in Sebastián's presence, it was not forgotten.
Many pretended to be his friends, but they did so only
for their own advantage, as the king so favored him.*

*It was because he knew of this ignominy that Don
Lorenzo refused to marry you, although the stain did
not guard you from his bestial desire. When he threw it
in your father's face, Sebastián lost all use of reason,
and the old tyrant honor ruled again. You were your
mother's daughter, after all, and once again his honor
was destroyed. It had been restored for him by the Holy
Inquisition, which had burned it clean. Now the
retribution would be at his own hands, and, though he
had loved you, he went mad at seeing the old shame
once again, and nothing could have saved you from his
wrath. You were doubly guilty, from your birth to a
tainted mother, and from your violation by a brutal
man.*

*One last thing I would say. Do not believe that your
father did not suffer all his life for his treatment of
your mother. I believe that many times in later years
he did ask himself if what he had done was truly out of
honor, or even duty to the Church. If he had tried to
help your mother, he could also have been accused. And
so, perhaps to mask his suspicion that cowardice had*

*prompted him, he made for his conscience a shield of
honor to protect him against his own misgivings. He
could tell himself that it was her family's falsity that
had wounded his honor and caused him to abandon her.
I think it was this self-deception that he saw threatened
when you were defiled. It had become his all, and he
had to defend it, even against you, his only love.
Perhaps it was the old doubts, too, that caused him in
the end to submit to his own demons.*

*As you have seen, I send you another document here.
It is a translation of a letter your mother received from
her mother, and the night that she told me her history,
she entrusted the original to me. Even then the paper
and ink were deteriorating, perhaps from the many
miles it had traveled, and the conditions in which it
had been hidden. I decided to have the letter translated
into Spanish from the Portuguese, so that at least I, if
no other, could understand the message there. Some
words I guessed must be Hebrew, and so I was in a
quandary about whom I might approach to translate it
for me. I finally decided to ask a man who had been
one of your Tío Emilio's friends. Though he was
already quite advanced in years, he was a scholar who
was fluent in Portuguese. I knew that he would do this
favor for me, and keep it secret. I do not know how he
was able to translate the Hebrew words. Nor do I
understand what he tried to tell me about using the
name God in his translation, so that non-Jews would
understand what was meant.*

*Having told this tale, I am now truly spent. I have at
last fulfilled my word to tell you of your family's
heritage and Margarita's unjust fate. Of my own life,
there is not much to tell. I continued with my work*

with those who needed my help, using what I had learned from Emilio to ease their pain. I have lived to grieve for all whom I once loved. I rejoice to know that you live, and that you have a daughter, but how I wish that I could have spent my life with you! It is so long that I am alone. Now I am quite ill, and I know that when this letter reaches your hands and eyes, I will not be found among the living.

So, my child, I tell you go with God for now and ever. I have faith that one day you and I shall meet your mother, and we will be restored to one another in that place that the Lord reserves for those who have truly kept His law of love. My blessings upon you, Juliana, all your life.

Your loving tía,
Ana Torres López
17 May 1687

42

RACHEL

A secret heritage. Even as I sat holding Ana's letter in my hand, it was as though I looked at myself from another place and time. Juliana's mother, too, had kept a secret, but hers was a dangerous legacy. I knew from my study of seventeenth-century Spain that what had happened to Juliana's family was a possibility, but we can distance ourselves from what is learned from literature and history. We can't clearly conceive of individuals whose beliefs and ways of being are so different from our own. They are so distinct from us in our modernity. It's easy to think of them as having never existed, not as we exist.

My mother had read these papers, and she said that she had failed, as Ana had failed. Ana blamed herself for not finding Juliana, but did my mother judge her so harshly? And for what perceived fault did my mother blame herself?

Was my mother's task the same as Ana's had been: to pass on secret knowledge, the truth of Juliana's heritage? I longed to be able to tell her that she hadn't fallen short, that I had found her papers, that I had discovered the secret. Yet, why hadn't she told me any of this sooner? Why had she left me to fumble on my own? And why had she addressed the papers to an unborn granddaughter?

I had to know Juliana's reaction to this news, and what was contained in the other letter Ana had sent her.

43

Juliana

22 October 1687

I believed that, cocooned within these walls, I was
sheltered from all outside harm. What could happen in the
world that could encroach upon my refuge? Once again,
life has taught me that our assumptions are but vanity.
Though she was taken from my life before I could know
her, the manner of my mother's death torments me more
than ever her absence did. It hangs about and chokes me,
as the lingering smoke from an *auto de fe.*

I grieve for my *tía*, who shall soon be gone from this
world, but at least she dies of a natural cause, and who
better than she, who strove to help those in pain and
sickness, to know that illness and death overtake us all? I
grieve for Silvia, who never returned to those whom she
left in Madrid. I can only try to shape my mind to believe
that she found some happiness in the countryside, a
retreat that must have seemed foreign to her. For my
father, I cannot grieve; though I once thought I forgave
him, his treachery was far greater than I could ever have
surmised.

My beloved *tía* would have me understand, and forgive,
perhaps so that the poison of his betrayal does not finish
the carnage that he began so long ago. Yet I find no room
for mercy inside this heart, which has withered to a thing

that serves me only to preserve that which we call life, for want of a better word.

25 October

I have put off reading the translated letter that my *tía* sent me. Since it is from my mother's hidden heritage, I cannot help but think that it will be a tale of sorrow, but I must read it, for she would have wished it.

44

Solomon

Last Will and Testament of Solomon Abravanel
Lisboa, 1512

Dear Ones,

I leave this testament for your children's children and beyond, that they might know who I have been and who they are, being proud of the ancient blood of our fathers that runs through our veins, and the faith that is in our hearts. I fear for them, for it seems that our God has said that for His chosen people, nothing shall be easy.

All my earthly goods, which number few here in this land, I leave to you, my beloved children. As you read this, do not grieve for my death, for the sorrow of this life and your dearest departed mother have long since called me to my grave. You know, my children, that this patrimony is not great. It seems that whenever we have prospered, the Lord has found ways to remind us that this is not what matters. What I bequeath to my descendants is the testament of my life. You know of this, my children, because you have lived the sacrifices with me. To this day, I carry within my mind, as a

*hidden brand, the image of my poor little children
holding on to the cart I pulled, with all that remained
of our earthly goods, bags upon your small, bent backs,
because a bit more food could mean we would survive.
More than sorrow, your faces wore bewilderment, and
you looked to me for answers that I did not have. To
this day, I do not comprehend the evil in men's hearts,
and perhaps I should rejoice that I do not.*

*To all who come after me, know that we are one, for
as we trace our lineage back, so too do we trace it
forward, and I love you, though you are yet unborn.
For who would not love the seed of his seed? Know that
for our people, study and wisdom in the service of God
are the greatest good. Strive always to learn and
understand, and when you study our sacred writings
and ways, you perform your duty twice over. Cherish
knowledge above all but God, for your thoughts cannot
be taken from you.*

*If ever you are forced to leave your home, look for
company in those who have gone before you, and know
that you share a suffering that we have endured for
generation upon generation. Has it never struck you
that Moses is one of our most revered fathers, he who
led us out of misery, only to wander for forty years
and never to be allowed entrance to the Promised Land?*

*Our family has for many generations lived on this
peninsula, yet even here we have not found a home, for
nowhere have we discovered a place that welcomes us.
Five centuries ago, fleeing the Muslim conquerors in
Andalucía, our great poet Moses ibn Ezra wrote, "I am
weary of roaming about the world, measuring its
expanse; and I am not yet done. . . . My feet run
about like lightning to the far ends of the earth, and I*

move from sea to sea. Journey follows journey, but I find no resting place, no calm repose."

My grandfather, as a boy, saw the great massacre of 1391. Both parents brutally murdered before his eyes, and he saved only by the "mercy" of a Christian who did not wish to kill a child but whose conscience did not prick him to release an orphan into the cruel world. This child, along with his older sister, fled Sevilla, but the disease of hatred and murder spread over the land. Córdoba, Toledo, Barcelona, Valencia, untold thousands killed. The Dominicans and the Franciscans stirring up hatred against the Jews. The Muslims then were not as prosperous as we, so we alone were named sorcerers and devils.

In the year of my father's birth, 1412, the Pragmática imposed a formal quarantine against Jews throughout Castile. We had always chosen to live with our own people, for comfort and safety, but what had been choice became law and smothered us. Live in walled ghettos, do not leave the country, do not move to another town. Clerk or judge, you are denied your place. Physician, do not minister to Christians. Housekeeper, do not work in Christian homes. Wear a black coat, adorned only with a red "Jew badge." A litany of rules like a cruel mockery of the Lord's commandments.

Denied a way to support ourselves, we were reduced to miserable poverty. Faced with starvation, my father's family mortgaged their communal lands and then pawned their Torah crowns. This was the cruelest turn of all. They denied us our goods, our lives, and they sought to deny us our very selves. All Jews over the age of twelve were required to attend conversionary

*sermons three times a year. And with many, our
enemies succeeded.*

*Thousands submitted to baptism while their faithful
brethren wept. Some, perhaps, believed, but most could
no longer bear the hardship and humiliation. The
"redeeming" waters were their only escape, and many
who withstood the pressure did not condemn them for
their weakness, for who is so strong that he knows he
will not succumb tomorrow? As our great poet Solomon
Bonafed wrote, one could not "erase these pleasant
names from my doorposts," for "their names are
engraved upon my brow."*

*Many "New Christians" chose to retain their old ways,
and we did not shut them out. The learned men of the
faithful debated with the apostates. Even among our
own wise men there was disagreement over whether
those who had accepted the new religion to save their
lives, whom we called anusim, might yet retain their
Jewishness, unlike the meshumadim, who had
apostasized for different reasons. We shared courtyards
and friends, and many conversos participated in our
festivals. They observed the Sabbath and slaughtered
their animals according to the Law of Moses. They did
all of this, and also climbed into positions within the
government and prospered in their business ventures.
At times they sought to atone, with the rituals of their
new religion, the abandonment of their old.*

*Yet I must accept that some came truly to believe in
their new faith and changed their hearts as they
changed their names. Names like Santángel, Montoro,
Valladolid, González, San Pedro, de la Torre, Goto
became their new selves, and many gained fame and
fortune from them. Solomon Halevi became Pablo de*

*Santa María, and Joshua Halorki, Gerónimo de Santa
Fe. Even in my time the people spoke of these two
men, though Halevi, at forty years of age, had
converted when my father's father was but a child.*

*Halevi had been wealthy and respected, erudite in
Talmudic studies and Maimunist philosophy. Many
called him Rabbi. Yet he forsook all of this and became
a priest, a doctor of theology, and bishop of Burgos.
They say that his writings reveal his true belief that
Jesus was the Messiah we all awaited. Halevi and
Halorki engaged in a literary debate that lasted for
years, and finally, in the year of my father's birth,
Halorki came to believe that Christianity was truth.
Kaddish services were intoned for him. Yet those who
mourned him were not dead for him, for he worked
against his people all his life. It seems he was sincere,
and this shook our people mightily. Those conversos
who spoke against us from their own sense of shame,
we could understand and reject. Those who were
sincere caused some to doubt their own belief. Perhaps
we were awaiting a Messiah who would never come, for
he had already died upon a cross.*

*There were times when the persecution eased, as
monarchs found they could not do without our skills in
government and finance, law and medicine. Our
learning had been the savior of our souls, and
sometimes of our bodies, though the positions our skills
bought were soon envied and the cycle began anew.*

*When I was a young man, it came to be that even
those who had submitted to baptism found that it was
not enough, and Old Christians persecuted New. The
price that they had paid for peace had been great, and
now that peace was forfeit to the Inquisition. Our*

faithful watched as those who had betrayed themselves were in turn betrayed by their new Christian brethren. They suffered prison, punishment, and fire. Death was termed "relaxation," and those who were "reconciled" found a slower death—one of destitution. Many were burned alive. Some were even condemned after death, and their heirs' goods confiscated by the Crown. A few repented their own faithlessness and embraced death as their own redeeming punishment. Some plotted their rebellion, and they were caught and burned, or their hands were severed from their bodies and they were left to bleed to death.

Ferdinand and Isabella, the Most Catholic Monarchs, rid their land of Moors and set to rid it of Jews as well. Often have I wondered whether they truly believed that one could bring faith through sword and flame. I submitted to memory the proclamation of 1492, for we would live its effects, and I wanted in my mind the words also, the words that condemned and exiled. We believe in the power of words. As homage to my people, I would not forget. "All Jews and Jewesses, of whatever age they may be, that live, reside, and dwell in our said kingdoms and dominions shall not presume to return to, or reside therein, or in any part of them, either as residents, travelers, or in any other manner whatever, under pain of death." Christians could not speak with us or befriend us, lest they suffer excommunication. It was a double bind, for those few who might follow their own Christian teachings and show mercy to their fellow man would be denied fellowship and redemption by their church.

That is not to say that there were many who so wrestled with their conscience. Most were glad to see us

*go. They coveted our goods and profited by our
expulsion. We could take whatever we could carry, with
this exception: no money, no gold, no silver. People
sold a vineyard for a donkey, a house for a horse.
Christian love of fellow men was reserved, it seemed,
for fellow Christians.*

*Many were the accusations against us. The Jews
torched Christian homes. The Jews cursed Christian
churches. The Jews defiled communion wafers and
flogged crucifixes. The Jews murdered Christian
children. Some believed this. Perhaps men, seeing the
evil in themselves, find it everywhere they look. Then,
too, I grieve to write it, many who accused were New
Christians, lending veracity to the absurdities. Their
guilt would not let them look upon righteous men but
caused them to spew forth like animals. Yet animals,
they say, do not betray their own.*

*Thousands fled north to Navarre, but no farther, for
France was closed to them. Tens of thousands took to
the south to the sea, to Italy, North Africa, or to the
east, to the lands of the Ottoman Empire. Tens of
thousands to the west, we among them, to Portugal.
We clogged the roads and seaports, and some pitied us,
and some mocked. Our rabbi told us to sing to keep our
spirits up, but our songs were lamentation. The last of
us left Spanish soil on the ninth day of the Hebrew
month Av, the day we fast to remember the destruction
of the Temple of Jerusalem.*

*King João II let us in, and those who had managed to
smuggle money with them paid a thousand cruzados for
an eight-ninths-residence permit. But he also wanted us
to convert. Had we sacrificed our home, only to
abandon our faith now? Most of us journeyed to the*

mountains to the north, where we have worked to this day in poverty and sorrow.

My last wish is that you hold fast this story of our family, and pass it on to those who will come after. Though it is a tale of much woe, know, my children, that you have been the wellspring of what joy I have known in this life.

Solomon Abravanel

45

Juliana

1 November 1687

I thought that my heart could feel no new sorrow, but the sufferings described by Solomon, though he lived so long ago, torment me. He writes to those who will come after, and so he writes to me. I have truly inherited this legacy of pain.

9 April 1688

It is some months now since I learned of my mother's unjust demise and my father's first treachery. I have struggled with this new truth: I am a Jewess. I have come to not only accept, but to enfold this legacy within me, with all of its tortured history. Though some would say that I am less, I know myself to be more than I believed, containing the sad story of Spain within me. It could be said that this lineage of mine brought me to this New World, which will embrace those who were born to it, and those of us who came, to create its own new heritage.

RACHEL

Now my bond to Juliana was even stronger, as we both read a heart-wrenching history of those who came so long ago. Even having been raised within her father's household, with its beliefs and prejudices, Juliana was able to welcome this new part of her identity.

For once, though, I found Juliana too optimistic. The New World has not always been just to those who were born here, nor to those who came.

There now remained only a few more pages of the diary.

47

Juliana

16 August 1689

I have lived within these walls for nearly thirty years, chased here by the violence of one man and the injustice of another. Life here passes so slowly and uneventfully. Our battles are those of the soul. We struggle to maintain our faith in God, in our sisters, and in ourselves. We struggle to find the beauty and happiness that can exist for those of us who have been placed outside the timeless cycle that most women know, of birth, love, and death, and of seeing our daughters pass through the same stages that we have known. I have, more than most of my sisters here, known what it was to be a woman in this sense. Yet I will never see my daughter renew herself in love, repeating the creation.

1 December

A new letter came today from my correspondent Sor Juana. She and I have been writing to each other with some regularity over the past few years, though I fear that I gain so much more from her missives than she from mine. Perhaps it is just that she is glad to know of another who seeks to gain knowledge, though I fear she thinks too grandly of my level of learning. She has at times sent me some of her essays, and I must confess that they are often too difficult for me to follow completely.

In truth, I much prefer her poems. There is one poem in which I have sometimes sought a vengeful refuge. The poetess says that men are foolish for accusing women, for do they not see that they are the cause of that for which they blame us? How apt this seems to be, and how well it fits my own experience. I was condemned, even by my own father, for a man's sin against me. Now the knowledge of my father's betrayal of my mother compounds his guilt a thousandfold in my eyes.

8 April 1690

It is very seldom that I speak with my Mercedes, and then it is only in general terms. She seems uncomfortable in my presence, or perhaps it is only that she is indifferent to me except in my role as her superior. I have never discovered how to close this distance between us, how to let her know how I care for her, for I fear that she might question my uncommon interest. While we both live in the only home that she has ever known, I do not see a way or a purpose in telling her of her true origin. In truth, I fear that anger, rather than loving acceptance, would be her response. I also recoil at the thought of our community discerning the truth. If we were cast out, I do not know where we would go, a woman and her mother cast adrift. I must also admit that my pride in the position that I hold here is of value to me, and I would rue its loss. And so I keep my daughter in ignorance.

The illness that struck Mercedes in her childhood has never returned, nor has there been any identifiable lasting harm. She fits in well here, and I must admit that she seems content to live the life of a nun, though I do not know her well enough to judge whether she is happy.

10 November

I have lived this life among women, and with a daughter who has not known me. This is one of God's ironies, that I, who grew up in a world of men and never knew my own mother, must live always with women. I did not know how.

Through the years I have returned at times to that darkness to which I descended when first I came here. During those long, shadowy days, they did not know if ever I would find my way back again. Later, some told me they believed the fiend had been fighting for my soul, and that my mumbling was some distorted message from my place of struggle. Others were simply unusually kind to me afterward, and embarrassed by my previous unseemly behavior.

The first time, so long ago, a doctor was called in. He said I suffered from melancholia due to an excess of black bile. He bled me to try to bring my humors back in balance, and Madre Superior became so worried at my paleness that she forbade him to return.

Once, Madre Mónica told me that she had the singular notion that what had happened to me had indeed been an illness, but one beyond any doctor's power to heal. She said it was an illness of the mind, and that, just as a strong body is needed to fight off the bad humors of the body, so, too, is a strong mind needed to fight back from the abyss I had approached.

Each time I have managed to emerge, some times taking longer than others. I learn nothing from these struggles, not even how to avoid or better defeat them. And always I carry the dread that I will succumb to the next assault. All that I lost haunts me still, and I do not know whether my life has brought me recompense.

21 June 1691

I have a growth within me that seems to swell each day, and I know that not much time is left to me. To distract myself from the pain, and to reflect upon my life, I have read all that I have written here over the years, and I have come to a decision. I will send Mercedes forth into the world, free of these confining walls, to live the life of a woman, a life that was denied to me and to my mother. I do not believe that she will welcome this, for she has no idea of the outside world, but I will command her, as her abbess and as her mother. I do not wish the injustices of our time and place to curtail her life, as they have imprisoned mine. I do not wish our line to wither here.

4 August

Twelve days ago I spoke to Mercedes, revealing to her the truth of her birth and enjoining her to leave the convent. At first, it seemed she could not grasp what I was telling her, but then, as understanding came, she passed from astonishment to anger and resentment that everything she had believed of her life had been a lie. She seemed not to lament that she had not received a mother's love from me, but rather to abhor the choices I had made, without granting that I had seen no other path. She did not wish to leave the only home that she had ever known, and spoke of her desire to take her final vows, but I called upon the obedience that she owed me, and she could not stay in opposition to her abbess. I hope that in time she will come to forgive my ruling in this matter and accept her new life. I hope that she will allow herself joy.

I have made arrangements as best I could for her. In my duties of overseeing the business of the convent, I have come to know a man of the world whom I trust. I have asked him to aid Mercedes as she leaves the shelter of her home and to help her find a husband. He does not know the reason for any of this, and I am sure that Mercedes will not tell him, for she feels shame at the truth of her life. He recognizes that I do not make decisions lightly, and that I have never asked of him a favor. I have full faith that he will carry out my wishes.

Mercedes leaves tomorrow and will take with her these writings, and my instruction to pass them on, to be forever shared with the girls and women of our blood, so that they may know something of the life that I have led. Perhaps someday my descendants, reading of my plight and of my choices, will find it strange that there was a time when men were so violent against women, and that women were blamed for it. Perhaps there will be a time when religion is not used as a weapon.

As for tomorrow, I do not worry that the others here will guess our secret upon her departure, for I do not look for my child to weep as I wish her farewell. Any tears that Mercedes may shed will be for the life that she has known here, and for those sisters with whom she has been close. My need to preserve our secret has ensured that I am not among that circle. I have observed that she can be a proud woman, and her bitterness toward me, I believe, will also dam her tears. I have buried my love for her for so long that I have no doubt that, in the company of others, no tears shall rise to my eyes upon seeing my child leave me forever.

Now, though, in the solitude and black night of my room, my grief comes upon me, like a familiar specter.

5 August

My most precious Mercedes,

I have not slept at all, for today you leave me. Having now read of my life, and the choices I have made, I hope that you will come to forgive me. I fled Spain to save my life, and thus ensured your survival, too. It may be sinful arrogance, but I am proud of how I faced what could have been a fatal adversity. I will not let our history end here, in this place that has been restraint as well as refuge. Perhaps one day this story will find itself in a kinder world.

You may not credit it, but know that I have loved you from before your birth. I believe that you will be able to find fulfillment in the life to which I send you, as you were able to find contentment in the life here, which I also thrust upon you. Go forth, my daughter, to share our fate, that other women of our blood may find some wisdom or compassion in our story.

I am always your faithful mother,
Juliana Torres Coloma

RACHEL

I sat amid the papers I had now scattered, grieving for the death of a woman I had never known, a woman long since turned to dust. I felt a mother's love toward Juliana, this woman I had come to know from the time she was sixteen years of age. I wanted to see her as faultless, as someone who had no choice but to do exactly as she did. Still, I couldn't help but ask what would become of Mercedes. Juliana had condemned her own daughter to a life without a mother's love and then sent her out into a world that she had never known.

The time had come to read all of these papers, to search for the clue that would solve their mystery.

49

Mercedes

Mexico City, 1738

To my granddaughter Luz,

I write this, having just wrested from you a promise to accept the papers I will leave explicitly for you upon my death, and to follow all of my instructions written here. You have shown some responsibility as you have approached womanhood, at least more than my other female offspring of your generation, and for that reason you were chosen. Remember the vow of silence that you have just given me, and divulge these secrets only in the manner I here prescribe. The task that I assign to you is a shameful one, but one to which you must submit, as I submitted, many years ago. I have tricked you by forcing you to promise something, the substance of which you could not imagine.

As I have kept to myself all these years the oath my mother pressed upon me, so I enjoin you to do, until the day when you compel a granddaughter of your own to take up your burden. She must make the same vow that you have made, to accept the papers upon your death. In her old age she will identify the granddaughter who will assume the task and extract the same pledges from her, to begin it all again.

I swore to my mother to pass these papers on. As you read them, know that I am the Mercedes of the diary of Juliana, or Sor Teresa, my Madre Superior, as I knew her. She commanded me to vow to pass on these writings, forcing me to forsake the only vows I had always longed to make. Yet I have "interpreted" a part of my sacred oath. That is how I have avenged myself, in some small part. I am certain that it was her intention for me to give these papers to my daughter, but those were not her precise words. She said only, "Preserve these papers, and pass them down through the female offspring of your family, my own descendants. Perhaps in some small way it will help them to understand some other woman's life, even if they can never know her in this world. It will establish a link for them, and for me, with women of the same blood, something I always longed for but never had." But was not I that link, though I had lived my life not knowing it?

She wished to affirm truths that should have been her shame, and mine, and that of our family, but she did not understand it as such. Still, I have crippled the fulfillment of her desires, without breaking my word. While I am alive, no other living person will know the true circumstances of my birth. No one will ever be able to discuss the nature of the papers with another living soul. I have clung to life much past what is common, so that I could thwart my mother's desire by waiting for you, a granddaughter, to fulfill her command. In my bitterness, I have triumphed, at least in this small way.

So that you may understand why I have perpetrated this small treachery, I will tell what you need to know of my life, and of my mother. All of my life had been spent in the convent, a serene life, and I had looked forward eagerly to taking my final vows and becoming a full-fledged member of the community. One day I was called to the abbess's room. I was puzzled, because I had heard that she was ill, and I could not imagine why she should desire to see me. In fact, I had reason to believe that the abbess found me unworthy, for although I tried with sincere devotion to fulfill all of my duties and to make myself deserving of being a bride of Christ, time and again I had been denied the privilege of taking my final vows. I searched my heart for some offense that I might have unwittingly committed, but I could discover there no possible reason for this summons. I was so sincere then in my desire to be holy, before my mother so cruelly used me.

I rather timidly entered Madre Superior's room and found her alone. She bade me to sit down, and I did so. I suppose she sensed that I was agitated, and she told me not to be frightened. She slowly leaned back, closed her eyes, and began to speak in a low voice of some secret that she was about to lay bare to me. I was, quite naturally, confused, not only about the substance of the secret, but also about why she should have chosen to tell it to me. Then she opened her eyes, and searched my face in an intense manner, as though looking for some clue or comfort there.

"What I have to tell you concerns you in a most direct, personal way. It will affect everything that will happen to you for the rest of your life. Do you know how you came to this convent?"

I confessed to her that one of the older sisters, Sor Beatriz, who had taken care of me when I was young, had one day told me that, as a baby, I had been left at the convent gate, with a great deal of money and a note. I was the child of a nobleman and his wife. They had come to the New World full of hopes, but the wife had died, giving birth to me, their first child. The husband was so racked with grief that he could not bear to see the babe, a constant reminder of his beloved wife. He could not send the child back to relatives in Spain, for he had become estranged from them. He hoped that his contribution to the convent, and the dedication of his baby daughter to a religious life, would, in some way, expiate his own guilt for having abandoned his child.

"Yes," the abbess answered, "that is correct. I know of the letter, and of its contents. I know, because I wrote it."

In my surprise, I rose from my chair, but she continued.

"I have avoided you all these years so that no one would ever see anything in my eyes, would ever suspect. You are descended from a most worthy family, but from a mother who could not give you a name, because she had only her own name to confer. She had no husband. I am your mother. Do not condemn me. Perhaps, after you have read these papers, you will begin to understand."

But I did not understand then, nor do I understand even now, how she could have divulged to me such a loathsome truth, with which I have lived ever since that day. And, further, having told me that she was my mother, she asked me to swear to her to keep the

papers, to preserve them, and to pass them on to our
female descendants. I stuttered that I could not keep
the last part of the promise, that I hoped soon to take
my final vows.

"You must leave the convent and make for yourself a
real life, with children who share your blood, and with
whom you can share your sorrows and your joys."

"But I love my life here," I protested. "I love Our
Lord. I have been happy here."

"I have not been so," she whispered, so faintly that I
could barely hear. "Swear to me. Give me your sacred
oath before God. Swear to me, as I am your mother,
and as I am your abbess."

I did as she asked. I could not refuse her twofold
authority over me. It is because of that day that I have
lived an embittered life, never able to show my feelings.
My husband would not have tolerated such gloom in his
wife, though he was a better man than most, to have
taken me without a proper background. I showed him
the letter, which had been saved for me at the convent,
and he was satisfied. He was much older than I, though
I myself was old for a bride. He was kind to me in his
way, and gave me children, but such was not the
happiness I had sought.

My mother wrote of a hope that her writings would
someday find themselves in a time when the way that
men treat women, often with violence and injustice,
may be a thing of the past. But from what I have seen,
there is no abatement of these cruelties. Being out in
the world has taught me that life holds much ugliness
of which I never dreamed, so safe and secure in my life
in the convent. What right did she have to banish me?

And so, child, I have determined much of the future course of your life, as mine was determined for me. You must marry and have children. Perhaps you will not regret this. You will be like most girls, who have no real choice.

Your grandmother,
Mercedes Torres
In the Year of Our Lord 1738

50

Luz

Mexico City, 1790

To my granddaughter,

*I hardly know how to write this letter to you. In so
doing, I am striving to fulfill a promise that I made to
my grandmother Mercedes Torres when I was young
and understood nothing of its implications. I wish that
I could at least tell you this in person, to somehow
soften the blow more than my grandmother attempted
to do with me, but my daughter, Sofía, is leaving
Mexico City with her husband, and she will not return.*

*Can you begin to imagine, I wonder, what it is like for
a mother to know that she will never see her child
again? Though she is a woman grown and wed, I
cannot tell you of the loss I feel already, knowing that
soon she will be gone forever from my sight and my
embrace. I shall never again hear her voice or gaze
upon her beloved face. When I see her, at times I seem
to stare at the place where she is standing, trying to
root her presence to that space, as though I could in
future return to the memory of her there. But that is
not possible, and I shall not see her pass through the
stages of womanhood, nor shall I hold you in my arms,
my own daughter's daughter.*

*In giving this to your mother to take with her, I am
trusting that she will one day bear you, a daughter.
Your mother is the youngest of my children. All of the
others are grown and married with children of their
own. As much as I love my grandchildren, they are all
boys and I do not believe that I can pass this legacy to
them. I believe that my great-grandmother Juliana
meant for her life's secrets to pass through the women
of her family. I cannot know how men would view what
happened to her, or what she did as a result. I cannot
know whether I can trust a man to deny his own
importance so much as to keep the secret and be but a
link in an unknown chain.*

*I base my mistrust of men's true honor not only on
what I have read within the pages I bequeath to you,
but on my own life as well. When I was but a girl, not
yet imagining what it would be like to enter marriage,
I heard my parents speaking of the mistreatment my
older sister was receiving at the hand of her husband. I
later learned that my loving father had aided my sister
with a civil suit against the husband. Though she had
this right under the law, there were few women who
dared. Very few prevailed in these kinds of cases, and
my sister was no exception. In fact, her husband was
so angered at my sister's action that he beat her until
she died, and still he beat her corpse. The fickle laws,
which offered to give recourse to women, then punished
her murderer but little, because he argued that her
disobedience and disrespect had so fueled the passion of
his anger that he could not control his actions.*

*Knowing of my sister's fate did not prompt me to wish
to enter the married state, and my parents' grief
tempered the usual insistence that a girl find a husband*

when she comes of age. I wished that I could enter a convent, but the solemn oath that I had made as a girl prevented me from following that path. I have no regrets on that account. My parents were happy when I married your grandfather, a friend of the family whom I had known for years to be a gentle man whom I could trust with my well-being. The life I have led with him has had its sorrows, but never any caused by him, and the life he gave us has given me the joy of my own children.

I have instructed your mother, Sofía, that she must teach you how to read, as I taught her myself, as my grandmother Mercedes commanded that I also learn this skill that is not always deemed necessary for a girl. I have made your mother swear to me that she will give these papers to you, having never looked at them herself. She is to extract from you a vow to pass the contents of the package only to your own granddaughter. When you have read this letter and the papers that go with it, you will understand as much as is possible of a message left so long ago. The manner in which I was raised, and in which my mother was raised by my grandmother Mercedes, would have led me to disdain the revelations from the writer of this journal. Instead, I believe that I have learned compassion, and that things are not always what the world deems them to be. I hope that you will find a like understanding.

Believe in yourself, my child, and the goodness of God to enable you to someday pass on these writings to your own dear granddaughter.

All my love,
Luz de Porres Yañez
1790

51

Dolores

Missouri, 1844

My dearest Elizabeth,

I will place this letter, along with a diary and certain
other letters, to be found among my things after I am
gone. There will be strict instructions for the person
who finds the package to deliver it to you, and to you
alone. You are sixteen and about to be wed, and I do
not wish to burden you with the knowledge within these
papers just yet, though I fear it will not be long before
they fall to you. The doctor tells me that I have not
much time left in this world of joys and sorrows,
though I have only just reached my forty-ninth year.
Only your grandfather knows what I am suffering, and
that is as I wish it.

I will tell you the story of how these papers came to
me. When my mother, Sofía, first told her mother,
Luz, that her husband wished them to move to Santa
Fe, Luz reacted most strongly. My mother loved Luz
very much and believed Luz's reaction to be caused by
her mother's love for her. However, Luz entrusted
Sofía with a package and said that she must not open
it but save it for the daughter she must someday bear,

*give it to her secretly, and make her swear to follow
the instructions therein. My mother spoke to me of her
feelings of hurt and betrayal at her mother's command,
and I believe that in that moment I, who was yet to be
born, fell from grace in my mother's eyes.*

*My mother nevertheless kept her word to Luz and gave
me the papers when I married, extracting from me an
oath to obey the instructions I would find in them. She
said that she gave them to me, rather than to my
sister, because I was the first to wed. My sister was
already promised to the brother of my new husband, but
perhaps my mother simply wished to rid herself of the
papers, to discharge her duty and be finished.*

*Not even your mother knows any of this, and although
it pained me to not share this history with my beloved
daughter Isabel, I had to obey the sacred oath that I
had made, though it had been wrenched from me when
I was also just a young woman. You must now decide
whether you will be able to keep the promise that I
demand of you by leaving these papers to you. If you
cannot lock the secret of these papers in your heart, to
be spoken of only to your future granddaughter, then
you must give the packet, unread, to another of my
granddaughters and bury your knowledge of their
existence forever.*

*I pray, however, that you decide to take on the task of
preserving and secretly handing them on to your own
granddaughter. I hope that you have felt my love all of
your life, and that your cousins did not discern the
extra feelings I had for you. I decided early on that you
would be the one to inherit this responsibility, which is
both honor and hardship.*

While I most sincerely charge you with upholding this

*promise that was first required of our ancestress so
long ago, I must confess that I did falter, and though I
do feel guilt at not having followed the letter of my
vow, I tell myself that my treachery is not so great.
After all, my twin, María, and I have always felt that
we are but an extension of each other. Our mother
Sofía's choice of me to receive the papers was an
accidental one, and they could easily have gone to
María. Therefore, contrary to the requirement of our
great-great-grandmother a century ago, I shared the
papers with my sister.*

*I also justified my defiance because of something my
mother told me. She said that when she and my father
left Mexico City and made the six-month, arduous
journey along El Camino Real de Tierra Adentro to
Santa Fe, she almost lost the papers in a river
crossing. In that eventuality, might not a second copy
have preserved the message of the pages?*

*As the years passed and María and I had children, we
didn't think much about the papers. Then, in 1824, my
husband told me of his intent to take us to Missouri. A
few years earlier, some traders had begun to make
regular journeys from Missouri to Santa Fe, and now it
was his intention to join with one of these groups on
the return. He felt that he and his brother, who would
remain in Santa Fe, would better benefit from the trade
if one of them worked from each end of the trading
route. My husband and I did not know exactly when
there would be a caravan returning, and we would be
called upon to pack what we could and forsake the life
that we had known.*

*Now the matter of the papers came to the forefront.
María and I decided upon a course whereby the stories*

within the papers would be preserved by both of us. We set out to copy all of the writings. It was agreed that I would keep the originals, for in this way, we told ourselves, we were not straying as far from the vow that I had made. And so we proceeded, stealing moments from our busy lives as wives and mothers. María was able to copy more than I, for as it became clear that our time to leave with the traders' group neared, there was much to be done in preparation. We finished only a few days before my departure. If you can imagine what it means to leave a twin, you will know the sorrow that I felt, but a woman must cling to her husband.

As the years in Missouri passed, and I saw my Isabel marry an American, and you were not even taught to speak my mother tongue, I decided that I must translate all of the writings into English, lest their meaning be lost. Those who would receive the papers would otherwise be passing on an indecipherable legacy, devoid of meaning. I am glad that I took this task upon myself, for in not just copying out the words, as María and I had done before, but in struggling to convey their message in another language, the pages became part of who I am. Thus, it is as though I have lived two lives, my own, and that of a woman so long ago. What she felt, I felt, and from how she endured, I perceived how to endure.

So these words from our past I bequeath to you, my child. My life has not been an easy one, but I somehow find a strange solace in knowing that so it has always been. A woman lives her life subject to the whims of God and men. But there are rewards, too, and you are one of my most precious. I hope that your trials are not many, and that you find strength in what you read here.

Your loving grandmother,
Dolores Martín Luengo
1844

52

Lizzie

To my darling Jenny, and to those who will read this letter after you,

I have given you a hard task in handing over these papers to you. I know from experience. It's not easy keeping a secret. Sometimes the temptation to tell was so powerful I could barely stand it. But I made a solemn vow, and I didn't want to risk retribution by breaking it. If you find you have to talk about it, you can always tell your old grandma, can't you, even after I'm gone?

As the others have done, I thought I'd add a little something of my own here, to be passed along with the papers. I fancy the idea of knowing someone else will be reading my words long after I'm gone. What I have to say won't be that interesting, but people being the curious creatures they are, I imagine they'll read it right through.

Everybody always thinks that just because a person has been around awhile, they have a store of wisdom hiding inside, just itching to get out. Sorry, but that's not the case here. Some of what I write here, you'll already *know, Jenny, but I'm putting it in just the same, for those who will come after you.*

I've always pretty much liked to share my every thought, which is why telling no one about these papers has been a heavy burden. I never could keep from chattering away, especially to my mama. She'd be bone tired at the end of the day, and I knew she longed to go to bed, but she was almost always patient, even if it was in a pained kind of way. She'd at least pretend she was listening, while she'd be finishing up some last chore. That last bit of darning could have waited till the morning, but since I kept on talking, she'd always find something to keep her hands busy, since her ears had to be. Guess she always hoped to get a head start on the next day, as though a woman doesn't always have a never-ending supply of something that needs doing. Sometimes I even felt sorry for Mama. She was so tired, but I just couldn't help myself. It seemed like the day just wasn't real, didn't count, till I'd had the chance to tell her all its highs and lows.

Even after I was a grown and married woman and my grandma Dolores had passed to the other side, I kept on telling Mama all about my day, because by then I had received the papers from grandma and had taken on the secret that she left for me. Maybe at that point I was trying to make up for the guilt I felt at not telling Mama about the papers. Maybe, if I just told her everything else, the sheer weight of trifles could outweigh that one big, important secret.

I didn't get my chatty nature from Mama. No, she was more tight-lipped than a child caught stealing. She talked, but hardly ever about herself. Even if we asked her a direct question about her past, she'd usually give

317

only some answer that never satisfied. For a long time I thought it was just lack of something interesting to tell, but later I figured maybe it was something else. After I'd seen my share of this life, and Mama was long gone, too late to search out the answer in her eyes, I puzzled it out that maybe Mama had too much to tell. Maybe there was something sorry there. Maybe she was afraid that once she started, she wouldn't be able to stop, and whatever it was would come out like a beast and devour her. Maybe that was it, but I'll never know, because Mama wouldn't tell.

I have the opposite view of things. I reckon that if you don't let out those things that are hurting you, that they'll just take deeper root and grow and grow inside you like an oak, until you are nothing but a hard old trunk. Still, Mama did manage to move her branches to us children when a wind came upon us. Happiness and song still nested in her boughs.

Jenny (and all of you whose names I'll know only from looking down from heaven), I hope you find something that helps you in these papers. What I found comforted me was knowing I had some different kind of people inside me, people I never could have dreamed up. It kind of made me feel better about something Mama used to say about me. I was always good at seeing things from somebody else's point of view, and Mama thought that I must not have a very strong character, since I was so easily influenced by other people's ways. I worried about that for a long time, but I've come to think that it's not so bad to see things from behind other folks' eyes. Oftentimes it helps them, and what else are we put on this good green earth for, if not that?

I hope you will treasure Juliana's words. I love knowing so much about someone who lived so long ago, and without whom we would not be here. How could such a woman have had a daughter like Mercedes, though, who defied her own mother and made things harder for all of us than they were ever meant to be? Still, growing up without knowing there was a mother loving you might do a certain damage to a soul.

Well, my hands are starting to give me fits, and my eyes aren't doing well either, so I guess I'll say my one last thing. My life hasn't been much different from most folks like me. In fact, for my first thirty-seven years, I figured I was pretty blessed, or at least lucky, one of the two. I often wondered why God let me off the hook so easily. Sometimes I felt like I should creep around, lest He see me and remember that He'd forgotten to let me suffer some. Well, I guess I didn't have to worry, because He remembered me, all right.

My hardship came right at the end of the War Between the States. And who could I have been to be left untouched? You might think that being here in St. Louis we didn't have things so bad, but you'd be wrong. See, we didn't rightly know if we were North or South, so we couldn't even pull together. My own sympathies were for the North, of course, never having owned slaves in my life, nor seeing the right of it. All my children felt like I did, my never having been one to keep that type of thing to myself, especially if I felt I was in the right. My twin boys both went off to war when they were seventeen, and at least they both fought for the right side. That was something to be thankful for, since it was not uncommon here in Missouri for two brothers to take up arms against each other. It was

*as though those boys wished to aim their rifles at each
other's hearts.*

*My boys went off together, but they never came back.
In some ways, you could even say I was lucky I got the
word. Lots of folks just waited and waited for their
sons to come home. But what's better: giving up hope
little by little, or all at once? I don't know. Thank God
I had your mama, or I don't know how I'd have gotten
through. Even now, after all these years, I have some
mighty dark days.*

*Once again, Jenny, I'm begging your pardon for giving
you the hardship of the promise you've made to keep
silent about this amazing gift. I believe you'll get
something from it, though. At least you know you're
one in a line of women, all of whom have been or will
be a part of you. I've been finding contentment in just
that, now that I figure I'm about to meet up with some
of them. Remember, we're all always there for you,
even if you don't know each one's particulars. We're
all there, that line of women, stronger than any army
men can dream.*

Your grandmother,
Lizzie Bates Compton
1881

53

Jenny

My dearest granddaughter,

First, I thank you for fulfilling your oath, as I know you will do. I would not have chosen you had I not been certain of this. Second, I want to tell you that I am sorry for requiring the secrecy that was demanded of me. Believe me, I know what it was and will be like for you, as did my grandmother before me. You will long to share what you learn from these papers, but your sacred oath forbids that. I want you to know that I chose you not only because of my confidence in your strength, but also because I love you so very much.

These letters and diary are your heritage, a heritage the meaning of which you may spend years trying to decipher. Indeed, as I have reread them at different points in my life, I have taken away something different each time, since as we get older our experiences constantly remake who we are. Remember this my dearest, dearest child: the papers form a link with the past, with the life, with the innermost thoughts of another woman who lived centuries ago, and with those who came after her. Consider the possibility that perhaps the link itself, even devoid of its own particular content, is worth some of the anguish of keeping the secret.

I could say much more to you, my darling, of the love I feel for you, and of what you might feel over the years, after you have read the diary and letters. But I do not think that is the intention of the writers. I believe that each woman is meant to experience the papers in her own world, though their worlds may have few similar circumstances. I am grateful to all of the women in this unbroken line, that they have carried the message for us, that they have not let our link be severed.

Some of the letter-holders have given some details of their own. I find that I haven't the heart to review my life here. You will know many of the important things about me from your mother. When I look back, I find that the milestones have to do with my children. I suppose that's true of most women.

Of my husband I will say that a marriage that started with love ended with emptiness and recriminations. I don't know whether that would have happened if we hadn't lost our only son on the fields of France during the Great War. One tells oneself that one must take joy in one's remaining children, but their presence sometimes seems to be only a reminder of the absence of the one you have lost. Perhaps that is why I was able to love you so much, because I saw nothing in you of your uncle.

I hope that you never live through a war like we did, though the news from Germany seems every day more concerning. I wish you an easier life, as I suppose every generation wishes for those who come after, but I don't have much confidence that it will be. Although outsiders may rank the sorrows and problems of others as lesser or greater, when they are yours you will suffer, even though they may not have the weight of others' difficulties. Still, as we know from Juliana and those who have come after her, women endure.

Enough of that. I just ask you to remember how I loved you, how we shared those quiet moments together that were so precious to an old woman who otherwise could only have lost herself in painful memories.

Your loving friend,
Grandma Jenny
May 10, 1936

54

RACHEL

All of this was too overwhelming. I would have a lifetime to reread each letter, to think about what it meant, to try to imagine what it must have been like to live through each writer's experiences. But for now I was caught in wondering about their connection to me. This last was a letter signed by a Grandma Jenny, and she would have been of an age to be my mother's grandmother. But Helen never talked about a Grandma Jenny. Could Jenny be Grandma Scottie's first name? According to the records I'd found, her first name was Janet, not Jenny or Jennifer.

I pulled out the baby book that I had bought, since Ned and I weren't having much luck agreeing on a girl's name for our child. The book not only listed names but gave their meanings, their histories, and even their popularity. I looked up Janet. In Scotland, Jess and Jenny were common pet forms of the name Janet. Janet Maude Scott's father was born in Scotland. Jenny was Janet Maude Scott Meades, born in 1866, my great-grandmother.

55

RACHEL

I went back to my desk and frantically searched through all of the papers I had spread out. I knew that I hadn't missed another letter, but how could Helen not have left anything of her own like all of the other women had done? Had she been taken too soon? Was that why she said she had failed Juliana?

Then it hit me. Of course there would be no letter—not for me, anyway. My mother was supposed to give the papers to her granddaughter, and she didn't have one. She had left the package as a contingency, in case something unexpected happened, but maybe she was waiting to write her letter. She was only seventy-two. Maybe she hadn't wanted to think about her own mortality just yet.

But how could a promise she had made to keep a secret seem so important that she couldn't share it with me, or even with Gabe, since it didn't seem like she was going to get a granddaughter? I could feel myself reconstructing between us the defensive wall that I'd had recourse to over the years, when I'd sensed that she was holding something back from me and I had not reached out, knowing that I would be rebuffed. Even in death, I had to make myself angry with my mother in order not to be hurt by her.

The next morning, I decided that I had to do something more than just keep running everything through my head over and over. I would go see my cousin Carol again. I called her to ask whether I could come over after my classes that day, and she said that yes, she'd make a point to be home by then.

I taught my classes mechanically. Sometimes I wonder whether the students have any idea of how much preparation and effort I put into my lessons, but on that day, I would certainly have forgiven them if they had thought I wasn't even paying attention myself.

When I got to Carol's and she and I sat down with a soda, I didn't know what to say. Usually I rehearse difficult conversations beforehand, but I hadn't even come up with a way to begin.

"Are you all right, Rachel? You look so tired—haunted or something." That seemed like a strange, though perceptive, thing to say. I just looked at her, not knowing where to start. She must have taken my silence to mean she had overstepped, because she started again.

"Are you having any luck with the family-tree project?"

"A little, but it hasn't given me all the answers," I said.

"What kind of answers?"

"It's just that I was hoping to find an explanation."

"For what?" asked Carol.

Finally I decided just to go ahead and ask what I assumed would be a fruitless question. "Carol, have you ever heard anything about some secret papers in our family?"

Carol took a drink of her soda, then slowly and deliberately put the can back on the coffee table and said, "Yes."

"Yes?"

"Yes. Wait here a sec, Rachel."

"Wait here for what?"

"Please, Rach."

After a few minutes, Carol came back to the room, holding an envelope. I got up and grabbed it from her hand, recognizing my mother's handwriting: "To be given only to the granddaughter of Helen Jordan Pearson when she reaches the age of fifteen. Not to be opened by anyone else."

I fell back onto the sofa. "What does this mean?"

"Rachel, I'm sorry, but I don't know . . . I found it in my mom's stuff after she died last year. I just really didn't know what to do. After all, my mom had apparently kept this letter for Aunt Helen, and I didn't feel ready to go against the instructions on the envelope. When you came over the last time, I almost told you about it, especially when you started asking me what I remembered of our family background, and whether there were any old papers. It all seemed so weird, and it was still so close to when Aunt Helen died, and why wouldn't she have addressed it to you? And then when you said you were pregnant . . ."

"You were going to wait years and years to maybe be able to give it to my child, who might be a daughter?" I couldn't control my voice anymore, and I didn't want to.

"Yes. No. I don't know. I'm so sorry, Rachel. I'm just so sorry."

"I can't believe you kept this from me!" I turned and walked out of Carol's house.

I probably shouldn't have driven in the condition I was in, but I did. I knew that Ned was working late and that Gabe had track practice, so I'd have the house to myself. I went into my home office and closed the door. I opened the letter that was not addressed to me.

56

Helen

St. Louis, 1990

To my dearest granddaughter,

I've entrusted this letter to my beloved sister, Sandy.
It's my safeguard, in case I should pass away before
you are born. I've asked Sandy to keep it for me until I
ask for it, which would be when you are fifteen years
old. If Sandy survives me, she or her daughter Carol
will hopefully follow the instructions on the envelope. I
haven't left this letter for your mother, because I don't
want her to know that I've kept a secret from her for
her whole life. This has been harder than you can
imagine for me, and at times I felt myself pulling away
from her, afraid I'd be tempted to reveal too much.

I have, over the course of my life, asked myself why I
have adhered so strictly to the vow I made to my
grandma Jenny to keep the letters secret from everyone
except my own granddaughter. It was a promise not
only to my grandma, but to God. Still, in my
adulthood, I have not been a very religious person. I
believe that part of me felt that I had no right to go
against this contrived tradition, for in a way it would

be betraying all of the women who kept the promise, to make light of the sacrifices they had made to maintain their silence. Who was I to so arrogantly disregard the strictures they had lived up to? Now that I have reached the age of seventy and still have no granddaughter, I question my decision.

In those first years, I maintained my silence equally from my love of my grandma and from a vague fear of some dire consequence. By the time I became a woman, it was habit and almost seemed a part of who I was. If I gave away this secret, was I giving away part of myself? When I married, I didn't tell your grandpa Daniel right away, and then, as time went on, I felt it would be too hurtful to all of a sudden tell him I'd been keeping secrets from him. As your mother grew, I longed to tell her, but how could I? Then both of us would have a secret from Daniel, and I couldn't do that to either of them. When Daniel died, Rachel took it so hard and was angry with me for a long time, because she had missed the last few moments with her dad. I was afraid of what it would do to our fragile relationship to tell her that I had kept something from Daniel for our entire married life.

I've always treasured the feeling of having been chosen as one more link in a chain of connection going back over three hundred years, to the first time Juliana wrote down her thoughts in a notebook. Even more amazing, I am only the sixth in this line: Mercedes, Luz, Dolores, Lizzie, Jenny, me. When I think of all that has happened in the world in that time, of all of the miles traveled, of all of the joys and sorrows, it's almost beyond comprehension. And yet, because of the faithfulness of this handful of women, we know something of the life of a woman who lived so long ago. We are a part of all of them, our foremothers.

Sometimes I wonder whether Mercedes's plan to dilute the message of her mother's life worked instead to preserve it. Maybe the very secrecy and conditions that Mercedes demanded instilled in each of us the realization of a great responsibility, that without us, the papers would be lost forever.

Having said this, I'm not going to ask you to keep the secret. I wouldn't be unhappy to think that my Rachel would, after all, know why at times I seemed to pull back. I would love for her to share in the revelations here. Maybe you will want to show your brother, my dearest Gabe, too. My sister, Sandy, and your cousin Carol might also be included. After all, was there really any reason that our grandma chose me, instead of Sandy? I guess that I'm a coward, not having shared the writings myself, but encouraging you to do so. Still, I am breaking half my promise by not asking for your secrecy.

Please don't judge me harshly for keeping silent. I know that nowadays being open with thoughts and feelings is admired more than it ever was when I was young. Still, I hope you'll find what you inherit worth knowing, our family's line for centuries, and the lives of women who, like us, had some choices in life but also found themselves in circumstances that augmented or deformed them.

I'd also like to tell you a little something of myself, as other secret holders have done. I always loved my grandma Jenny. She would come to stay with us in the city in winter but in summer returned to her home in the country, so that she could be close to the place *where her husband had been buried, long before I was born. She used to let me brush her silver, silken hair, and try to put the tortoiseshell combs in it. I'm sure I often hurt her head, but she never complained.*

It was Grandma Jenny who taught me to love books. When my mom had scolded me for something, she would often then take pity on me and suggest that I might want to look for Grandma. I'd knock on Grandma's door, and she would usher me in, book already in hand, and we would escape. Perhaps she wasn't just introducing me to her favorite world. Perhaps she was also preparing me for the gift that she had very early on decided it would be my privilege to receive.

As the years passed, Grandma started to stay with us year-round, as even she admitted that her home in the country was too isolated. On my eighteenth birthday, in that hours-long lull between receiving everyone's morning good wishes and the evening's special supper and cake, Grandma asked me to join her in her room. As I had grown and no longer needed her to read to me, I had still spent many happy hours with her over the years, sometimes just talking, sometimes reading over letters that she kept in a large box under her bed. She would show me the old stamps and stationery, and also explain who the writers were and what relationship they bore to our family. She would read short excerpts from some, but only passages she thought would be of interest to me. Most of the letters were from friends and older relatives of hers already gone, and contained only the most superficial news, such as do most letters, which convey nothing of universal significance but somehow manage to give the recipient a general feeling of care and love.

Seated there in her old wicker rocker, Grandma asked me to get the box out. We had been through the letters so many times over the years, and I didn't really want to spend time on my birthday to look at them again, but I handed it to her. Grandma took out all of the letters, put them on the edge of her bed, and, with some difficulty, removed the bottom of the box. The "bottom" she had taken out, which I had seen countless times, with the old-fashioned Valentine's card pasted onto it, was false.

Grandma removed a fat, yarn-tied envelope, which had lain hidden beneath the smiling Cupid. I knew that here was something I'd never seen before. Grandma didn't open it, though, but leaned against the headboard of the bed, resting for a minute.

"These papers have never been seen by anyone else alive," she finally said. "No one, not even your mother, so much as knows of their existence."

I asked her if she had written them, and she just smiled and replied softly, "Only the newest one."

"You must keep these papers safe, and hidden. No one must know about them, not even your mother and father. After I am gone, you must open them up and read everything. Then you will know what to do. You must swear to do what I have told you."

"Yes, Grandma, but . . . I don't understand. Why must I keep it secret, and what if I can't?"

"Just remember that I was able to keep the secret, and that other girls and women long before us kept it also."

Somehow the intensity of Grandma's gaze, usually so soft and loving, compelled me to nod my head and

mutter, "I promise. Yes, Grandma, I swear," not at all
sure that I could be true to my word.

But I was. At first it was so hard, especially when
Grandma died a few days later. I read the diary and
letters, and for several days I barely spoke, which had
my parents really worried. I was so afraid of telling the
secret, I kept quiet. There was something else, though,
too. I was angry with Grandma. I was angry that she
had asked me to do something that seemed so hard.
Even now, it seems cruel, and it makes me feel bad to
say that, especially in light of the hardships she had in
life.

I've often speculated about why Grandma chose me.
Was it something she noticed in my personality that
made her deem me worthy? Or was it the background
she had given me? Or was it simply the convenience,
since she lived with us? I suppose it could have just
been chance that linked me to several other young
women who had been entrusted with some papers that
would confer on them, then and there, one last task in
life.

In reading over what I've written here, I see that I've
told you little of my life beyond the papers. If I'm gone
before I can share something of myself, you'll learn
about me from Rachel. Yet there is something that no
one else knows, and I want to share it with you, a
secret piece of myself to pass on. I loved a man before I
met your grandpa. The man's name was David.

Like so many young men at the time, David joined up
after Pearl Harbor. He was killed six months later. His
mother came and told me a few weeks after she got the
telegram. She apologized that she had not come sooner,
but said she had been unable to talk about it. I

remember thinking that I could easily forgive her, since it had given me that extra time of believing David was alive.

I found out later that he had died in the battle of the Coral Sea, on the USS Lexington, an aircraft carrier. I also learned that most of the crew were rescued. In war, you know that you may lose a loved one, that his chances are no better or worse than those of anyone else. But when I learned that most of the crew had been rescued, I questioned why he hadn't been spared. Why did he have to die in a place I had to look for on a map?

I met your wonderful grandfather in 1949. I never did tell him about David. If I wronged him in that, he never knew. You'll already know a lot about Daniel from your mother, who loved him deeply, as I did. You'll know that he was also taken from me at a relatively young age, and for a while I cursed God for choosing me for pain again. Now I believe that He didn't choose me. He doesn't catalog our sorrows.

It's still my hope that I will know you, but I've written this letter just in case. Because you are my daughter's daughter, I already love you.

Your grandmother,
Helen Jordan Pearson
October 2, 1990

57

RACHEL

I heard Gabe come in and call me, but I didn't respond. I didn't know how long I'd been sitting there, my feelings numbed, my mind running in circles. I'd thought I wanted to know the full truth, but now that I had it, I didn't know what to do with it. I couldn't even come up with how I was "supposed" to feel: duped by my mother or consoled because there was a reason for her aloofness? And why had she left the papers, all but this, in her house, where I was sure to be the one to find them if something happened to her? Another mystery I would never solve, another missing piece of the puzzle that was my mother.

Abandoned. Yes, that was what I was feeling.

I got up and went out to Gabe, whom, despite all her shows of affection, my mother had also scorned.

The next few days, it was as though I were on autopilot. I taught my classes, went to my office hours, bought groceries, ate with Ned and Gabe, but I wasn't really present. Ned kept asking me what the matter was, but I couldn't give him an answer. Part of me resented him for not having figured out sooner that something was really going on with me. I was hurt that he didn't press me harder to find out what it was, even as I pushed him away.

Besides, I couldn't tell him everything then. It would have required more than I had in me, and I didn't know how to articulate what I was experiencing. I had found these amazing papers. I had been betrayed by my mother and cousin. I had not been honest with my husband and my son.

I should have felt more of a connection to Helen, but instead I didn't feel connected to anyone. It seemed like I should do something, but I didn't know what. Finally, something I had read in one of the letters made me go looking in the place where I had stashed everything. It was in Dolores's letter. She had given copies of the papers to her twin sister, María, who had stayed in Santa Fe, as far as I could tell. Here was something I could do. I could go to Santa Fe and see if I could find any trace of María's descendants, to find the woman who also knew of our Juliana. I knew it was a long shot, but it gave me a reprieve from facing my own deceptions.

"Ned, I want to talk to you about something."

"What is it?" He was only half listening, and it annoyed me that he hadn't looked away from the basketball game on TV.

"I wondered if you and Gabe could do without me for a couple of weeks."

"What do you mean?" Now I had his attention, and I rushed into my well-rehearsed explanation.

"Just that. Gabe's used to spending time by himself when you're at the hospital and I'm at the university. You could scrounge up your dinners or go out. The only real problem is laundry, and I thought I could teach Gabe how to do it, even pay him a little something. It's time he learned anyway."

"Yeah, I guess we could manage, but where are you going?" I heard surprise and some hurt in Ned's tone.

"You know that article I've been working on, about the Mexican playwright Hernández?" Ned didn't immediately register recognition, and it was no wonder. This wasn't really an article I had been actively working on, but one that I had started, then put aside about a year ago. I had turned my attention to another Latin American dramatist, and all of my research time before my mother's accident had gone to that project.

"Well, through various sources," I continued, "I've found out that there are a number of books at the University of New Mexico that would be essential for my research. Some of the original manuscripts are kept there, and apparently Hernández made a number of explanatory notes that aren't in the published editions."

"But I thought you're always saying that the work should stand on its own, without any need of explanation from the author."

"I know. I have. But the notes may help me to see something in the text that I've missed." I knew this was contradictory, so I quickly continued, "Besides, I have to at least show in the article that I'm aware of them, or I'll be open to criticism. UNM also has some foreign journals that we don't have available here."

"But couldn't you get them on some kind of interlibrary loan?"

"No. The manuscripts they have are originals. They're not going to let those leave the library, much less travel halfway across the country. I really need to go, Ned. You know I'll be coming up before the tenure committee next year, and this article is one that is really critical if I'm to have a good chance. It has to be well received, and to ensure that, I have to be thorough."

"Okay. I guess we can be a couple of bachelors for a while. I'll miss you, though. Try not to be away any longer than you have to."

I relaxed but felt guilty as I kissed Ned. "I'll try not to be gone too long. I'll miss you, too."

I lay awake for several hours that night, reassuring myself that everything I'd said to Ned was true. Of course, I hadn't realized before that a visit to Albuquerque would be so crucial once I had returned to the Hernández article. I'd thought that I might ask a former student, who was doing graduate work there, to look into the materials and maybe send copies of things that might be useful, but now I could do a more thorough job and wouldn't have to impose on anyone else. Of course, all of this was a cover for my real reason for going to New Mexico: to see what I could find out about María's family.

Just before seven thirty, I looked over at the clock and turned off the alarm. Ned didn't have to be at the hospital till later that morning, and I quietly got ready and left for my nine o'clock Beginning Spanish class.

After class, I went to the chairman's office to perform the disagreeable task of getting his approval for my trip. In addition to everything else, I'd been working to get students' papers graded and to calculate their grades for the end of the quarter. One of the weeks I wanted off would be the end of the quarter break, but I needed permission to get someone else to cover my classes for the first week of the following quarter. I hoped I could find what I was looking for in two weeks. Neither the chairman nor my family would be very happy if it took any longer.

As I entered his office, the chairman seemed rather preoccupied with some books and papers he had spread on his desk. While he had long ago achieved tenure, he still published articles with a studied regularity, sometimes to the detriment of his department and his students.

"Yes, Rachel. What can I do for you?" he asked, his tone implying much less friendliness than his words.

I told him about my plan to go to the University of New Mexico and do some research for an article. He seemed surprised.

"I think that's a good idea. You know that I have always encouraged women faculty to travel for research." His next sentence immediately contradicted that claim. "Are you sure your family can spare you?"

I answered in an even tone, used to this kind of question, which would never have been put to my male colleagues. I couldn't help but think that if he himself had been more attentive to his own family's needs, his wife might not have left him two years earlier.

"I have that all worked out, thank you."

"Well, if Ned needs any advice, have him give me a call. I've got this kind of thing down to a science now."

"I'm sure."

The next quarter, I was supposed to teach the class on Latin American novels. Now all I had to do was ask Lorraine to cover for that. I could get a grad student to do my language classes for a week. Lorraine and I usually met for lunch in the cafeteria, next door to our building. I didn't see her at first, so I got myself a sandwich and sat at one of the small tables. I wasn't worried about asking her for this favor. Apart from being my friend, she enjoyed the challenge of doing a couple of classes in an area other than her usual field, nineteenth-century Spanish lit. She was certainly capable of it, since all doctoral candidates had to pass exams on all areas of Hispanic letters and kept up at least a semi-active interest in the other specialties.

"You're going where? To do what?"

"Don't give me a hard time, Lorraine, please. I need you to do this for me."

"Teach your Latin American Novels class."

"Yes, please, Lorraine! I've done all the prep, so you shouldn't have to do much work, other than just teach the class."

She looked at me skeptically but agreed. "Okay, sure. But when did you decide you needed to go to UNM? You've done lots of articles before without gallivanting all over."

"I know, but this one is different. Besides, I need to get away for a while. Be by myself."

"I hear you. I never could understand how you married people get anything done. I mean, how do you think with all those people around?"

"All those people? Lorraine, it's just Ned and Gabe."

"I know, but still. Of course, I'm not saying that if Mr. Wonderful appeared right now to sweep me off my feet, I'd turn him down. I'd just make it clear that I need a lot of private time."

"Good luck with that!"

"Speaking of Ned and Gabe, how are they going to manage without you?"

"Not you, too! I just got through explaining to the chair that they'll do just fine, thank you very much."

"Great! That means that you can go with me to those meetings in New Orleans next fall."

She had me, she knew it, and she walked away in triumph. "See you later, Lorraine!" I called to her retreating figure. "And thanks for taking my class!" She just waved, without looking back.

58

RACHEL

I concentrated on relaxing as the plane began to taxi down the runway, gathering speed for takeoff. During childbirth classes many years before, I had made the invaluable discovery that relaxation is something you can teach yourself. I willed my stomach to be still. It wasn't that I was afraid of flying; I simply didn't like to be airsick. The bouncing of the plane often made me ill if I didn't go through the ritual of concentrated calm.

I tried not to think in precise terms of what it was I was doing. Much of my resolve rested on the obscure possibility of finding some very distant cousins, and I had so little to go on. Dolores's twin was named María. Dolores had signed her letter "Dolores Martín Luengo." I assumed that at that time, she and her sister had followed the system of using your father's family name, then your mother's, and of not changing your name when you married. So I would be looking for María Martín Luengo in Santa Fe. Dolores had written her letter in 1844, and she was already a grandmother, so that gave me a rough time frame for María, too. I considered myself good at research, but not this kind of research. Given that I had so little to go on, this was more like divination.

I leaned back in the seat, pulled out the magazine from the pocket in front of me, and settled in to work on the crossword puzzle. As I filled in the white squares among the black, my concentration deepened, as though filling in all of the spaces would be an omen from some unknown power. I had most of the puzzle completed but was stuck on one long word. The adjacent words indicated that the last three letters were *ion*. "Period of time." The obvious answers surfaced first. Minute, hour, day, month, year, decade, century. But none of these ended in *ion*, and none of them had enough letters. I counted the staring boxes. Ten. I sipped the juice the steward had brought, and stretched my perspective. Span, season, era, epoch, eon, interim. I stared out at the clouds below. Several possibilities ended in the correct letters. Duration, intermission, dimension. Across the aisle, a little girl was telling her mother that her ears hurt, and her mother told her to open her mouth very wide and try to yawn. "It worked, Grandma," she told the woman on the other side of her. Trifling as it seemed, I envied that girl, flanked by mother and grandmother, surrounded by the protection of their love. That was it: *generation*.

Filling in my discovery, I found that the surrounding words were suddenly clear, the long word having supplied the clues I needed. I closed the magazine and returned it to the pocket, glancing at my watch. The time had passed more quickly than I had realized. My mind must have wandered as I was contemplating the puzzle. I leaned back, focusing on the relaxation I needed for the landing.

I was glad to be arriving while there was still light. We were approaching the Albuquerque airport. I looked out the window and saw the dry terrain and the hills in the distance, turned golden rose by the setting sun. So different from home.

I'd taken a room at a hotel near UNM. I checked in, then called to tell Gabe and Ned that I'd arrived and that I missed them already.

59

RACHEL

I found the library for the humanities and was there when it opened at nine o'clock. The white plaster walls became adobe in my midwesterner's mind. The wooden beams and murals on the walls provided a very different atmosphere from my own university's library. It was appealing and inviting. As a teacher, I am to be a lover of learning, and a library is a source of knowledge, catalogued and compartmentalized for us, there for the taking or the borrowing. The library can open the doors to unimagined journeys of the mind. I had always loved the quote from philosopher Daniel Dennett: "A scholar is just a library's way of making another library."

My research on Hernández, the purported reason for my journey to New Mexico, went well. The library really did house some original manuscripts. I thought that the marginal notes supported my theory that Hernández's interest in Mexican identity was at least as important to her as her desire to portray what it meant to be a woman. Many male critics had written off Hernández as a playwright beneath their level of study, because she examines what it is to be a woman in her society. By emphasizing her interest in the meaning of being Mexican, I was hoping to bring about further discussion of her works. Comparing her with such writers as Octavio Paz or Carlos Fuentes, I hoped to reintroduce her to male scholars.

I knew that some of my women colleagues would feel that this approach was a betrayal of Hernández's sincere exploration of her female identity, and would say that the study of women writers was better left to women, who can more readily understand their concerns. But this seems shortsighted and restrictive. We would never tolerate our exclusion from the study of male authors. Nor will I accept the excuse of male critics and teachers who shy away from women writers, saying that they feel unempathetic to their themes.

Having concluded my scholarly research, I could procrastinate no longer. I realized that looking for María would be even more difficult than looking into my own ancestry, and I also kept coming up against the fact that I hadn't been able to go back any further than the second half of the nineteenth century. For this search, I would have to start with María, who I believed had been born in the early nineteenth, or even the late eighteenth, century. Would the records even exist going back that far? I would go to Santa Fe and start what I hoped wouldn't be a fruitless search.

When I checked out of my Albuquerque hotel, the chatty desk clerk asked where I was headed next. When I told her, she insisted that I should take 14 and go the Turquoise Trail, rather than just drive up 25, as most people did. The Turquoise Trail could take me half a day if I stopped at some of the scenic spots along the way, as she recommended, rather than just the trip of a little over an hour on the shorter route, but she assured me that I wouldn't regret it. I decided to follow her advice and got out my New Mexico map to make sure I knew how to go.

New Mexico's license plates say LAND OF ENCHANTMENT, and I had always been a little cynical about that title, but even from the outskirts of Albuquerque, I found that I agreed with that moniker. At home I loved the green of the trees in summer and dreaded the gray of winter. Here, the desert colors of copper, sienna, and umber lent the landscape a dreamlike beauty. I felt like I could be two places at once, gazing into the distance, where rain moved across a mesa miles away, while I was in sunshine.

I decided not to take the side trip to Sandia Peak. I'd heard that at well over ten thousand feet in altitude, it didn't always provide a clear view, as the peak could be shrouded in clouds. Besides, though I had decided to take the less direct route, I did still feel some urgency now that I was getting closer to starting my search for María. As I drove on, there was a sign for a town called Madrid, and it seemed somehow more than serendipitous. As I continued along the road, nearing Santa Fe, another sign announced El Camino Real de Adentro National Park. Dolores, María's twin, had mentioned in her letter that her parents had traveled from Mexico City to Santa Fe via El Camino Real de Adentro. I was journeying in the land traversed by Juliana's descendants.

After checking into a hotel in Santa Fe, I wandered along the streets of the historic plaza. I went into a T-shirt shop and bought shirts for Ned and Gabe. Perhaps I was trying to allay my guilty feelings for leaving them, for keeping them in the dark, for not missing them enough.

The beautiful old buildings of the city exuded a sense of history and invited fantasies of being another person in another time. After dinner, I decided to attend a ghost tour that evening. The guide took us on a fascinating excursion, bringing alive those from the past whom one could never know. I didn't really need that reminder, though—there were voices that haunted me already. I was alone with other women's memories.

The next morning, I made my way to the Santa Fe County Clerk's office. When I got to the front of the line and told them what I was trying to do, I got a skeptical look and directions to the room with the microfilm. The clerk, Frank, told me that it would be a painstaking search, since the records had simply been photographed, then put on the microfilm. The records from that time were often baptismal records. There was little categorization, other than into twenty-year periods. I settled in with the first box he directed me to and started to work.

Dolores had written her letter in 1844 and at that time already had a granddaughter who was sixteen years old. I decided to start my search for Dolores's and María's birth records around 1780. Of course, Dolores and her own daughter could have gotten married and had children at a very young age, so Dolores and María could have been born as late as, say, 1798. I was at first pleasantly surprised that there were, in fact, some records of births from as far back as the period I had guessed would be the appropriate time, but the tedium set in before long.

Late that afternoon I found María Martín Luengo. Her mother was listed as Sofía Luengo de Porres, and her father as Juan Martín Morales. Dolores's grandmother had signed her letter as Luz de Porres Yañez. This had to be my María, born July 3, 1795, baptized July 5.

My elation began to wane as I realized that finding the record of María's birth proved only that she existed, and I had already ceased to doubt the authenticity of the papers. What drove me now was a desire to share the reality with another woman of Juliana's line.

Again I was faced with the difficulty of trying to go forward in official records. I had found a record of María's birth and baptism, which had her parents' names, but of course there was no indication of who came after her. Would I need to search through the records for a child whose mother was listed as María?

I went back to the clerk. Things were pretty dead in the microfilm room, and I noticed that he was reading what looked like a history book. I asked whether he was studying history, and he said that he was a grad student in history at UNM, and drove up twice a week to Santa Fe to work in the records office to make some extra money. I told him my dilemma, and he seemed glad of the diversion.

"I'd suggest looking through the marriage licenses as the next step, although that would assume she got married. Then, once you found that and had her husband's name, you could also look for land deed transfers, and that should tell you about children they had, too, probably just the boys, though. That could get tricky, anyway, since for this period they would initially be under Mexican rule, and some of those records are in Mexico City. After the Treaty of Guadalupe Hidalgo in 1848, when Mexico ceded this area to the United States, the original landowners were supposed to be able to keep their land, though that didn't always happen. I don't know—it might be just as easy to go through looking for births with her as the mother."

I had known this wouldn't be easy, but this was discouraging. I couldn't stay there indefinitely.

"Do you know anyone I could hire over the next few days to help me look?" I asked, doubting that would be possible.

"Well, I could do some hours, and maybe some of the other grad students I know would be willing to help."

I latched on to the idea before he could change his mind. I gave him the number at my hotel, and we agreed to meet at the office the next day at nine o'clock.

The next few days were a roller coaster of hopeful hints and devastating dead ends. But in the end, with the help of Frank and some of his friends, I found a family I believed to be the descendants of María. I didn't know what degree of cousins they would be, and I didn't care. I just hoped someone in the family had papers passed down from María, copies of the pages passed down to me from Dolores, papers that included a copy of Juliana's diary.

I felt as if somehow Juliana and all those women in between were looking down and smiling. Some of María's descendants were living in Albuquerque.

60

RACHEL

I called an Elena Ríos. I didn't know whether she would be the right generation to have received the papers, or even the right line of the family after so many generations. The odds that she would be the correct person to know about the papers were very low, and I would be revealing the secret. Still, I had to know. After all, I was also the wrong person to have possession of the papers, and I had experienced many feelings and phases as I read through them, but even after reading Mercedes's letter demanding secrecy, I hadn't ever felt guilt. I assumed that I would have to make a lot of calls before I found the right person, and that I might never be successful. I guess I was hoping that the people I called would tell their extended families about the crazy lady who had called, and that my story would finally ring true to someone.

So I was astonished when Elena immediately knew what I was talking about. I had somehow managed to find the keeper of the papers on my first call! To Elena, it seemed that the most incredible part was that I had put in the effort and had been able to track them down. She invited me to come for dinner the next night and said that she would invite a few other family members, too. She didn't seem to understand my surprise at this, but I wondered how she would explain to them who I was and how I had found them without revealing something of the secret of the papers.

The next evening, as I followed the directions Elena had given me over the phone, I found that I was rising into the foothills on the outskirts of Albuquerque. I parked beside a beautiful home. It didn't seem more than a couple of decades old, but it mimicked the architecture of the older Spanish buildings. I knocked.

"I'm coming!" I heard steps approach the door and felt someone regarding me through the peephole. A short woman about my age, with a round face, dark hair, and black eyes, emerged from the shadow of the opening door.

"Elena Ríos?"

"Rachel?"

As I nodded my head, she gathered me into the home. I could see from the entryway that there seemed to be a series of large, high-ceilinged rooms, all with windows on two sides, one looking out at the view of Albuquerque and the mesas in the distance, and one side opening onto a beautiful courtyard.

"I'm so glad to meet you! I can't tell you how excited my mama is. When I told her about the diary you found, she couldn't believe that it could be the original of the one we have. I guess you've figured out that the book we have from our ancestress María is a copy of the one given to her twin, Dolores, in the 1820s. So you have the original, from the seventeenth century? I can hardly believe it! Have you brought it with you? Could we see it now? But I'm not letting you say anything."

I could barely follow the torrent coming from Elena, and by the time she had finished, the room was filled with

351

women and men, girls and boys of all ages. I leaned in closer to Elena and spoke softly.

"But isn't this all supposed to be kept secret, passed on from grandmother to granddaughter? I must admit, though, that is not how I got the papers. I found them in my mother's things."

Elena furrowed her brow. "What do you mean? Oh, you can't be saying that your family has followed the mean-spirited directions given by Juliana's daughter, Mercedes? Mercedes, Mercies—if ever someone was misnamed!"

"Well, yes, my family has followed her instructions. I wouldn't even know about them if my mother hadn't died before I could give her a granddaughter."

Elena could see the stricken look on my face. "Oh, I'm sorry, I didn't mean to make light of the difficulties the women in your family must have had in keeping the secret. Maybe because María was never meant to have the papers, our family never took Mercedes's stricture seriously. We've always shared the papers with all of the family, girls and boys both. Considering the way the family has grown, this crowd here is only a small part of those of us who have read the papers."

Elena's family had prepared a most delicious meal, and everyone had questions for me to answer: about how I had found them here in New Mexico, how the papers had come to me, and how many of their extended family lived in Missouri. For them, there was no smothering secret, only their connection, to one another and to those who had gone before.

Elena's family, too, had written letters to add to Juliana's diary, though without the missing generations of my accounts. After her extended family had left, with hugs and promises to come the next day and tell more tales about their family, Elena and I stayed up late into the night. We wondered together at what Juliana's life was like before the rape. We imagined what it would be like to live in a convent and be besieged by doubts that would have been roundly condemned. We discussed whether Juliana's wish that her diary would one day find itself in a more just and tolerant time and place had come to pass. We, too, would send it into the future, and hope for a more perfect world.

We read each other's letters, pausing now and then to make a comment or ask a question. As she bent in concentration, I studied Elena's open face, so different from mine, yet across her nose and cheeks a sprinkling of freckles like my own. This kind woman and I would reunite our families, so long divided, now joined by Juliana.

EPILOGUE

RACHEL

St. Louis, Missouri, 2014

I am in my seventh decade, and even my discoveries are now long in the past. The original papers reside in the university library, along with a copy. My daughter, Julie, has a baby girl of her own, and Gabe a son and a daughter.

I stumbled onto a treasure that I know belongs to all of us, even though centuries of vows made by other women would have denied us that right. When I returned from New Mexico, I shared the gift of my past with Ned and Gabe. When Julie was old enough, I told her about the papers I'd discovered before she was born. I've used the papers to connect my daughter and my son to their heritage, so that they may know the strength of their foremothers and take courage from their lives. When they are old enough, my grandchildren will receive this legacy, whether or not I'm here to give it.

When I reflect on all that the letters have meant to me, I struggle to articulate their power. There is a longing to have known Juliana. How can I better imagine her life during the years-long periods of silence? How did she go from doubting novice to abbess? How could she bring herself to command her only child to leave her?

And the others—all the others who came after her. What joys and sorrows did life hold for each of them, outside their connection to the diary, and what did it mean to them? All of these women are now a part of me, a part I never suspected, never dreamed.

And for my mother herself: the explanations in her letter didn't satisfy. What did the diary and letters mean to her? How did they shape her? Why did she keep her vow, a trick on Juliana herself, who would have wanted each of us in the line to know her through her diary? I'd like to think that she came close to telling me, but that's just my wishful thinking. I'll never know my mother's yearnings.

But I am thankful. Like Juliana so long ago, I am more than I had believed. She and all the others have been resurrected. I even showed the papers to Lorraine, my closest friend. And who knows? She may be related to Juliana, too, somewhere along the line. Three centuries of descendants. We are vast and myriad.

ACKNOWLEDGMENTS

I am profoundly grateful to those who fostered in me a love of books, and who gave me the confidence to write and to put my novel out into the world. Thank you to all of you!

The Tuesdays at Two group accepted my writing and helped me learn that given a deadline I could come up with something new every two weeks, even with a writing prompt like "fond." I'm so glad you invited me, Vicki Stadelman.

Michael David Lukas, you took time to meet with me when I was still writing and hadn't begun to realize what the whole publishing journey would look like. Being taken seriously by someone who had already so successfully gone down that road gave me hope that I would make it.

Martha Hoffman, I appreciate that you took so much time to closely read and analyze my manuscript. Your insightful suggestions made my novel better.

Brooke Warner of She Writes Press, your initial words of encouragement carried me through the final push to finish this book. I can still repeat your words verbatim. I so admire the dedication you give to each and every book that She Writes publishes. Annie Tucker, my developmental and copy editor, not only did your suggestions greatly improve my manuscript, your enthusiasm about my work carried me through many challenging moments. I can also quote from sections of your letter by heart.

Shannon Green, my She Writes Press project manager, you were patient with all of my newbie questions, and kindly and efficiently guided me through the publishing process. Julie Metz, you and your design team came up with a cover that perfectly reflects my novel. Tabitha Bailey and the team at BookSparks, you found great ways to get my book in the public's eye.

She Writes Press authors, your wisdom and generosity have been a revelation to me. You so graciously share your struggles as well as your triumphs.

For decades I have cherished the discussions of my AAUW Oakland-Piedmont book group. You have taught me that not everyone loves the same books, and that's okay. A special thanks to Marge Slakey, who showed her faith in me as she quietly kept asking me how my book was going.

Angela Kucherenko, I've loved our long discussions about what it means to be a historical fiction author.

Diane Rawicz, the writing events we attended, and the times we obsessed together about our writing, were part of why we have become friends.

My mother, Sybil Romano, showed me that books can be a passion that can carry one through all the stages of life. I can still hear the enthusiasm in the voice of my father, August Romano, saying, "Listen to this!" as he read a newfound favorite paragraph in the latest John Steinbeck novel he was reading.

To my sister, Ellen Romano, it has meant so much to me that you have always, always been there for me. Thank you for all of our talks about family dynamics and secrets. Maybe you see a shadow of some of that in this story. Your writing has inspired me, from the first poem you wrote when you were six.

Thank you to my children, Ben and Kate D'Harlingue, who took my writing project seriously, even when I abandoned it for years. Ben, you commiserated with me over the difficulty of sitting down and getting words onto the page, even as you lovingly encouraged me to keep going. Since you read mostly nonfiction, you offered a different perspective, which I treasured. Kate, you buoyed my spirits by telling me that this kind of book really could work, even giving me examples. Your reaction to my novel touched my heart.

My beloved grandchildren, Liliana and Oliver Norman, playing with you, reading to you, and listening to you, helps me to put things in perspective and remember what is important in life.

Most of all, thank you to my wonderful husband, Art D'Harlingue, for not only indulging but encouraging all of my varied interests over the years. You stood behind me when I said I didn't want to look back at the end of my life and wish I had tried to write a novel. There must have been times when you thought I'd never finish it, but you never let on. You patiently supported me and listened to the never-ending details about the road to finishing a book, and then getting it published. Your support and your love mean everything to me.

ABOUT THE AUTHOR

REBECCA D'HARLINGUE has done graduate work in Spanish literature, worked as a hospital administrator, and taught English as a Second Language to adults from all over the world. The discovery of family papers prompted her to explore the repercussions of family secrets, and of the ways we attempt to reveal ourselves.

She shares her love of story both with preschoolers at a Head Start program, and with the members of the book club she has belonged to for decades. D'Harlingue lives in Oakland, California, with her husband, Arthur, where they are fortunate to frequently spend time with their children and grandchildren.

SELECTED TITLES FROM SHE WRITES PRESS

She Writes Press is an independent publishing company
founded to serve women writers everywhere.
Visit us at www.shewritespress.com.

The Black Velvet Coat by Jill G. Hall. $16.95, 978-1-63152-009-9.
When the current owner of a black velvet coat—a San Francisco
artist in search of inspiration—and the original owner, a 1960s
heiress who fled her affluent life fifty years earlier, cross paths, their
lives are forever changed . . . for the better.

Estelle by Linda Stewart Henley. $16.95, 978-1-63152-791-3. From
1872 to '73, renowned artist Edgar Degas called New Orleans home.
Here, the narratives of two women—Estelle, his Creole cousin and
sister-in-law, and Anne Gautier, who in 1970 finds a journal written
by a relative who knew Degas—intersect . . . and a painting Degas
made of Estelle spells trouble.

Portrait of a Woman in White by Susan Winkler. $16.95,
978-1-938314-83-4. When the Nazis steal a Matisse portrait from the
eccentric, art-loving Rosenswigs, the Parisian family is thrust into
the tumult of war and separation, their fates intertwined with that of
their beloved portrait.

The Island of Worthy Boys by Connie Hertzberg Mayo. $16.95,
978-1-63152-001-3. In early-19th-century Boston, two adolescent boys
escape arrest after accidentally killing a man by conning their way
into an island school for boys—a perfect place to hide, as long as
they can keep their web of lies from unraveling.

The Vintner's Daughter by Kristen Harnisch. $16.95,
978-163152-929-0. Set against the sweeping canvas of French and
California vineyard life in the late 1890s, this is the compelling tale
of one woman's struggle to reclaim her family's Loire Valley vineyard
—and her life.

The Sweetness by Sande Boritz Berger. $16.95, 978-1-63152-907-8. A
compelling and powerful story of two girls—cousins living on
separate continents—whose strikingly different lives are forever
changed when the Nazis invade Vilna, Lithuania.